Me, Shakespeare and the Anti-Love Club

PACIFICA ACADEMY DRAMA SERIES
BOOK ONE

CHRISTINE MILES

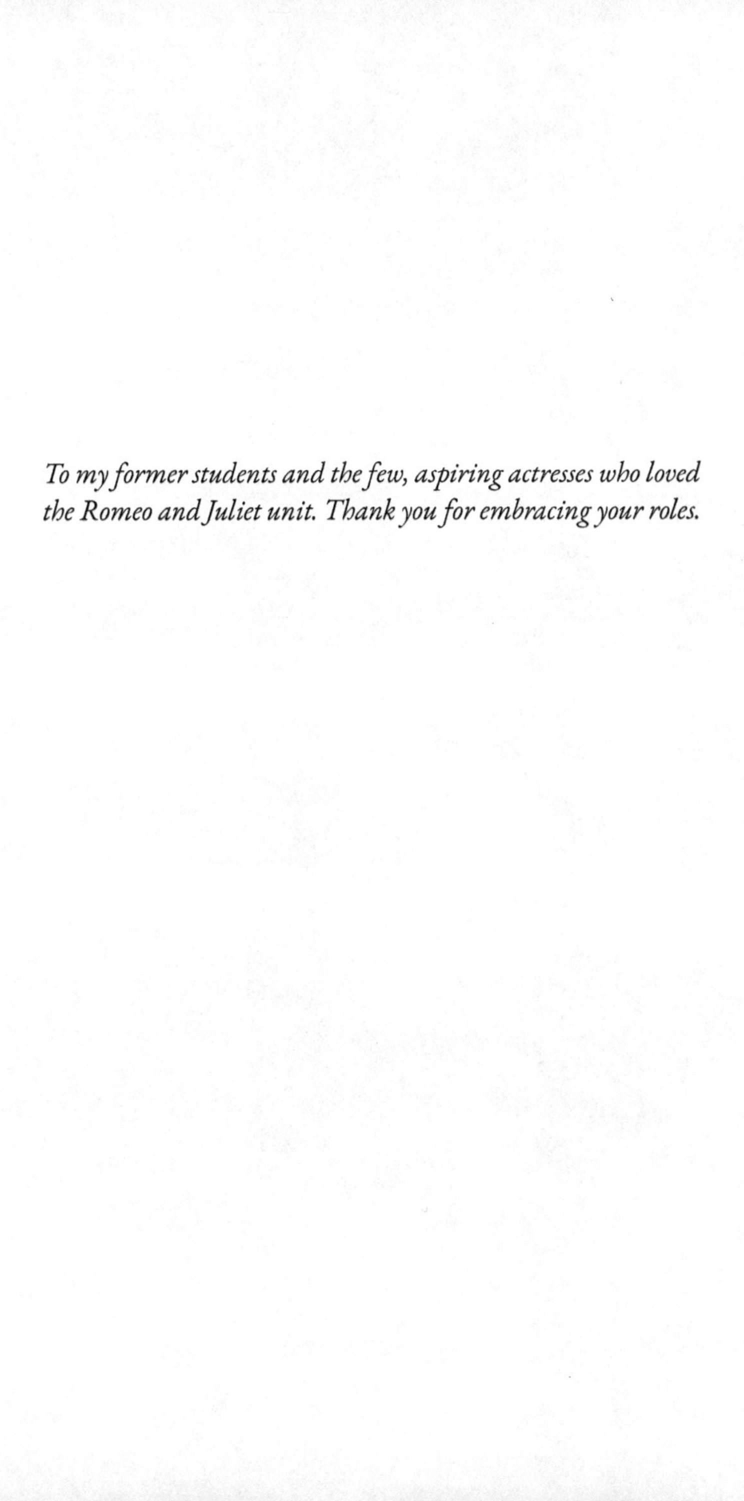

To my former students and the few, aspiring actresses who loved the Romeo and Juliet unit. Thank you for embracing your roles.

＃ Books by Christine Miles

Adult Contemporary Romance

Timing is Everything Series

Last Time We Loved (Book One)

First Time We Laughed (Book Two)

The Time We Met (Book Three)

This Time It's Forever (Book Four)

Smart is Seriously Sexy Series

Off-the-Charts Chemistry (Book One)

Passion Under the Microscope (Coming Winter 2024)

Young Adult

Pacifica Academy Drama Series

Me, Shakespeare and the Anti-Love Club (Book One)

The '68 Camaro Between Kenickie and Me (Book Two)

Teddy Brewster's Hold On Me (Book Three)

Silver Bells for Me and (Saint) Nicolas (Book Four)

You and Me Dancing to Gershwin (Book Five)

Summer in Winter Wonderland (A Cozy Mystery)

Chapter One

Be a Part of William Shakespeare's Epic Tragedy
Romeo and Juliet
Auditions will be held Tuesday, the 5th, in the auditorium,
starting at 3:15 SHARP.
Open to all grade levels.
Please note, British accents are not required.

This is what I'd been waiting for. Juliet Capulet. My dream role in the best love and hate story ever written. The Theater Department hadn't done a Shakespeare play in years, and Mr. Peters had finally chosen one for the big fall production.

Since I was alone in the school's auditorium lobby, I closed my eyes and envisioned myself on stage, dressed in a red Elizabethan gown. I imagined the sides of my long, chestnut hair swept back in a fancy braid, with a few wisps framing my face. Kind of like Claire Danes's hairstyle in *Romeo + Juliet*. Not my favorite movie version, but even I couldn't deny Leonardo

DiCaprio and Claire Danes had been perfectly cast. Their chemistry had sizzled. And having chemistry with cast mates was so important. Especially in a play like *Romeo and Juliet*.

I visualized a few of the boys who were really talented and active in theater, as Romeo. But then the auditorium doors to my right flew open, as did my eyes. A herd of fellow juniors spilled into the lobby, their chatter and laughter echoing throughout the large space. They ambled by me, one kid after another wearing Pacifica Academy's strict uniform of khaki skorts (girls), khaki pants (boys), white polo shirt, and navy-blue cardigan.

My best friend, Meghan Vaughn, followed them while she pulled her phone from her backpack. Once our eyes met, she smiled, and shook her head.

"I almost texted you when I saw this." She stopped next to me and pointed at the poster hanging on the wall between the two sets of auditorium doors. "But then I remembered you're working in the Theater Department as your elective this period." She quickly tapped out a text. "Talk to me, Kass. What do you need to get ready for the audition?"

I focused again on the poster. "I've been preparing for this since the sixth grade."

I not only wanted this role, I needed it. Getting Juliet would surely cinch my acceptance into the competitive Youth Summer Drama Session at the San Francisco Theater Company next year.

She tilted her head toward the auditorium, her dark hair pulled into her perpetual tight ponytail. "Well, I'll admit Mr. Peters's Reader's Theater class *might*, actually, be fun."

Meg was an athlete and loved being a cross-country runner —not a theater student.

"But I won't be taking him up on the extra-credit offer for his classes." She shook her head again, her ponytail swishing. "Some twenty extra points to anyone who just auditions for

Romeo and Juliet. He said something about wanting to see new faces."

I glanced at her.

What did that mean? New faces for the smaller roles or the big roles, too?

"But I'm sure he wasn't thinking about his talented regulars when he said that," she swiftly added.

The same auditorium door flew open. And tall, somewhat dark, and ridiculously adorable Justin Richardson strolled out. Well, J.R. But I'd never called him by his nickname.

He once said he liked me calling him Justin. I stopped that thought before more followed.

His eyes found mine. I couldn't stop myself from noticing how the muted sunlight coming through the lobby's glass doors brought out the green in his hazel eyes.

He tried on a smile as he, for some reason, headed... straight...for...us.

Meg turned her head far right and whispered, "You knew this would happen at some point today so just be cool. And breathe."

I started my deep-breathing exercise. The one I did to control pre-performance nausea.

We hadn't seen each other since That Night over two weeks ago. When our perfect, passionate five months together abruptly ended the moment he chose someone else.

He focused on Meg, then held out a piece of notebook paper folded into what looked like an actual note. "You dropped this on your way out."

He had the kind of voice a girl wants to hear as she's lying in bed at 1:00 in the morning, with her phone plastered to her ear, and buried under blankets in an attempt not to wake her sister. As much as I hated to admit it, I really missed hearing his voice. And the all-over body warmth I always felt while we talked about everything.

Meg, the best, best friend imaginable, snatched the note and muttered, "Thanks."

He looked like he wanted to roll his eyes, but then his gaze found me again, and I searched his face for regret. And that he missed me. Missed us. Until his too-perfect mouth curved into a smirk.

"You're lookin' good, DQ."

I narrowed my eyes.

DQ, his nickname for me that I now hated, being short for Drama Queen, not Dairy Queen. And no one—not even him, for the most part—looked good in our school uniform.

I looked Public Enemy #1, my new nickname for him, directly in his eyes. "Oh. I'm sorry. Did you say something to me?"

His smirk faded, and an emotion I couldn't read flashed across his face. "Have you always been able to cause a room's temperature to drop below freezing?"

I leaned forward. "No. It's a brand-new superpower I received after—"

"O-kay." Meg waved her hand between us, as if dicing up the tension. "Retreat."

His mouth formed a tight smile. "I do have a more important elsewhere to be." He adjusted his backpack over his shoulder, then turned left, and sauntered into the school's busy main building.

"Remind me of what I ever saw in him." But it was a rhetorical question.

"Kassidy, don't even go there." Meg linked our arms and we started walking in the same direction as him. "You've been there and done that scene. A few times."

"How could I forget he was taking Reader's Theater, too?"

He'd also chosen the class as an elective at my enthusiastic urging. He'd seemed so interested in hearing about theater and all the plays I'd done as we became friends last year.

"And I'll continue ignoring him like I did today." Meg hugged my arm to her side. "Now that you've seen him and gotten all that over with, you can really start moving forward. Like getting the part of Juliet?"

"Right." I took a head-cleansing breath, the jerk-face and our past leaving my mind as I released the air. We wound our way through students heading to class. "I need to focus on what's really important. Auditions are next week, and I always thought Juliet's monologue from act three, scene two, would be the perfect audition piece." An eruption of laughter from some boys forced me to loudly finish, "It's after the Nurse tells her Romeo killed Tybalt."

"Okay. And I'll be here."

Jade, a pretty little redhead in our class, suddenly walked out of a classroom, her head angled down. She veered right, without looking up, and disappeared behind a group of kids.

I glanced at Meg. "It looks like Jade's having a tough first day back."

Meg growled and said, "That's because Gavin dumped her in a text message a few days ago. Then he posted a selfie and that he was 'free at last' on Snapchat."

I stopped walking. "He did *what*?" It came out almost as shrill as those same boys went around us.

"How have you not heard about this by now?"

"Meg, I've been kind've caught up in my own stuff." I'd also been avoiding social media since the humiliation of That Night. "Are *all* the boys in this school complete jerks?"

"Not Owen." Her expression softened. "And I know I'll see him later, but I miss him. We so weren't ready for school to start."

I nodded and tried to smile as we started walking again.

After my summer with *him*, I'd felt the same way about school.

"But," she added in lowered voice, "J.R. and Gavin are definitely assholes."

And on that, she was definitely correct.

* * *

I walked into my room and stepped over a small pile of my sister's clothes right by her unmade bed. I shook my head as I stopped at my neatly made bed, diagonal from hers, to drop my backpack. I then turned and stepped toward the desk she and I shared. My Vision Board hung directly above the desk.

My eyes landed on a special picture. One of the few I had with me, my dad, and my mom. She, dressed up as Eliza Doolittle, held me on her hip with my dad standing close beside us.

I'd inherited so much from my mom—petite figure, dark hair, blue eyes, and a love of and talent for acting. I'd been so young when the picture had been taken and had no memory of seeing her in that show. And the usual sadness of not having the memory filled me up.

I wanted her to be here so she could see me continuing what she started. I loved acting, but it had also become my way of staying connected to her. Always.

I smiled at the picture, at her, then glanced at the flyer for the Youth Summer Drama Session I'd pinned to the board. Getting into the summer program would increase my chances of being accepted into a college with an excellent theater program.

I wouldn't let anything, or anyone, interfere with me getting one of the most fantastic female roles written for the stage. I needed to stay focused and not think about *him*. Or how I'd imagined my junior year—our year—going up until

That Night. When I'd stopped being good enough for him. I'd stupidly lived in the Land of Blissful for five months.

The front door opened and closed, and I turned from my board.

A few seconds later my sister Michelle bounced into our room and flung her backpack on her bed. "Telling Mom what play you're doing this year?" she asked.

I smiled and took the few steps back to my bed. "Sort've. And he chose an awesome one." I sat on my bed's edge and she dropped beside me.

She smiled, her braces shining from the sunlight filling our room. "So what's Mr. Peters doing? A comedy? The last two plays were soooo depressing."

"He chose a tragedy."

She groaned.

"A Shakespeare tragedy called *Romeo and Juliet*."

She squealed and threw her arms around me. Being thirteen, almost fourteen, my sister was into bouncing and squealing.

While we hugged, rocking each other from side-to-side, Dad appeared in our doorway, and looked exhausted from his shift at San Francisco General.

"Can I assume from the squealing your first day went well, too?"

I knew what Dad really meant and prepared myself for the questions.

My sister leaned back. "Did you see the stupid jerk-face?"

I sighed. "Yes. But he was alone." Thank goodness.

My deep breathing wouldn't have helped me get through seeing *them*.

Dad walked into the room, his dark eyes full of concern. "Anything else happen?"

He was probably wondering if I'd sent Public Enemy #1 to the nurse with a black eye.

"We exchanged mutual hatred." He looked relieved, and I added, "Don't you think the school would've called you if I hadn't been able to control myself?"

He opened his mouth to say something, paused, nodded, then said, "But you're okay?"

A little over two weeks ago was the first time Dad dealt with a daughter who'd just had her heart annihilated. But he'd brought me a box of tissues and held me tight while I sobbed into his chest. Once my emotions were somewhat stable, he left and came back a little later with my favorite ice cream, Rocky Road, and an extra-large spoon. Which had made me smile.

I missed my mom. But he was the Best. Dad. Ever.

"Daddy, I'm fine. And I have absolutely amazing news." All of us needed to focus on something way more important. "Guess what play we're doing this year."

"I...would have to say...I have no idea. But isn't Mr. Peters due for a comedy?"

I opened my mouth to answer when Michelle screeched, "*Romeo and Juliet*!"

Dad made two fists, then raised his arms in the air. "Finally, Shakespeare." He opened his hands, and my hands met his for a double high five. "When are auditions?"

"Tuesday."

"And your audition piece?"

"Got it. I just need to practice."

"I'll be here to help." He pointed at Michelle. "It's your turn to unload the dishwasher."

She released a heavy sigh, stood, and mumbled, "Here I go."

Dad's long shifts as an ER doctor meant Michelle and I shared several chores around our condo. At least they came with a weekly allowance.

"Kassi, are you sure you're okay?"

I shrugged and nodded since I didn't want him to worry. But his question brought back all the heartache that consumed me for days and my chest tightened. During those days, I couldn't stop replaying our big summer moments. And picturing them *together*. Then Meg and my sister dragged me from the condo one day to go shopping, probably at Dad's insistence. And that's when the fury had hit. So I was being honest when I said, "I'm more angry than anything else."

He nodded and leaned down to kiss the top of my head. "I'm going to get cleaned up."

"Working on your book tonight?" He was writing his first cat-and-mouse crime novel.

"I'm too worn out. In fact, I'm so worn out how does pizza sound?"

"Sounds great." Once he left, I faced my bookcase headboard and reached for my copy of *Romeo and Juliet* from freshman year English.

I had some math homework to finish, but later. Much later. Working on my audition piece would also keep me from thinking about Public Enemy #1.

And the fact I never expected to start my junior year with a broken heart.

Chapter Two

I pressed the button that would open the downstairs door of my building. Meg had offered to come over after her cross-country practice to help me rehearse Juliet's monologue. We were also going to do some homework. Three days into the school year and our teachers were already loading us up with work. But when she walked into my condo, I gasped and my heart rate sped up. Because she was sobbing.

"Owen's...*cheating* on me," she wailed, followed by a hiccup.

I closed the door behind her and asked, "Meg, what on earth are you talking about?" I'd just seen her at school a couple of hours ago and everything had been fine.

"I...don't know...what happened." She hiccuped and sniffed. "Where's...your dad and...sister?"

I took her hand and quickly led her into my bedroom. "She's in the living room doing homework and Dad's not home yet." I closed and locked the door. "Meggie, what happened?"

She dropped to my bed, her tears flowing from her eyes. "I

saw him…just now. After practice. With *Brandy Espinosa*. He had his arms…around her."

My face hardened. Owen Garrett was supposed to be one of the "nice guys." He also happened to be Public Enemy #1's best friend—my eyes widened.

Had that jerk-face's rotten behavior caused this?

I sat beside her. "Did you confront them?"

"No. I was too shocked." She sniffed a few times. "My sister has a Dammit Doll…still in her room. It has black yarn for hair. I think I'm going to take it and turn it into a Voodoo Doll. I'll use really long pins, too." She roughly wiped her nose.

"You don't believe in that stuff."

She hiccuped. "But it hurts. And I want to make her hurt. And that asshole. Why would he do this to me?"

I put my arm around her, and she rested her head on my shoulder.

Helplessness consumed me as she shook from her weeping. She'd probably felt like me right now when I went through this over two weeks earlier. Then I remembered what Gavin had done to Jade.

What was going on at Pacifica Academy? Was an outbreak of broken hearts running rampant through the school? Were there other kids trying to put *their* hearts back together?

If so, that was completely unacceptable.

"Meg, between me, you, Jade, and the others we don't even know about, something has to be done about this."

She took a shaky breath. "What…do you mean?"

I stayed silent as I searched my mind for an answer.

* * *

I breathed in the salty, humid air as I walked to school. The city's typical, morning haze filled the sky. It looked thinner than usual and that meant the sun would be out before noon. Because of the thin haze, I could see the top of the Golden Gate Bridge.

We lived a block from Alta Plaza Park, the high school only a couple blocks from there. It seemed like today would be the perfect day to go to the park, stretch out on the grass and continue to work on my oh-so important monologue. And as of today, I started listening to my Visualization Playlist, visualization and positivity being the key to acquiring one's most important goals. Right now, I had Kelly Clarkson's "Stronger (What Doesn't Kill You)" on the highest volume I could stand. Not one of the newest songs in my playlist, but the lyrics fit my mood and brilliant idea I'd come up with hours after my distraught best friend left.

When I reached school, I pulled my phone from my sweater pocket, stopped the music, and rushed into the building while removing my earbuds. I not only had to tell Meg my brilliant idea, but I had to see how she was doing.

I found her at her locker sluggishly loading her backpack. She glanced at me and my heart clenched. Her eyes were bloodshot, and her nose and cheeks were red.

"Owen blew up my phone last night with texts. I finally told him I saw him with Brandy. And if he wanted to keep his male parts safe, he'd better stay far away from me."

"What did he say?" I asked quietly since other students were also at their lockers.

She looked at me, her eyes becoming wet. "The messages stopped."

I frowned. "That brings me to my brilliant idea."

"Finding a second Voodoo Doll and dropping them both into acid?"

"No. We're going to start Pacifica Academy's first-ever Anti-Love Club."

She continued looking at me, her eyes blinking rapidly.

"Meg, those of us who've been spurned by Cupid's love-tipped arrows need to take back our hearts. And pride. Show love we don't need it to be happy. You, me, Jade—"

"Kass, I love your support and loyalty and tendency to go overboard. But that seems a little dramatic. Even for you. And that's only three people."

"But there has to be more of us. In fact, I was walking behind Natalie the other day and overheard her talking to her friends about her messy break-up with some college guy."

"Do you really think Natalie Carlisle would join this club?"

"It's worth a try. Because she, like us, sounded angry and just done."

Meg closed her locker door and faced me. "Do you even know how to start a club?"

"I don't hear you saying no to joining me on this necessary emotional journey."

"That's because I'm still stuck on the fact you're absolutely nutso."

My shoulders slumped. "I'm going to do this, with or without you, because I know it's the right thing. But it would be easier if I had my best friend as vice president."

She gave me blatant stink eye. "I can't believe you're pulling the bestie card."

"Please, Meggie? I promise it'll be exactly what we and everyone else in our club will need to move on without shedding anymore tears."

She took a deep breath, then released it in a burst of air. "Because I love you and your insanity, I'll do this with you."

I quietly clapped my hands before pulling her close for a hug. "To answer your question, I thought I'd start with student council."

* * *

JFK—or Joshua F. Kilpatrick—was a senior and president of student council. Between his name and his dad being a state representative, everyone knew where he was headed.

I tracked him down in the crowded, noisy cafeteria at lunchtime. He was sitting by himself and reading *The 7 Habits of Highly Effective Teens*.

Of course.

I sat in the chair across from him. His untouched lunch of a peanut-butter-and-banana sandwich sat in front of him. I tried to ignore the sweet smell. And seeing the sliced banana poking out from the sandwich's sides.

He dragged his cobalt eyes from the book and stared at me, not smiling.

"Hi." I held my hand out for him to shake, which he did after a few seconds of wary hesitation. "I'm Kassidy Pashen. Junior. And I want to start a club."

He, with an air of annoyed boredom I didn't appreciate, closed his book. "Right. You're the drama girl. I recognize you from the plays. Aren't you J.R.'s ex, too?"

I was fine with "drama girl." I loved and felt proud of my theater accomplishments. But I straightened at "J.R.'s ex," which scratched a still very vulnerable wound.

"What kind've club do you want to start? Because we have many. That have nothing to do with drama."

If this JFK wanted to make it in politics beyond the walls of Pacifica Academy, he needed to work on his people skills.

"My friend and I want to start an Anti-Love Club."

I could tell by his expression he didn't know whether to laugh or shoo me away. Maybe he wanted to do both. But I maintained my firm eye contact and posture.

At that moment, Public Enemy #1 entered the cafeteria

with his cheating buddy, Owen, and of course they decided to walk by us. The enemy met my unyielding, hostile stare, but his stare held more humor. Jerk-face. Owen at least turned red and looked away.

The moment they passed by, I refocused on my objective. "How do I start my club?"

He leaned back in his chair. "If you're determined to go through with this, you'll have to find a teacher willing to be the advisor."

Hmm. In my excitement, I had forgotten that pretty big detail.

"Then, if you actually find one," he continued, making it clear he didn't think I would, "you'll need to put in writing the club's name. The advisor's name. The president's name and any other officers. The club's purpose or mission. How often you plan on meeting. And how many members you have. Because you need at least eight members to even start a club."

Meg and I would have to do some serious sniffing around and recruiting, too.

"Put it in student council's box in the school office. If you meet the requirements, we'll approve it and you should be able to have your meetings in the teacher's classroom."

I stood. "Okay. And thank you."

"Uh-huh," he grunted as he opened his book.

We could totally do this. Now I needed to find my heartbroken best friend.

As I left the cafeteria, I literally bumped into Sloane Chaplin.

She took a step backward. "Watch where you're going, DQ."

Public Enemy #2 and the theater rival I wanted to slap for many reasons, one being she'd used *his* nickname for me. And, just my luck, she was with her equally delightful best friend, Brandy Espinosa, captain of the girls' varsity volleyball team.

"I'd rather be Queen of Drama than Queen of Peroxide." Thank you for that one, Meg.

Brandy's almost black eyes narrowed into slits. "What did you say to her?"

Public Enemy #2 held up her right hand. "Don't bother. Because I'm glad we ran into each other. I thought it would be great fun to tell you the news personally."

"There's nothing you have to say I'm interested in hearing." Especially if it pertained to her and her new...boyfriend. I started to walk around them.

"Just thought you'd like to know I'm also auditioning for Juliet," she practically sang.

I halted, then slowly turned. Someone bumped against me on their way into the cafeteria. But my eyes never left Sloane.

We'd been rivals since sixth grade, after I got the part of Tinkerbell in *Peter Pan, Jr.* I could still remember her tantrum, even though she'd been given the bigger role of Wendy. I also vividly remembered her flaunting getting the Queen of Hearts in *Alice in Wonderland* in seventh grade. I'd gotten the Duchess and had really wanted the Queen of Hearts. But I'd been the one celebrating freshman year when I snagged the big part of Rhoda Penmark in *The Bad Seed*. She'd ended up with a very small part. She hadn't auditioned for *The Crucible* last year.

Our biggest difference was I sounded like Mumble the penguin from *Happy Feet* when I sang. I somehow hadn't inherited my mom's singing gene. And Sloane, the daughter of Mrs. Chaplin who led the two choirs and directed the spring musicals, was a natural-born singer.

"Being Juliet will be my way of showing you you're not the only one who can act."

She almost sounded jealous. It didn't change the fact she'd

caught me off guard. So I said the first argument that popped in my mind. "But you're *blonde*."

The two exchanged a how-pathetic-is-she look.

"I can go back to my natural hair color when I get Juliet. And I'll get it. My mom is having her friend, a professional actress who played Juliet, help me with my audition piece."

I straightened to my full, five-foot-four height. "In so many ways you're not good enough to be Juliet." A little lame. But I still deserved an A for articulating the insult.

"Whatever." They turned to leave, but Public Enemy #2 stopped to glance over her shoulder. "Between going after and getting Juliet, and J.R. finally snapping out of it when it comes to you, this year is starting out perfectly." They disappeared into the cafeteria.

* * *

"They're such bitches," Meg hissed. "They walk around here like they run this place."

She'd texted I would find her at a table buried deep in the silent library. I suspected as of today we'd be avoiding the cafeteria for as long as possible.

"She and Brandy need to be taken out. Immediately."

Meg sounded like a mob boss wanting to execute a hit. The ones that ended in a massacre and were a way of sending a message to others if they were thinking about wronging the family.

She gave me a tiny smile. "But good job for basically telling Sloane Chaplin you're not afraid of her. Especially since she and J.R. are now—"

"Please don't say it. I can't even think about that right now."

Unfortunately, Sloane was my equal when it came to acting. If she managed to get Juliet, I could lose the Youth

Summer Drama Session. A huge part of me would also feel like I'd let my mom down. All that, combined with Public Enemy #1 falling under her questionable spell, would cause my heart to finish withering, then die.

"I knew I'd have to nail my audition. But now I have to be extraordinary."

"And you will be. Can you imagine Queen Peroxide, who's really only good in the musicals, trying to do Shakespeare justice?"

"You're right. She'll be out of her comfort zone. Which should give me an advantage." I hoped. "So," I began since we needed a subject change, "did you...see him? Today?"

Her lower lip trembled. "We passed each other once, and he didn't look at me."

I pressed my lips together before saying, "We need to start recruiting for our club. JFK said we need eight members to start it." I paused, then added, "And a teacher-advisor."

She winced. "Really?"

"We can do this. We can get Jade and I think we can get Natalie. With us that's four. And boys get their hearts broken, too. Remember last year when Rachel broke up with Nate before the Hearts Afire Dance? Because she was tired of him not dressing nice for anything?"

She nodded, and I said, "I still don't think he's fully recovered from that humiliation. And that's where we need to focus our recruiting efforts. I'll think about which teacher we should ask. There has to be one in this school who will understand and appreciate what we're doing."

"Okay. Start this afternoon?"

"Yes. Forming the Anti-Love Club has officially begun."

* * *

After school, I stood on Nate's left side, Meg on his right, as he dug through his locker.

"It sounds like a girl's club," he said above the hallway's student-traffic noise. "And I'm the star pitcher on our baseball team. I got a rep to uphold."

I said, "You can't stand there and say you've forgotten what Rachel did to you."

"It's also no secret she started dating your friend," Meg added. "Or ex-friend."

Nate was cute in a blond, boy-next-door way. But right now his face was stony.

"Are you saying this club is really about getting revenge?" He smiled, a bit wickedly. "Because I like the sound of that."

"Nate, this would be a school-sponsored club. Of course it would have nothing to do with revenge. Think of it more as a...support club."

He groaned. "That sounds worse than Anti-Love Club."

"What if we promise to find another boy?" Meg asked.

"And all you have to do is come to the first meeting. If it's too girly for you, you can leave with no hard feelings. Which is a perfectly acceptable compromise."

He cautiously eyed us. "Did you really get Natalie to join? She kind've scares me."

I lifted my shoulders. "She came off a little...strong. But she's not that bad. I swear."

He shut his locker door. "One meeting. And you promise you'll find another guy?"

Meg crossed her heart.

"Then I'll give it a chance. But only because I like you two. And Jade."

Meg and I hugged him, and he turned the color of a stop sign.

"I'll let you know when we're having the first meeting," I said before we walked away.

"Do you think Nate had a point?" Meg asked. "About the whole reputation thing?"

"How is our club going to be any worse than Chess Club?" I smiled. "Meg, we already have five members and only need three more. It'll be great. I promise." My smile grew. "This is exactly what our school needs."

Chapter Three

"Back, foolish tears, to your native spring...your tribe —*tributary*—drops belong to woe, which you... mistaking...offer up to joy. My husband lives, that Tybalt would have—"

A quick knock interrupted my practice, followed by, "Kassi, get out here. Right now."

I glared at my reflection and went to the door.

Dad's face exuded frustration. Michelle's, on the other hand, radiated triumph at her success. She'd been trying to get me out of the bathroom so she could take her shower.

"Why can't she use your bathroom?" I snapped at Dad as I headed for my bedroom.

"Hey. Watch the tone. And you've been in there long enough."

I tossed my copy of *Romeo and Juliet* onto my bed and dropped beside it.

My emotion had been right on, but I kept stumbling over the lines.

Dad had followed me and stopped in the doorway.

"I totally suck." I grabbed my throwing kiss emoji pillow

Public Enemy #1 had surprised me with on our one-month anniversary. And that I didn't have the heart to shred.

"Yeah." Dad walked into the room.

I looked up, and tears from frustration and the memory of him giving me the pillow filled my eyes.

"You probably do right now since you've been practicing most of the weekend." He pulled out the desk chair and sat. "Honey, you need to take a breath and clear your head."

Tears slipped from my eyes and I used the soft pillow to brush them away. How I despised Sloane. And the fact I'd allowed her to get into my head. That was focused on my audition tomorrow afternoon. I'd hit the pause button on everything else, including the club.

"I've been meaning to tell you this but was waiting for the right time. Which I do believe is now." He paused, then said, "Your mom was Juliet in our college's production."

My eyes widened, and I wiped away the remaining tears. "Really? I thought she was only in musicals."

"It was the only time she went after a leading role that wasn't in a musical. And I helped her the night before *her* audition since she was looking and feeling like you are."

"But she got the part." I sniffed. "It sounds like she got every part she wanted."

Another reason I had to get Juliet. I wanted to make my mom proud. The only other part I'd gone after, and gotten, had been Rhoda Penmark. I'd lucked into my somewhat big part in *Peter Pan, Jr.* because our music teacher told me I resembled a brunette Tinkerbell.

"Not this time."

Perfect. And if this was supposed to be my dad's idea of a pep talk, I'd feel better curling into the fetal position and crying myself to sleep.

"It's kind of a funny story." He smiled. "Your mom got Lady Capulet and the Juliet understudy. The girl who was

Juliet found out, a month into rehearsals, she was three months pregnant." He laughed. "She was stunned and for obvious reasons had to give up the part. But your mom was glowing the day she took over the role of Juliet. And she was breathtaking." He looked right at me. "Just like you'll be."

Altogether different tears hit my eyes. "No offense, but I really wish she was..." My voice cracked and he rolled toward me.

He gathered me in his arms. "I wish that, too. I know she would've loved being the one to help you through this. But I hope I'm doing okay? And that story helped a little?"

I laughed through my tears. "Yes. And I swear you're doing a great job."

He released me and rolled the chair back toward the desk. "Are you ready to do this?"

I nodded, wiped my face again with the pillow, dropped it, and stood.

Because my mom had been through this and ultimately succeeded, I'd succeed, too.

I snatched the copy of *Romeo and Juliet*, which Dad snatched from me.

"I need this." He opened it to the oh-so important page. "Anytime you're ready."

I closed my eyes, took a breath while picturing myself as Juliet in this emotional scene, and on stage with Mr. Peters as my audience. I then released the air and opened my eyes.

* * *

"But with a rearward following Tybalt's death, 'Romeo is banished' - to speak that word...is father, mother, Tybalt, Romeo, Juliet." I stepped closer to the stage's edge and pretended to be looking out from her balcony. "All slain, all dead. 'Romeo is banished': There is no end, no limit, measure, bound—" My mind went blank, but it recovered the end of her monologue before panic hit. "In that world's death...no words can that woe sound." I turned my head right, as if her Nurse was standing by me. "Where is my father and mother, Nurse?"

Silence followed, and I looked forward and quietly released the air in my lungs.

Mr. Peters, a slight man with dark, curly hair, sat in the house's center section, second row. He started talking to his favorite stage manager, Angelina, now a senior.

The auditorium was my happy place. Except on audition days. The emptiness of the stage and house made it feel extra silent. And lifeless. It was also pretty intimidating being the only person on stage and Mr. Peters's sole focus. For a thirty-one line monologue.

He finally faced me. "Thank you, Kassidy. The cast list will be posted on my office door by noon tomorrow." He looked down at his clipboard. "Can you send Sloane in next?"

I forced my mouth into a smile. "Yes. Thank you, Mr. Peters."

I, with amazing calm, walked down the stage left stairs. I, also amazingly, walked up the aisle, without glancing their way. But when I reached the doors I started trembling.

Coming from the silent auditorium, I felt a little unprepared for the lobby's noise. It was about half-full of students practicing while anxiously waiting for their turn to audition.

I spotted Meg to my left. She jumped up from the floor when she saw me. She waved me over, but I shook my head. Mr. Peters had given me a horrible job and I had no choice but to—that's when I spotted *them*. To my right. Sitting together on one of the few lobby benches. She looked focused on her opened copy of *Romeo and Juliet* as he stared straight ahead.

Up until now, I'd been lucky. I really hadn't seen them together since school started. Not eating in the cafeteria had contributed to that. So my heart almost stopped at seeing them sitting close on the bench. Like That Night. I also couldn't ignore the only reason he could be here was to support...her. I had imagined him, many times, doing the same thing for me.

The tears hit with fierceness, but I blinked them away.

I headed their way and my trembling doubled in strength. The moment I reached them, he sat upright, then started roughly wiping his palms on his thighs.

"How'd you do?"

"Why do you even care?" she loudly protested.

Although I had to give him credit for looking and sounding genuinely interested in how my audition went, I glanced at her. I said with more confidence than I felt, "I crushed it. He wants to see you next." I pivoted on my right foot and marched toward Meg.

She gave me my backpack and we walked into the main building.

"I was trying to get you out of there. Why the hell did you go talk to them?"

"Mr. Peters asked me to get her—" My voice caught on the emotion and a few tears trickled from my eyes. "I really hate audition days. And seeing them didn't help."

"At least you saw them after it." Meg hooked our arms. "Boy, did J.R. turn out to be a real dick. Like someone else," she nearly snarled. "I wanted to go punch him after he walked in and sat next to her." She squeezed my arm. "But you blew Mr. Peters away, right?"

With my free hand and sweater cuff, I blotted my eyes and cheeks, and mouth that now tasted salty from my tears. "Maybe. All I can say is I went with a vulnerable approach and didn't choke." I'd tripped over tributary—what was it about that word?—and had briefly drawn a blank at the end. But those were minor mistakes in a monologue written in iambic pentameter.

"All that means you were freaking awesome. When is he posting the list?"

"Noon tomorrow." Which meant I had a long, sleepless night ahead of me, made worse by what I'd just seen.

* * *

I muffled what felt like my billionth yawn of the morning because my night had been sleepless. And filled with images of them happily together and her prancing around the stage as Juliet. Those thoughts caused my stomach to twist for what also felt like the billionth time.

I glanced at the wall clock and stifled a groan. Forty minutes until lunch. Until finding out if my life would take a spectacular turn or come to a bitterly swift end.

Ms. Simmons was going over our first writing project of the term. As much as I liked English class, I couldn't get through it today without a distraction.

I reached into my backpack and withdrew a spiral notebook. I'd written **ANTI-LOVE CLUB** on the cover. We now had Jade, Natalie, Nate, and another junior, Lexi, who'd caught her boyfriend with another boy over the summer. I cringed at the memory of her still shocked and humiliated expression. Our most recent recruit was Warren, our only senior, who had come out last school year. Meg enlisted him based on his confession he was done being crazy about another senior who would never feel that way for him. Poor guy.

We still needed one more member and we needed a teacher. But who?

Meg and I would have to brainstorm at lunch, but after realizing my fate when I saw her in exactly—I peeked at the clock and my head dropped to my desk—thirty-eight minutes.

"Kassidy, is there a problem?"

I felt everyone's eyes before I sat up and smiled. "No."

Ms. Simmons nodded. "I know the cast list is being posted today, but I would appreciate your full attention until class is over."

She returned to the Smart Board, every classroom's electronic whiteboard, and I kept my eyes on both. As I watched her, though, I remembered her being one of the few single teachers. There had to be a good reason for it since she wasn't unattractive for a middle-aged woman. Average height, slender, had short, stylish brown hair, and wore reading glasses.

Hmm. An idea I'd run by Meg.

She dismissed us a few minutes early, and I grabbed my backpack and fled the room.

As I sprinted toward the Theater Department's office, located downstairs and on the other side of the building, I managed to dodge students and remove my phone from my backpack. Meg had already texted *I'm almost there* to which I hastily replied *On my way.*

The office was in chaos when I walked in and I saw Public Enemy #2's blonde head.

I started to shake when Meg emerged. Our eyes met, and I didn't know how to read her confused smile. Then my rival broke through, followed by two weepy girls. She stopped in front of me. And if she had the power, I would've burst into flames. Which meant one thing.

My shaking stopped and my stomach righted itself. I smiled, sidestepped her, and Meg grabbed my hand. She bulldozed her way through kids. And there it was on the door. Bold.

Juliet Capulet-**Kassidy Pashen/Understudy, Bree O'Neil**

I squealed, threw my arms around Meg, and jumped up and down.

"I knew you'd get it," Meg said as she bounced with me. "But keep reading."

Something about the way she said that caught my elated attention. We released each other, and I tore my eyes away from her to continue reading the list.

Romeo Montague-**Drew Chang/Understudy, Justin Richardson**

My eyes tripled in size and my joy evaporated. "But—What—I don't understand."

He had never—not ever—auditioned for the school plays. He was a soccer star.

"Oh, it gets better. Keep going."

Juliet's Nurse-**Bree O'Neil/Understudy, Maddie Harrington**

Lady Capulet, Juliet's mother-**Sloane Chaplin/Understudy—**

I looked at Meg. "Of course." On the massive bright side, she obviously hadn't been good enough to be my understudy, even with the "professional coaching."

I turned my attention to the Montague side of the cast list and froze when I saw it.

Mercutio, kinsman to the prince/Romeo's friend-**Justin Richardson—**

"He got Mercutio, *too*? Nononono. How? This doesn't make any sense."

"He must've taken Mr. Peters up on his extra-credit offer. And been really good."

"But he's not an actor!"

Meg took my hand and led me away. My outburst had caught everyone's attention.

He was an extremely talented piano player, but almost no one at school knew that about him. But that talent had nothing to do with acting. And Mr. Peters had cast him in an important supporting role? And as the Romeo understudy?

"No. This—this has to be a mistake." I looked at Meg. Then another reality hit. "Oh. My. God. Meggie, please tell me my enemies did not just get cast with me in this play."

She hugged me. "I'm sorry, but you need this." She pinched my arm hard, and I pulled away. Then anger replaced my shock.

I went for the doorway where I ran into Drew and Bree, seniors who were now my cast mates.

"Hey, you." Bree smiled. Until she saw my face. "Did he give Juliet to Sloane?"

"I can't talk right now." I moved around them and headed for the cafeteria.

"Kass, please don't do anything nutso," Meg called.

How could he invade my theater world? He knew how much all this meant to me.

And I really couldn't believe the jerk-face had done this after choosing my rival.

I entered the full, noisy room and paused to scan the tables until I found him sitting with Owen and two other soccer players.

I narrowed my eyes and marched right toward them.

The second I reached their table I said, "What do you think you're doing? Do you think this play is a joke?" I glanced at his buddies who had stopped their obnoxious chewing in response to my sudden, clearly unfriendly arrival.

He set his sandwich down. "That was fast. Is flying your other new superpower?"

"Just answer me." I didn't care my voice had risen. Or that we were being watched.

"Okay." He stood. "I'll be right back."

They nodded, their dumbfounded expressions changing to amusement.

He clasped my shoulders, angled me forward, then steered me, gently, in the direction I had come from.

I not-so gently shrugged off his hands.

When we reached the quieter hallway, I stopped and rounded on him. "Mercutio? And the Romeo understudy? How did you of all people manage *that*?"

He shrugged. "I guess I'm that good."

I crossed my arms. "Can you control your ego long enough to have this conversation?"

"Only if you do it first."

I glared up at him and leaned forward. "Justin Richardson, I don't know what you were thinking when you auditioned for this play. But believe me when I say if you and your new...girlfriend...ruin this for me, you both will regret—"

"Newsflash, DQ. This isn't about you." He also leaned forward, his hazel eyes hard. "I auditioned because I wanted the extra credit. And maybe I wanted to try something different. Is that okay with you?"

I remembered all of his interest when I talked about the plays I'd done. And he did have a performer side to him. But why would he try out acting *now*?

"I never thought I'd be good enough to get a part." He straightened, his irritation transforming into...panic? "Mr. Peters pulled me aside after Reader's Theater to explain his casting and what it meant to be an understudy. To make sure I could handle it, I guess." He laughed, but it wasn't out of humor. "And don't worry, DQ. I won't *ruin* anything for you."

He'd never talked to me with such nasty sarcasm. Even during our arguments, which started happening before That Night. And his sarcasm stung every part of me, but I maintained my hard stare. That's when a memory from yesterday appeared in my mind.

He'd not only been in the lobby to support her, but he'd also been waiting to audition. It's probably why he'd been wiping his hands on his thighs.

"Are we done now? I need to finish eating because I have to go meet up with—"

"Yes. I certainly wouldn't want you to keep the magnificent Sloane Chaplin waiting." My nasty sarcasm had rivaled his, but saying those words had caused my shaking to return.

He took a step back. "Congratulations on getting Juliet."

He walked back into the cafeteria. And I wondered how on earth I would get through the next several weeks without committing two justifiable homicides.

Chapter Four

Meg and I approached Ms. Simmons's classroom after school. She, sitting at her desk, wore her reading glasses while rapidly typing something on her computer.

We looked at each other, Meg nodded, and I knocked on the doorframe.

Her head shot up and she removed her glasses. "Hi, ladies. What's up?" She reclined in her chair as we walked toward her desk.

I forced myself to give her my biggest smile. "We were wondering if you'd be our advisor for a club we're starting. It would be Pacifica Academy's first-ever Anti-Love Club." I now more than ever needed this club and really, really hoped she'd say yes to this.

She looked confused, then her eyebrows nearly reached the ceiling. And I wondered why everyone I talked to about this club looked at me as though I had strangled Cupid, and his ghost was flying around my head.

"And what's the purpose of the club?"

"To bring together other students who have had their

hearts crushed, and are dedicated to taking them back and showing love who's really—"

She held up her hand. "I think I get it. But why did you come to me?"

Meg and I exchanged a quick, uncomfortable glance.

"Well..." Meg began, "this is kind of a small school and because of that we know you're...um...single."

"And thought that you might...maybe...understand..." My voice trailed off as Ms. Simmons shook her head, almost sadly, and my face became warm.

She pursed her lips as she stared at a spot on her desk.

I eyed Meg. It looked like she might also be thinking this hadn't been such a brilliant idea. There could be many reasons why she was single, and I pictured my dad. She could be in his situation. Brokenhearted, but not because of deliberate hurt caused by the other person.

We continued standing there, the awkward silence turning painful. But that's when she straightened, placed her reading glasses back on her nose, and refocused on her computer.

"I have to admit I do like the club's originality. Count me in, ladies."

I grabbed Meg's hand and squeezed.

Ms. Simmons looked up. "When are you planning on having the meetings? I would think you'd be pretty busy with *Romeo and Juliet*. Congratulations, by the way."

"Thank you. And Friday afternoons. For thirty or so minutes. Can we start this week?"

Meg had somehow found and recruited a freshman named Paige. Meg said Paige had asked a boy she liked in her math class if they could be study buddies. He'd responded by bursting into laughter, then walked away with his friends who were also laughing.

What was *wrong* with the boys at this school?

"That shouldn't be a problem. But I can promise you the meetings won't go past four."

We backed away from her desk and I said, "Thank you so much, Ms. Simmons."

"You're welcome."

We collapsed against each other once we were in the quiet hallway.

"I can't *believe* she said yes. So what now?"

"I'll get it typed up and printed and stick it in student council's box tomorrow. And we need to let everyone know about the first meeting. I also have to tell you my two more brilliant ideas for our club. We should make flyers, too. How about this weekend?"

She shrugged. "Okay. It's not like I have a date. But how are you feeling now? About...you know."

My stomach had been queasy all afternoon. "I'm dreading it." I had never—not ever—felt that way about being in a play. "But after tomorrow, it has to get easier. Right?"

"Maybe. I have to get to cross-country practice. I'll see you later."

We parted ways at the school's main entrance and exit. And the moment I stepped outside the memory of *his* betrayal hit me. My empty stomach clenched. At the memory of my breath disappearing before I felt the piercing pain in my heart. Seeing them outside, all cozy, at Owen's birthday party two weeks before school started.

That had to be what it felt like when a person was actually stabbed in the heart.

I removed my earbuds from my backpack and plugged them into my phone.

No, we hadn't been getting along that day or That Night. Or even the day before. Maybe because we'd been inseparable and became caught up in us the second school let out for summer break. Maybe our intense months together caused the fizzling. And, maybe, the fizzling prompted him to choose her. Because I'd been too much for him after all. Too much of a DQ. And now I was stuck with *them* for the next two months.

He'd taken that much time to prepare and audition, apparently very well, because he "wanted to try something different" this year? And for extra credit?

Seriously, how was any of this fair?

I twisted my earbuds into place and tried to focus on my deep breathing, my music, and the warm, sunny day. But my shock and irritation forced my memory into our past.

He'd come from a different private middle school. I'd figured he was a conceited jock, based on his soccer reputation and the stupid attention he received from girls. So we'd been nothing more than classmates. Until our sophomore year Bio teacher made us lab partners.

He'd sat next to me and said, "Hi. We've never officially met. I'm Justin Richardson. But almost everyone calls me J.R."

"I know who you are," I'd replied without looking at him.

"*Are* you a poet who doesn't know it?"

I'd smiled at that. "Clever."

"I try. And I know you played the psycho little girl in last year's play."

"Guilty."

"I—" He'd laughed. "I liked that play. You were really good."

I'd peeked at him and quietly said, "Thank you."

That had been it for interaction, outside of quick smiles and "Hey" at the beginning of each class. We hadn't really talked again until, about a week later, we started dissection.

"Mrs. De La Rosa," I'd said from my seat beside him, "I don't understand how these dissections aren't considered a gross violation of earthworms."

Everyone, including Mrs. De La Rosa, had stopped to look at me.

"I'm not following you."

"These poor invertebrate animals were doing nothing but enjoying the earth. Until they were dug up and killed for the purposes of being cut open, so we can study their anatomy. How is this lesson fair to earthworms and applicable to life?"

I'd heard the snickering. Even *his* shoulders had been shaking with quiet laughter.

She'd given me that teacher look before saying, "Kassidy, my classroom is not a stage. So please save the dramatics for Mr. Peters." She'd then returned her attention to the board.

"You're kind've a drama queen, aren't you?" he'd said at the end of class.

"I was merely trying to get her to see it from the earthworm's point of view."

"Believe it or not, I meant it as a compliment." He'd given me a crooked smile. "You say what you think and have no fear about it. It's...pretty cool. Your last name fits you."

My face had flushed, which had caused his smile to grow. Afterward, he'd started calling me DQ, but only when he caught me being, well, me.

I'd slowly fallen for his charm and the fact he seemed surprisingly down-to-earth, after that day. But I now wished I'd had the sense to keep him away from me. Because he'd turned out to be a phony player who deserved to be banished from Pacifica Academy for his crimes.

* * *

I texted Dad and Michelle earlier with my Juliet news but had left out until now the other casting. And they were staring at me as we ate sandwiches from our favorite deli.

"Wow, does that suck for you," my sister said before returning to her sandwich.

We were sitting at our small dining room table right off the kitchen.

"I didn't know he acted," Dad said.

"He doesn't."

Yes, he'd performed many times in front of an audience for piano recitals but, despite his gift, he'd stopped doing those when he turned thirteen. Now, he played for himself and avoided classical music. Because that was his "mom's thing." Not his.

"Well, he must have been pretty good, considering what Mr. Peters gave him."

That's the part I couldn't shake. Everyone knew Mr. Peters chose his cast very carefully. He not only considered a person's talent and audition, but also looked at personality and physical attributes, as well as maturity. Mrs. Chaplin cast her musicals the same way. Though everyone knew she favored her daughter. Maybe that's why most of us who were active in theater felt more honored when chosen by Mr. Peters for his plays.

But how could Public Enemy #1 have been that good in his audition?

"Honey, are you going to be okay with all of this?"

"I have to be. And it's not like we have any scenes together. Rehearsals start tomorrow and that's going to be the hardest part." Seeing *them* every afternoon, talking quietly and laughing together like they had been That Night, would be like feeling the piercing pain in my heart over and over.

"That's what's concerning me. Spending that much time together after everything—"

"Dad, I have no choice." I sat up. "I'm perfectly capable of being a professional." And certainly the Anti-Love Club would help me get through this.

It had to at this point.

"Kassi," Dad quietly began, "I know the other casting isn't what you expected. But I want you to know if your mom was here she'd be really proud of you. Just like I am."

I loved hearing him say that, and I gave him a soft smile. "Thanks." Though I knew my mom's experience as Juliet had been nothing like mine would be.

I had what I wanted. Juliet Capulet. Having the part made me feel closer to my mom, too. And being Juliet would put me one giant step closer to a spot in the Youth Summer Drama Session. But I couldn't ignore my dread when I envisioned the upcoming weeks.

Chapter Five

"Rehearsals are here, Monday through Thursday, right after school until around five. You must attend every rehearsal. But I know that stuff happens and we'll deal with it accordingly. Okay?"

Most of the *Romeo and Juliet* cast nodded at Mr. Peters.

We were occupying the first two rows of the house's center section. I sat between Drew and Bree. And I knew, because I couldn't stop myself from looking, my enemies were sitting together at the end of our row. They were between David, a senior and our Friar Laurence, and Cody, another senior, our Prince Escalus and *Mercutio's* understudy.

"*Romeo and Juliet* is running the second weekend of November. We'll have our typical Friday, school matinee, then our first evening show. The final performance will be Saturday night. We'll be spending a lot of time together and you need to think of each other as family." Mr. Peters paused to take a swallow of his water. "And I can promise, like any large family who spends too much time together, you will get sick of each other. And me. But all we can do—and in the words of Walt Disney—is 'keep moving forward.'"

More nodding.

"Good. Now, most of you know each other, but I want to introduce the new faces. A few of them took me up on my extra-credit offer."

I groaned silently.

"I'll start with our Mercutio and Drew's understudy. J.R. raise your hand. And wave."

His arm went straight into the air and he received enthusiastic applause when he turned to wave at everyone...as if he were on a Macy's Thanksgiving Day Parade float.

"I can't believe he auditioned that well," Bree grumbled as the applause ended. "Maybe Mr. Peters was tired by the time J.R. auditioned for him and will come to his senses?"

I loved Bree. We bonded during *The Crucible* last year. I'd been Mary Warren and she'd played Elizabeth Proctor, the part I'd actually wanted. But with her light brown hair and eyes, and calm personality, she'd really looked and done well with the part. I knew she'd be great as the Nurse. And thank goodness she'd been assigned as my understudy.

"I guess we'll soon find out if he really is any good."

"Next up is our Count Paris. Noah, if you'll also raise your hand and wave."

Noah, a sophomore, of course had to mimic *his* ridiculous wave as everyone clapped. Other new faces included a new student named Michael, a junior and our Lord Capulet, and Barrett, yet another junior and our Lord Montague. Other newbies were lower class men, our Citizens of Verona, but some had also snagged understudy for the smaller supporting roles.

"All of you have a lot of work to do. Memorizing Shakespeare isn't easy. But I wouldn't have chosen you for this play if I didn't think you could do it. Which leads me to our Romeo and Juliet." Mr. Peters looked directly at me and Drew. "I'm expecting great things from you two."

Drew grabbed my hand, stood, and pulled me up. "We got this, Mr. Peters," he said as the applause started. He then raised our hands and made us bow before sitting back down.

He could be the class clown, but it made him fun to work with. He was also talented, always prepared and, in his own goofy way, pretty cute. He could sing, too, and had been perfectly cast as the Scarecrow in last year's spring musical *The Wizard of Oz*.

Mr. Peters held up his worn copy of *Romeo and Juliet*. "All of you should have this. It needs to be with you until you learn your lines and blocking. So, take out your scripts and a pencil. We need to cut dialogue here and there for appropriateness and run-time purposes."

"And here we go," Bree said as she reached into her backpack.

I smiled at her. With Drew as my Romeo and Bree as my Nurse, maybe this wouldn't be so bad.

* * *

"'You Give Love a Bad Name.'" I faced our six members. I felt confident the club would catch on when we started posting flyers for it around school.

I had written the song title, with Ms. Simmons's okay, on her Smart Board.

Enter brilliant idea number one that came to me while in the car with Dad who kept the radio on his favorite eighties and classic rock station.

"A Bon Jovi song that came out a long time ago and that we feel is perfect to be our club's theme song. We can play it every time we get new members. Any objections?"

Meg and I were answered with silence and four blank stares. Ms. Simmons, sitting at her desk, had her lips pressed together and appeared to be fighting a smile.

"I hate old music." Natalie tore her eyes from her phone. Her close friends were other uber-rich kids, but Natalie had an edginess to her which caused many kids to be, well, afraid of her. The fact she was tall and striking, with long black hair and dark eyes, didn't help her edgy image. "I don't even know who Bon Jovi is."

Warren, whose fun, easy going personality made up for his average looks, smiled at us. "Well, I think it's an inspired choice."

"I like it, too." Nate shrugged. "It has my vote."

A good sign, considering he still looked uncomfortable. Despite Warren's company.

"Me, too." Lexi, a quiet, pretty, and *natural* blonde, tended to be kind to all Pacifica kids. Even if they didn't deserve it. "I don't know that band or song, either. But the title sure seems to fit us."

"Maybe you could play it for us?" Paige timidly asked.

I'd never seen Paige before this meeting. She was curvy with a round face and seemed somewhat...fearful? And I wondered if she felt intimidated being "the baby" of our club.

"That's fair." Jade, sitting next to Paige, gave her an encouraging smile.

I looked at Ms. Simmons. "Can we bring up YouTube?"

She smiled. "Sure. But only because I know that song has clean lyrics."

I erased the board while Meg went to Ms. Simmons's laptop, which controlled the Smart Board. Within seconds, she had the YouTube link up and selected. As the commercial played, she upped the computer's volume. And we waited. Then the video, from a long time ago, filled the screen, the crowd started cheering, and the song's opening lines exploded from the board's speakers.

I watched our club members watching the video of the band jumping, dancing, and running all over the stage. The girls' eyes were wide. It looked like they didn't know what to think of the band's spectacle. But Warren and Nate were bouncing their heads with the music.

At about the song's halfway point, Meg paused the video.

"So," I said with my brightest smile, "now that you've heard the lyrics are we agreed?"

"It still has my vote," Nate mumbled.

"And I still think it's an excellent choice," Warren stated.

The girls nodded while looking at each other, as if they needed permission to like the song. Even Natalie consented with a curt nod and shrug.

"Good. Now that we have that out of the way, we need to talk about what's next." I gestured to myself and Meg "We came up with a very important club activity for tomorrow night. A first step to really moving on. Does anyone have plans?"

And enter brilliant idea number two.

"My friends have dates, so hell—I mean no." Natalie glanced at Ms. Simmons who had her head angled down, and I felt certain she was pretending to be absorbed in grading.

"I have no life." Paige slouched in her chair. "I'm definitely free."

"I've decided it would be best," Lexi softly said, "considering my unique situation, if I kept a very low profile from now until forever."

Ms. Simmons's head snapped up and she frowned at Lexi. "That's a pretty strong statement. Whatever happened couldn't have been that bad."

"You'd be surprised." She turned cherry red, then quickly looked down at her desk and started playing with a lock of her long hair.

Ms. Simmons went back to "grading."

I said, "Does that mean everyone is available?"

"Why not?" Natalie muttered. "I've sworn off all guys from now until forever."

Warren nodded. "Same here. So I'm up for whatever tomorrow night."

"Jade? Nate?" Meg asked.

They looked at each other, and Nate shrugged. "Yeah."

Another good sign.

"What did you two have in mind?" Jade cautiously asked.

"It's a surprise and it'll be great. Meet us at Meg's house at seven. And make sure to bring something important that represents the person who gives love a bad name."

Chapter Six

I stared out the passenger-side window of my dad's Volvo SUV. I had my license, but with this being our only car, and with him on call, the car was his. Meg lived close enough to walk, but Dad didn't like me or my sister out walking past 6:00.

"If I ask why you have that picture, would you tell me?"

I glanced at him. "Probably not."

He and Michelle didn't know about the club. My sister had a big mouth, which meant Dad would find out, and I didn't want him to worry. He might see the club as me not taking everything that happened with Public Enemy #1 very well, and he had enough going on.

"It's a Polaroid," he tried again. "Must have been taken during the summer?"

I nodded and looked down at the picture I'd taken of *him* in June. Two weeks and four days after my sixteenth birthday, and when I'd received the camera from Dad. I'd fished the photo out from a storage box underneath my bed containing several other pictures of him, and us. I didn't feel comfortable putting them through Dad's shredder. Yet. But this photo was different.

I'd taken it the day we'd played tourists at Fisherman's Wharf. I'd snapped the picture just as he'd given me his crooked smile that made my stomach do about ten somersaults. We'd later gotten caught in an unpredicted rain shower and ran back to his car. He drove us back to his big empty house—

"Honey," Dad said as he stopped in front of Meg's house, "don't do anything that you might regret later."

How did parents know when their kids were up to something?

"I'll see you in a couple hours if I don't get a call."

Yes, I'd chosen the picture because it was my favorite one of him. But it represented so much more and for that reason it had to be sacrificed tonight.

Meg opened the front door of her Victorian-era home— her parents were in real estate—and greeted me with, "I didn't think my parents would ever leave for that party."

I followed her into the house's grand foyer with a beautiful wood staircase that led up to the second floor. "Is everything ready?"

She closed the front door. "It's all set up in the back."

They had a patch of land for a backyard, and the neighbors were awkwardly close, the norm for living in the city. But if we did this right, they would think we were barbecuing.

"What'd you pick?"

I held the picture out, and her eyes widened.

"Wasn't it taken *that* day?"

I nodded, and she pulled me in for a hug.

"Like Owen, I thought J.R. was different."

We released one another, and I became determined not to shed one more tear for that jerk-face. Then the doorbell rang, which meant the time for The Purging had arrived.

After everyone showed up, we went outside and stood closely around the metal bucket. All of us held our items. Thank goodness it was nice enough to be in jeans and long-sleeved shirts, early to mid-fall usually being the city's nicest weather. If tonight had been rainy, we would have had to cancel this necessary activity.

"Are we ready?"

Everyone nodded, then Jade asked, "Are we doing what I think we're doing?"

Her wide eyes swept over our necessary Purging tools—the bucket, lighter fluid, matches, and a just-in-case fire extinguisher.

"Yes. I'll go first. And we should all do it the same way for maximum benefit." I held up my picture. "This is a picture of him I took on a day that turned out to be very special." My voice cracked on the words. And at the vivid memory of us. In his bedroom. Exchanging shy smiles as we, after pausing our head-spinning kissing, decided to take our relationship to *the* next emotional and physical level. The first time for both of us.

It had been awkward. We'd been so nervous. But it had also been absolutely magic—I shook my head. Anger replaced my heartache. And stupidity.

Because I loved him and had believed everything he'd said to me.

"Justin Richardson." I held the picture over the bucket. "You give love a bad name." I dropped the picture into the bucket, then picked up the lighter fluid, held it upside down and squeezed. Hard.

"That's enough." Meg swiped the lighter fluid. She faced us and held up a ticket stub from a San Francisco 49ers football game. "This is from our first football game. His parents are season ticket holders. The Patriots beat us into the ground, but we were so focused on each other we didn't care." She sniffed a few times. "Owen Garrett, you give love a bad name." She released the ticket, watched it drift into the bucket, then added a squirt of lighter fluid.

Jade stepped forward. "The card from the first bouquet of flowers he gave me. Pink roses on my fourteenth birthday. My favorite," she added with a sad laugh. "Gavin Styles, you give love a bad name." In went the card, followed by a careful squirt of lighter fluid.

"All I have is a printed copy of an adorable selfie he took of himself and posted on Instagram," Warren declared. "And I would rather not show you who he is."

"No. Not fair." Natalie looked first at me, then everyone else. "That should be totally against the rules."

"You do know our exes and the details of our humiliating break-ups," Lexi quietly said. "I think I can speak for everyone when I say we're not here to judge you."

"Agreed. Suck it up buttercup." Nate held a little blue, stuffed dog with a bone in its mouth that said "I ruff you."

Warren released an exasperated sigh and showed us the picture.

My eyes grew. "Your unrequited love is Drew Chang?"

We all looked at each other, our mouths hanging open.

"I know he's as straight as Harry Shum, Jr., my forever celebrity crush, but there's just something irresistible about Drew." He focused on me. "Do you even know how superbly lucky you are that you get to kiss him—"

"Enough." Nate nodded at the picture. "Throw it in."

Warren did but failed to add more lighter fluid.

"Are you really going to burn that?" Paige barely tilted her head toward Nate's dog.

He shrugged. "I couldn't decide between this thing or the card that went with it. From our first Valentine's Day together."

Jade smiled at him. "I think it's sweet you kept those. But

it might be best if you chose the card. The dog is awfully cute."

"And he didn't do anything wrong," Meg said. "Maybe give him away?"

He dropped the dog and removed a narrow card from his back jeans pocket. It looked like one of those overly sentimental cards that went on and on about why and how much the person giving you the card was in love with you.

Nate held it over the bucket. "Rachel Marlowe, you definitely give love a bad name."

I'm pretty sure I heard him mumble the B-word as he added lighter fluid.

Natalie held out a mangled San Francisco Giants baseball hat. "This belongs to the asshole. It *was* his favorite hat. He once told me that every time he wore it, they won." She rolled her eyes then laughed, almost maniacally. "He tried to get it back, but I told him I gave it to my dog for a chew toy." She tossed it into the bucket. "Tanner Prescott, you are a self-absorbed dick who gives love a bad name."

"Should we burn that?" Paige, who was next, withdrew and pointed at the hat.

"It'll be fine," I assured her. "What do you have?"

"Just a copy of a picture." She held it out and open for everyone to see.

It was a picture of a blond gawky boy wearing braces and glasses.

"How old is that picture?" Natalie asked.

"It was taken when we were in seventh grade." Paige gazed at the paper. "I've known him since preschool. We used to be good friends." She sighed. "Until the end of eighth grade when he lost his braces and glasses and was suddenly considered 'super cute' by all the girls."

All of us glanced at each other as Paige continued staring at the picture.

She wasn't at all unattractive with her shoulder-length, dark-blonde hair, blue eyes and shapely figure.

"Throw it in there and dump lighter fluid on it," Natalie practically barked.

Paige dropped the paper and, arm stretched out, barely squeezed the bottle. "Landon Ellsworth, I thought you were my friend. But now you're a jerk who gives love a bad name."

Lexi also had a ticket stub. "From a community-theater production of *Rent*. His favorite musical." A soft, gloomy laugh followed. "It represents the day I should've figured out the truth after he said, many times, how much he loved the Tom Collins character. And the guy who played him in that show. I'm so *stupid*," she added, her voice nearing meltdown.

"No, you're not." Jade squared her shoulders. "Because that means we're all stupid and all we're really guilty of is loving someone who didn't deserve it."

"I guess, like Natalie, I'm lucky I don't have to see him every day at school." Lexi tossed the ticket into the bucket. "Cam Jenkins, you probably didn't mean to break my heart. But right now you give love a bad name." She hesitated, released a sad sigh, and added a squirt of lighter fluid.

Our bucket now held our items. And our emotions and experiences. There was only one thing left to do.

I picked up the matches, then looked at each of my club members.

"We should step back." Nate backed away from the bucket.

Everyone mimicked his movements but me. The club and The Purging were my ideas. So I needed to do the honors of dropping the lit match.

I removed a match from the box and swiped it against the side. The smoke went up my nose before I carefully held my hand over the bucket. I paused, then dropped the lit match.

An enormous flame roared and burst from the bucket, and I jerked my arm backward.

And I heard a scream loud enough for the entire city of San Francisco to hear. Which caused the other girls to scream as loud.

I stumbled backward so fast I lost my footing and landed on my butt.

"Where's the fire extinguisher?" Nate yelled above the chaos.

I sat there, amazed, watching the flames almost reach the low-hanging leaves on the Vaughn's only backyard tree. I could also smell the lighter fluid and smoke, and the burning paper and hat. That's when the crystal-clear mental image of us explaining Meg's house had accidentally burned down because of The Purging filled my head.

"I can't get the pin out!" Meg screeched.

The fear in her voice snapped me out of my daze. I got on all fours and crawled toward her. But Nate ripped the fire extinguisher from her hands. He pulled out the pin, aimed the hose at our bonfire and frantically started spraying. Within seconds, he'd doused the fire. And a long, stunned silence fell around us. Until we heard the sirens.

* * *

"The Purging."

I just finished explaining everything to the younger fireman, glaring at us. The other two, older firemen were trying to muffle their laughter. I hoped that meant we'd get out of this with no more than a slap on the wrist. The paramedics had already left since we weren't hurt.

The younger fireman continued glaring at me and my club members. They literally had my back. They stood right behind me with the exception of Meg. She stood at my right side, her face bright red.

"Your neighbors were extremely worried," he said to Meg.

Her face turned even redder and guilt settled itself onto my shoulders.

"One dispatcher reported that a neighbor who called said it sounded like girls were being burned at the stake."

"Well, obviously that person was wrong."

"Natalie, shut up," Jade mumbled.

"Where are your parents?" he asked Meg.

"They're at some party downtown and won't be home until late."

One of the older firemen stepped forward while fighting a smile.

"Tyson, leave' em alone. No one was hurt. Nothing burned"—he peered into our bucket that held the burnt, smelly remains of our various items now covered in foam—"except what they intended. At least you had the fire extinguisher handy." He released a quick laugh. "But you need to get this cleaned up. And your parents *will* get billed for us being called."

Meg's face paled, and the guilt weighed my shoulders down.

"Of course." I attempted my most apologetic smile. "We'll do it now. And we really are so sorry. We just got a little carried away with our emotions. And the lighter fluid."

He, and the other fireman who thought this was hilarious, continued laughing as they headed into the house. The unamused one gave us one more glare before following them.

Natalie rolled her eyes. "That guy needs to remove the firehose shoved up his ass."

"At least the other two were nice," Lexi said, twirling a lock of hair around her finger.

"God, I hope no one finds out about this." Jade gave us a

long look. "Maybe now would be a great time to come up with a pledge. Something along the lines of whatever happens in the Anti-Love Club, stays in the Anti-Love Club?"

"I wholeheartedly agree with that," Warren stated with a nod.

I nodded, too, as did the other members. But one.

As we heard the firetruck leaving, I faced my stunned and pale best friend. "Meggie, I'm so, so sorry. And will the stay the night and throw myself at your parents' mercy when they get home." Because they'd be getting a bill, we had no choice but to tell them everything.

And that meant Meg's parents would, most likely, call *my* dad.

Just. Perfect.

"I'll stay, too," Paige offered with a tentative smile. "I didn't have to add lighter fluid."

"You three shouldn't have to take this alone," Jade firmly said. "So I'm staying."

"Me, too." Nate shrugged. "This has actually been a really good time." He laughed. "Not that I'm saying I want a career as a pyromaniac."

He continued laughing and Warren joined him. Within seconds all of us—even Meg—were laughing. Really hard. Even though Meg and I would probably be grounded forever after tonight, the laughter felt fantastic. An unexpected part of The Purging that made me feel like I belonged to a new something special Public Enemy #1 could never infiltrate.

Chapter Seven

I stepped back from the activities bulletin board. I'd pinned our flyer beside a poster promoting the *Fall*ing in Love at First Sight Dance, our first one of the school year.

But it really sucked I'd made the flyers by myself. Because Meg and I *had* gotten in huge trouble for what happened Saturday night. The second I opened our SUV's passenger door Dad said, "You're grounded from all social activities not related to the play until further notice." Meg had been grounded, too. Which meant neither of us had any idea when we would be able to attend another meeting. So much for my brilliant idea. And based on what our fellow members had been saying on Snapchat, they'd escaped persecution.

I guess Meg's parents didn't know their parents as well.

"Anti-Love Club. I heard about this from JFK."

My frown deepened at the sound of *his* voice. On the plus side, it seemed the Anti-Love Club members had taken the what-happens-here-stays-here pledge seriously. It appeared no one at school had heard about us almost burning down Meg's house.

I eyed Public Enemy #1. He stood just behind me to my right side as he read the flyer.

Shouldn't he be on his way to Reader's Theater?

I worked in the Theater Department's office this period. But I could be a couple minutes late since Mr. Lowry, the technical teacher-director, was pretty low key.

My enemy looked at me, his expression a mixture of disbelief and exasperation.

"You can keep your opinions to yourself."

"Don't you think it's a little crazy that you, our school's Juliet Capulet, are promoting an Anti-Love Club?"

"Juliet is simply a fictional character I'll be playing and has nothing to do with reality."

"Fine." He again looked at the flyer. "But this is over the top. Even for you, DQ."

I wanted to say stop calling me that. But I loved how my name sounded when he said it.

Totally. Pathetic.

"I wouldn't expect you to understand. You really have no heart. Or soul."

That hadn't sounded as harsh in my head, and a twinge of guilt hit when he huffed and looked at the floor. He stood like that for a few seconds before lifting his head.

He faced me, his eyes filled with anger. "Does it feel good to assume you're right about everything and everyone?"

My guilt vanished at his tone. And the fact I wasn't in the mood for him. For this. "I don't claim to be right about everything and everyone. But I'm right about you because I, unfortunately, know you very well."

"I thought you did," he quietly said, as if he were talking to himself. Then his mouth curved into a smirk. He glanced at the flyer and back at me. "But you don't know anything about me, DQ. Not one bit."

He'd wanted his comments to hurt. And if words could slice a person, those wounds would be deep and gushing blood. But I also knew he was playing eye-for-an-eye.

Meg suddenly appeared at my side. "Oh, look, the alpha male has separated himself from his pack. Are you sure they can survive without you for more than five minutes?"

"I like it better when you're ignoring me." He started to leave, but stopped and looked at Meg. "Has it even occurred to you to talk to Owen? To get *his* side of the story?"

Meg drew back, her mouth slightly open.

Strongly sensing those questions might be directed at both of us, I said, "Why would she do that, since she knows what she saw?"

"Does she really?" he snapped at me.

As if this moment, already drawing attention from passing students, couldn't get any worse, Public Enemy #2 showed up. And pressed herself against him.

I tried, really hard, not to focus on her practically hugging his side. But I did catch his slight shift away from her.

"Why are you talking to her?" she asked, not bothering to hide her disgust.

I felt the near-overwhelming urge to go for Sloane Chaplin's throat as Meg said, "He was just leaving. You can get on your broomstick and leave, too."

She ignored Meg while giving our flyer a contemptible look as he started to leave. But she grabbed his hand, which seemed to startle him.

Public Enemy #2 pointed at the flyer. "That's the most pitiful thing I've ever seen."

I leaned forward. "That's because people like you only love yourselves."

I started shaking as Meg and I headed toward the theater's side of the school. I did my deep-breathing exercises until the shaking had almost stopped. I then glanced at my best friend. Who suddenly looked...guilty?

"Meg, if Owen didn't do anything wrong, why is he acting guilty and avoiding you?"

She nodded. "That's true. But I did threaten his male parts if he came near me."

"My ex-jerk-face was backing up his friend. You need to stay strong. We both need to stay strong," I forcefully added while I tried to forget what just happened. Particularly seeing their hands joined. But instead of intense pain, anger burned inside me.

I resented that for the second time in my theater career I was dreading a rehearsal.

* * *

Mr. Peters sat cross-legged in the middle of our large circle. He asked everyone with speaking roles to sit in a circle on stage, the extras having long been dismissed for the day.

Shane, a junior and our Benvolio, was reading his dialogue from the beginning of act one, scene four, when the boys are on their way to the Capulet's mansion for the ball.

The Capulets made up one half of the circle, the Montagues the other, with our Friar Laurence and Prince Escalus linking us at the bottom. At least, it was the bottom from where Drew and I sat. The rotten part about this arrangement was *she* sat to my right, Bree the only person separating us. To my left sat Drew, followed by Shane, followed by *him*.

Mr. Peters wanted us to spend a few rehearsals "trying to deliver our lines as if we were performing in the final show." So far, it had been a somewhat comical exercise as everyone tried to get used to the language.

"But let them measure us...by what they will...we'll measure *them* a measure, and be gone," Shane finished, followed by a laugh.

His looks reminded me of a Ken Doll. Not that he looked plastic. He just happened to be one of the cutest boys active in theater. He was also really talented. And would've been a much better choice for Mercutio.

"Give me a torch," Drew said, and sounding truly depressed over losing Rosaline. "I'm not for this ambling. Being but heavy, I will bear the light." He reached left, toward Shane and Public Enemy #1, and pretended to take a torch. The three then shared a laugh.

"Great," Mr. Peters said. "Mercutio you're up."

The enemy had been lounging in his chair, but quickly sat up. I'd been anxious for this moment, too. This being his first scene in the play. Not that delivering the lines while sitting down would demonstrate what Mr. Peters had seen in him during his audition.

"Nay, gentle Romeo...we must have you dance."

"Not I, believe me. You have dancing shoes...with nimble soles...I have a soul of lead, so stakes me to the ground I cannot move."

"You are a lover." He looked at Drew and smiled. "Borrow Cupid's wings, and soar with them above a common bound."

He had that line memorized?

"I am too sore enpierced with his shaft...to soar with his

light feathers…and so bound I cannot bound a pitch above dull woe. Under love's heavy burden do I sink."

"I like how miserable you sound, Drew," Mr. Peters interrupted. "Mercutio, go."

"And, to sink in it, should you burden love? Too great oppression for a tender thing."

I had to…reluctantly…concede he'd nailed the "I don't get it" aspect of his dialogue.

"Is love a tender thing?" Drew continued, then sighed. "It's too rough, rude, too boisterous…and it pricks like thorns."

Our *Mercutio* had paused, and to the point I lifted my eyes from my copy to glance his way. And immediately caught his hazel eyes, because he was staring. Right at me.

"If love be rough with you, be rough with love!" He broke our eye contact to look at Drew. "Prick love for pricking, and you beat love down." He followed that up with a quick wink and smile, then looked back at his book. "Give me a case to put my visage in. A visor for a visor. What care I…what curious eye doth quote deformities? Here the beetle brows shall blush for me."

"Stop there. J.R., make a note in your copy that's when you'll put on your mask." Mr. Peters sprung into a standing position. "Great work. We'll pick up here tomorrow."

Everyone slowly unfolded themselves from the metal chairs.

"Okay," Bree mumbled, "maybe Mr. Peters knew what he was doing."

I frowned. Because I couldn't believe he'd looked in my eyes during his "be rough with love" line. What did *he* have to be mad about? And though I hated being on this stage with my enemies, I really hated the fact Bree and Mr. Peters might be right about him.

Chapter Eight

Day one of blocking was always the worst, and the moment I walked outside I took a long, deep breath and slowly released the air. My eyes then landed on my sister, sitting on the step closest to the school's front door. She had on her turquoise Beats headphones and was bobbing her head in time to the music coming from her phone.

I tapped her on the shoulder, and she hooked her headphones on her neck.

"Dad told you to wait inside until we were done."

She groaned. "I was soooo bored and tired of being in there. It's too nice of a day. And there was only so many times I could listen to Mr. Peters say 'That's *not* where you belong.'"

I wanted to say it always looked like a hot mess when we started blocking. But I had to agree with her. It had been nothing but clumsy confusion because we had to imagine our spots on stage with all the scenery and props, and while we held our books so we could deliver our lines. All this had proven highly difficult for the newbies. Except for one. Public Enemy #1 knew most of his lines, too. Including his Queen

Mab monologue. Then again, it's not like Mercutio had that many lines, since he died about halfway through the play.

Thinking of him reminded me he would be coming out the same doors any second and, most likely, with *her* cemented to his side. "Let's go." I rushed down the remaining steps.

"I didn't get a chance to see when I was in there, but is jerk-face still doing well?"

"Yes." And that's all I needed to say about that.

Michelle seemed satisfied with my simple response. Or sensed my snide inflection. She put her headphones back on as we turned right at the corner to head east.

I pulled my phone from the front pocket of my backpack, then my earbuds. My Visualization Playlist might improve the crabbiness I'd been feeling at the fact *everyone* in school couldn't stop talking about Bryan Costello's usual We're in This--insert S-word here--Together party this Saturday night. A huge party Meg and I would be missing due to my oh-so brilliant idea.

I shook my head at the same time a gold sedan pulled up alongside us.

We were native San Franciscans and had heard the "Stranger Danger" speech. But I'd also watched enough *Datelines* and *48 Hours* with Dad that my instincts worked in overdrive.

I smoothly switched places with Michelle, walking on the outside, as the car's passenger window came down.

"Hi there," the man driving the car said.

He smiled, a bit too much like a Cheshire Cat for my comfort level. He had his blond, shaggy head angled left and down, while still managing to keep his car straight.

"Can you girls tell me how to get to Ocean Beach?"

Michelle then noticed the car. Her steps slowed and she removed her headphones.

"Turn around and go west," I responded as I looked away from him.

"Sounds easy. Can I give you two a ride somewhere first? You look like sisters."

His last comment hung in the air for a few seconds. Then every part of me felt violated. To the point I shivered.

My heartbeat accelerated as I gripped Michelle's hand and walked faster.

In the two years I'd been walking to and from high school, I had never encountered anything like this. Disgusting cat-call whistles, sure, especially when Meg and I were together. But none of those creeps had ever stopped.

"We're fine." I couldn't believe this guy hadn't swerved off the road yet. And was he the *only* person out driving today? The only other cars in sight were parked.

"I'm just being neighborly. You two look like you live around here, so I'm sure giving you a ride home won't be out of my way."

Those statements verified my suspicion his needing directions to Ocean Beach had been a giant ruse, and I halted. He slammed on his breaks.

I took two shaky steps back and faced him, while making sure Michelle stayed behind me. "We don't want a ride and if you don't leave us alone I'll call the police." I'd spoken loudly and showed him my phone. I hoped both might scare him off.

The creep actually looked startled. Then fast-approaching steps caught my attention.

I turned my head left and did a double take. Because it was *him*.

He stopped beside me, slipped his right arm around my waist despite Michelle being glued to my back, and lowered his head to kiss my temple. "Hi." He leaned back and, looking into my eyes, added, "Thanks for waiting." He tore his eyes from mine to bend down and look at our stalker. "Hey. Is there a problem?"

Stalker-Creep's smile became strained. "No. Just getting directions to Ocean Beach."

"Then you have what you need?"

"Yeah. Thanks." Stalker-Creep eased back into his driver's seat and reminded me of a snake slithering away from an unsatisfying hunt.

I shuddered at the image, and Justin hugged me a bit closer to his side.

I released a soft sigh of relief.

As we watched Stalker-Creep drive off, Justin relaxed his arm around my waist, then removed his phone from his left pants pocket. "Are you guys okay?" He had an eye on the car as he thumbed something onto his phone's screen.

And I realized he was getting the guy's license plate number.

"*Creeper.*" Michelle pried herself from my back. "I didn't think he was gonna leave."

My phone chirped and vibrated with a new text message. I glanced at the screen to find he had texted me the plate number. "Wait—You...still have my number?" I'd deleted his number, and some photos, That Night during a second fit of furious tears.

"I think we should call the police," he said.

"No. We can't." He and Michelle looked at me. "It's just..." I abruptly felt a strong urge to nestle deeper into his arm still around my waist. I also wanted him to give me a *real* kiss. But I couldn't have any of that. Not anymore. So I stepped away from him and his arm.

His face flushed and he took a step back.

"If our dad finds out about this," I tried again, "you know he'll never—not ever—let us walk anywhere in this city, alone, again." I already rarely drove anywhere. I couldn't lose my walking freedom.

"She's right." Michelle eyed him. "Never."

Frustration and anger flashed through his eyes. "But the call can be anonymous. And what if the guy has already moved on to other—you know what? I'll take care of it."

I stared at him.

"But right now I'm walking you guys home." He met my stare, unyielding and almost daring me to challenge him.

I hesitated, then said, with all the honesty I felt, "I think that might be a really good idea." Pride had no place in this specific situation.

His posture relaxed at the same time Michelle said, "Works for me."

We started walking. My sister had ended up between us, with him on the outside.

I stole a sideways peek at him. He looked left and behind us, and that's when I noticed he didn't have his backpack.

"Where did you come from?"

He glanced at me. "School." He went back to eyeing our surroundings.

Okay. Stupid question. Maybe that encounter had affected me more than I thought.

"But how did you know what was going on?"

"My mom was picking me up when I noticed you two. And the car. I threw my backpack in her car and told her I was going to walk home."

Michelle and I exchanged a wide-eyed look since he lived blocks away in the Marina District. His walk from our building would take him at least twenty minutes.

"How's eighth grade?" he asked my sister while still keeping an eye out for the guy.

"It's okay. I guess. I'm soooo ready for high school,

though. But I think I'm going to like English this year. We're reading *The Outsiders,* and I can't put it down."

Michelle, like our dad, was more into math and science. My two least favorite subjects.

He continued talking with her, his eyes on alert, and my pulse approached normal.

He'd always been good with Michelle since he also had a younger sister. But his sister, Beth, was eight years younger than him.

As we continued walking, Michelle's chatter filling the space between us, my mind drifted to him slipping his arm around my waist, followed by the brief kiss on my temple. An oh-so familiar display of affection I loved and that he'd started once our friendship catapulted into boyfriend-girlfriend status right before spring break. And much to the surprise of many kids in our class, including a specific someone he'd never looked twice at until—I concentrated on the much happier memory of us. Even though it was bittersweet.

Weeks of friendly banter had turned into a month of serious flirting after he'd stopped dating some girl from another private school. And all the emotional and physical tension led us to an afternoon right after school. In my bedroom. Where we were supposed to be studying for our Biology midterm. Dad had been at work and Michelle at a friend's house. He'd been scrutinizing my Vision Board when he noticed my special picture.

"That has to be you with your mom and dad?" He'd leaned in for a closer look.

"Yeah." I'd been sitting cross-legged on my bed, but something compelled me to get up and join him at the desk. "It was taken after her first performance in *My Fair Lady.* She was Eliza Doolittle. I wasn't quite two years old then."

He'd glanced at me. "How did she die? If you don't mind me asking."

My smile had slipped. "An aggressive breast cancer. I was four and Michelle had just turned two. We really only know her through stories. And photos."

"Wow, that's..." His voice had faded into nothing as he focused again on the picture. "She must've been really talented. So are you. I've liked watching you in the plays."

My face had become hot, and his crimson, before we shared a quick, awkward laugh.

"I think your bluntness is rubbing off on me," he'd said, not quite looking at me.

"It occasionally gets me into trouble, though."

He'd given me his crooked smile; the tummy somersaults had started weeks earlier.

"You're being honest. And there's nothing wrong with being who you are." His smile had, incredibly, turned shy. "I play the piano. I'm pretty good, too."

I'd been so stunned by his confession my mouth had actually dropped open.

"I get it from *my* mom." His smile had disappeared. "But I don't talk about it since it's private. Well, Owen knows. And a couple of my other good friends I've known forever."

That had snapped me out of my shock. "Why did you tell me? I mean, I'm flattered—"

"Because you get it. Being a performer. And I trust you." Our eyes had locked while he spoke, and we leaned closer together. "Do you know your eyes have green in them?"

I shook my head, and he'd hesitated for a breath before pressing his lips to mine.

They had been warm. Delectable. And he'd tasted like the mint gum he'd been chewing earlier. But as I started sinking into him and our unplanned kiss, he'd pulled away.

"I'm sorry."

I'd peered at him, and as the Justin Richardson fog lifted I'd asked, "Why?"

He had laughed. A bit nervously, too. "I pushed us past the friendship line."

I'd given him a shy smile, though in my head I was doing Snoopy's happy dance in response to *everything* he'd said and done in those few minutes. "What if I'm okay with that?"

The corner of his yummy mouth had curved into a mischievous smile. "Then I'd have to be as blunt and say..." He'd gently cupped my face, our mouths came together, and I'd felt like I was being kissed for the very first—

My foot caught on a raised section of sidewalk and I pitched forward. But he grabbed my arm before I landed on the concrete. When I'd steadied myself, I chanced a glance at him and my sister. He was fighting a smile while she wasn't bothering to fight her giggles.

He released my arm, and my face warmed to the point my body became hot.

"So," I asked when we were walking again, and in a desperate attempt to move beyond the mortification and my trip to our blissful past, "how's Beth?"

"She's good."

"How's everything going with your parents? Did they say anything about the play?"

"It's the same. And no. Not really."

His emotionless replies about his parents didn't surprise me. I was one of the few people who knew he had a fragile relationship with them. They weren't around much due to their careers. His dad was a big-time architect and his mom played piano in the symphony.

"What did your friends say about it?"

He shrugged. "They were surprised and laughed a little bit, but what would they say? They're my friends."

Okay.

I didn't know if I wanted to hear his answer to my next question since I really missed hearing him play. There were a few things I couldn't stomach the thought of him doing with *her* and playing the piano was one of them. But I had to know. "Been playing the piano?"

"No. Been too busy."

A part of me felt relieved. But then the irrational, jealous part imagined him being too busy with Public Enemy #2. The rational part, though, knew he also had to be on overload when it came to homework and learning his lines that included Romeo's. Thinking that didn't stop me from *wanting* to ask how he'd been busy. But thank goodness for my common sense.

When we reached our building's front stoop a few minutes later, Michelle sent him a quick goodbye wave and headed up the stairs.

I stopped and faced him. Our eyes met, and I didn't know what to say. Then more memories filled my head. Of us talking and laughing while he walked me to the downstairs door too many times to count. And all the kissing. Like we'd never see each other again.

"I'll wait to leave until you guys are inside."

His voice snapped me back to the present.

I gave him a hesitant, half smile. "Thank you. For what you did."

He gave me his crooked smile, and my stomach did its usual somersaulting.

"You were doing fine, DQ." He laughed softly. "As usual."

His compliment sounded genuine. And like the Justin Richardson I'd fallen for back in the spring.

I could only think to say, "Thanks," then walked up the stairs.

Once we were behind the downstairs door, I turned to wave at him. But he was gone.

Chapter Nine

"We're hungry." Michelle bounced up as I walked into the kitchen. "Where's Dad?"

"In his room. Writing. And he put me and Meg in charge tonight."

"Does that mean you're paying for the pizza?"

I stared at my sister's pink face.

She and five of her closest friends had been giggling uncontrollably while they turned our living room into the space for her pre-birthday slumber party. Her birthday was Monday.

She had her dark-blonde hair pulled up in a knot, and wore a pink and black pajama set. The T-shirt said, "I'm a teenager. To save time, let's just assume that I'm always right."

I smiled and pointed at the T-shirt. "Is that new? And he didn't leave me his credit card. So get in there and get out."

"Dad bought it for me as an early birthday present, because I soooo needed new pajamas for tonight." She bounced in the direction of Dad's room.

The buzzer then thundered through our condo. Seconds

later I opened the front door and Meg presented a covered pan.

"Brownies with walnuts. Your dad's favorite."

I shook my head. "You do know he's not the one having the slumber party. And how did you know he and your parents would say yes to this plan?"

Our plan being we were grounded so why couldn't we be grounded together here.

She walked into our foyer and closed and locked the door. "Your dad can be a pushover. And you know how much my parents like him."

Michelle skipped out of his room, then closed his door and went back to her friends.

Meg glanced at his door as we walked by and whispered, "Is the real-life Dr. McDreamy writing tonight?"

She only called him that when we were alone.

"Yes. And he put us in charge of Michelle's slumber party. It was one of his other conditions to you coming over."

That and we couldn't "put one foot outside this condo." And having Meg here, on this particular Saturday night, would be worth dealing with my sister and her giggly friends.

Once we were in the kitchen, she frowned and set the pan down.

"But he'll come out at some point. Right?"

I stared at her. "Meg, seriously. He's my dad."

Her silly, schoolgirl crush on Dad started when we were in middle school. It had gone away when she and Owen became serious after going to last year's fall dance together. But now that they, too, were no more, it seemed her crush had returned.

"He's good looking. For an old guy."

He could be considered a catch. Being tall—a gene Michelle inherited since she was already an inch taller than me —classically handsome and in great physical shape due to the almost daily workouts on his exercise bike. He made a good living, too. But his hours were sometimes tough. His patients also occasionally affected him since he often dealt with the rougher side of San Francisco. Dealing with the city's darker side had inspired his book.

"So," Meg quietly said, "kids are already showing up to Bryan's party."

I nodded.

Bryan, now a senior, threw this party and his end-of-year party--It's Finally Effing Over. Almost everyone went to his parties because he invited everyone. He, like Natalie, was uber-rich and his parents traveled a lot.

Meg and I went to this party last year. But his end-of-year party had been so much better. Because I'd gone with *him*. The night had also ended in an equally fun and dizzying make-out session in the car that lasted until right before my curfew.

I pushed the memory from my mind and said, "Sorry we're missing it."

She shrugged. "I'm sure he and Owen went."

I couldn't argue with her since *he* wouldn't miss Bryan's party. They were pretty good friends and soccer teammates.

"And not alone," she muttered. "It's probably better we're not there."

Something else I couldn't argue with. Or think about. Still, Bryan's parties were the most popular parties thrown during the school year.

Michelle and her friends then pounced on us and started to loudly call out their orders.

Meg and I looked at each other with wide eyes as their voices became louder. Then Meg sneezed. Probably because all of them smelled like they'd drowned themselves in perfume. The super sweet kind of perfume with a cutesy name like Pinkalicious.

I felt the beginnings of a headache from the smell and

leaned toward Meg. "I'm glad my dad let you come over tonight. But he definitely won this round."

* * *

Meg and I were curled up in our favorite spots on the cushy sectional couch in my living room when I caught Dad rushing into the kitchen with his empty plate.

"Hi, Dr. Mc—Dr. Pashen. Did you like your pizza?"

I smiled and threw popcorn into my mouth.

"Yes, Meg, thank you," he replied with a trace of exasperation.

"I made you—I mean, I made brownies. With walnuts."

"I'm full right now, but I'll have one later," he said, and escaped back to his room.

Meg returned to her phone. "Well, the party's looking like a typical Bryan rager. And it looks like Warren, Jade, and Nate are sticking pretty close together. That's good." She glanced at me. "But they wish we were there. And say hi."

Yikes.

"Natalie's there, too. But with her friends. I guess Lexi and Paige decided not to go."

I wasn't sure how much more play-by-play of the party via Snapchat I could stand. At least Michelle and her friends had settled down. And I'd opened a window to help get rid of their pink perfume smell, which had also helped my headache go away. All six of them were now stretched out on their sleeping bags, right in front of our massive television. But they were focused more on their phones than on the Netflix movie.

They were subjecting me, and because of my strong objections, to *Gnomeo & Juliet.*

I, being a total snob when it came to Shakespeare, felt the 1968 *Romeo and Juliet* was the *best* movie version. And I absolutely loved *West Side Story.*

"No signs of the two jerk-offs in any of the photos."

I was about to beg her to stop the torture when my phone chirped and buzzed.

I stuffed more popcorn into my mouth and picked up my phone beside me on the couch. And I stopped chewing when I saw the familiar number I'd long-since deleted.

I sat up and stared at the message. An image I couldn't make out.

"Kass, what is it?"

I finished chewing and swallowed. "I don't know."

I removed the popcorn bowl from my lap and swiped the message. I typed in my password and went right to my messages. Where I was confronted with a picture. Of them. Sitting very close and facing one another. He held a plastic cup —was he drinking? And she, also drinking, was laughing. At something he must've said.

The picture reminded me of That Night. And I couldn't breathe. Because of the piercing pain in my chest. Then the junk I'd been eating twisted inside my stomach.

"I need the bathroom."

I darted into the bathroom, closed the door, and headed right for the toilet.

After I'd emptied my stomach and flushed, I struggled to catch my breath. The picture of them wouldn't stop glowing in my brain, and tears burned my eyes.

The door handle jiggled. Meg slipped inside, and she closed and locked the door. She knelt beside me, and I couldn't stop my hot, soul-wrenching tears. Just like That Night after he'd eagerly dropped me off.

"I can't...breathe," I managed to say around my tears.

She frowned and picked up my phone where I'd dropped it in order to fling the lids open. She knew my password and was then staring at the photo.

"How could he do something like that to me? And after

what he did for me and my sister?" I moaned thinking about my moment of stupid weakness. Staring into his perfect hazel eyes and smiling as we stood outside my building.

She focused on me. "Kassidy, J.R. is many things. But he's not *this* cruel." She shook her head, her ponytail flying. "I know that bitch did this. Probably with Brandy's help. She must've, somehow, gotten his phone, saw your number—you said he still had it when you were telling me about Stalker-Creep—and they did this."

"But his password..." I rested my forehead on the toilet's edge and started my deep-breathing exercises.

We'd been sappy-love-song happy until we started arguing a few days before That Night. And he'd never shared his phone's password with me.

We heard a soft knock and, "Kassi? Are you okay?"

"Everything's fine, Michelle. Go back to your party. She had too much junk food."

I could just hear her retreating footsteps.

"Kass, he didn't knowingly send this picture."

I sniffed and said, "Maybe...maybe not. But he's still going to hear about it."

Chapter Ten

I marched into school and went to the second floor. I wanted to catch him before first period. And, as luck would have it and I cleared the steps, I caught a glimpse of him heading left, right before he disappeared from view.

I walked to the middle of the hallway, then followed—more like stalked—him. The hallway was somewhat filled with students at their lockers and on their way to class. But absolutely nothing would have stopped this confrontation.

Fury had long since replaced the Saturday night meltdown that would be my last.

"Justin Richardson," I called out, "I need to talk to you."

His steps came to a slow pause, which caused mine to halt.

Kids walked by us as he stood with his back to me. I could tell they were trying not to stare, and laugh, at the scene about to unfold.

His head fell back on his shoulders. He stared up at the ceiling for a breath before leisurely turning. And his physical appearance deflated me. But only a fraction.

With the uniform, his tousled hair and just enough dark stubble to be considered, well, totally *hot*, he looked like a preppie bad boy. But this morning's look wasn't normal for him.

"What do you want, DQ?" He looked at his watch as a very nosy boy accidentally brushed against him. "I've been here five minutes." His right arm dropped to his side. "What could I possibly have done to piss you off? Except invade your air space on my way to class."

I walked toward him, and not caring in the slightest kids were listening. Or that he, too, seemed to be having a bad Monday morning. Which was about to get worse.

"You act like some kind've Prince Charming to the rescue last week and then I get that picture from you Saturday night?" I stopped when we were in touching distance. And I noticed his normally hypnotizing eyes were bloodshot and heavy with exhaustion.

I tried, really hard, not to care.

"What are you talking about?"

I'd been prepared for his question and went into my phone. Not even ten seconds later I nearly shoved it into his haggard face.

He squinted at it, then his eyes widened, and his mouth slowly opened.

"What the fu—" He looked at me. "I don't know what that is."

I unleashed my most vicious stare. "Well, it's a picture of you clearly enjoying Sloane Chaplin's dazzling company—"

"Stop. I don't need your sarcasm." He again looked at my phone. What color had been in his face disappeared. He'd probably just realized the picture had, in fact, come from his phone. "I—" He released a frustrated sigh. "I had too much to drink at Bryan's party."

Although I'd already suspected this, his honesty surprised me. And the fact he really had drunk that much since he also wasn't a drinker. Something that had separated him from some of his friends and one of the many reasons I loved—no. I couldn't go there.

Still, the fact he'd let loose to that extent told me something big had to be going on at home. With his parents.

My heart longed to know the what, but I had to stay strong. For my own preservation.

"I somehow misplaced my phone. But then—" I actually saw the light bulb go on in his eyes. Which swiftly hardened. "I know by now that crazy head of yours has twisted that"— he pointed at my phone— "into something it's not. But do you *really* think I had something to do with that picture?" His raised voice was now causing attention.

I really believed he hadn't known about the picture. Knew Meg had to be right about it somehow being Sloane and Brandy. But those thoughts didn't help my anger. I also fully resented his "crazy head of yours" comment.

I lowered my arm. "Maybe you should keep better track of your phone the next time you decide to party with your girlfriend."

He took a step closer, his eyes now radiating apology that also held some...desperation? "Kassidy, I'm really sorry." His eyes hardened again. "But it pisses me off you thought I could do something like that. Especially to you."

We continued glaring at each other, and students continued walking slowly by us.

I believed his apology. But I couldn't find any forgiveness since I was sick of him, them, and the hurt I couldn't escape. Because he'd decided to "try something different" and go for extra credit he never would've needed with him being a smart, hard-working student. Another reason I'd fallen—incredibly hard—for him.

Thinking of the other reasons I'd fallen so hard, I backed away. "I'm really sorry I believed everything you ever said to me."

A muscle in his jaw started to pulse as I continued backing away.

"I also can't believe I'm stuck with you, and her, four days a week after school for the next six or so weeks. Both of you better stay far away from me." I spun from him and headed straight for my locker.

My dark mood hung onto me through the morning and right into horrible Advanced Algebra. That I had with Public Enemy #2.

I was doodling broken hearts, that I also colored black, in my math notebook, when I heard, "Earth to Kassidy Pashen."

I lifted my eyes and caught the T-Rex's aggravated look.

Mr. Thatcher, a bulky and balding man, was one of three math teachers who taught junior-year Advanced Algebra. And was the teacher no one wanted. Between his last name, imposing frame, and cranky personality, he'd gotten his nickname from previous students.

"Good. You are present today."

Several students, of course, giggled.

"Solve this equation for me."

I stared at the horribly complex algebraic equation he'd written on the Smart Board, then heard myself say, "Mr. Thatcher, I don't understand why we even have to learn this level of math if we aren't going to be a math teacher, engineer, or some kind of scientist or doctor. And I know I won't be pursuing a career in any of those things."

The laughter grew in volume as his face turned red. I also thought I truly saw a hint of steam coming from his ears and braced for one of his notorious tongue lashings.

"Other teachers may find your outbursts cute, Miss Pashen, but I'm not one of them. Detention, right after school, with me, in here. Don't be late."

My mouth fell open. "But I have rehearsal—"

"Not my problem. And they'll rehearse without you until

I decide you're free to leave." He returned to the algebraic equation.

I slumped in my seat and, without thinking, glanced at Public Enemy #2. And she gave me a satisfied smile as she mouthed "So. Stu-pid."

I wondered if she'd still be giving me her cat-who-ate-the-mouse smile if Meg pinned her down while I ripped out every one of her bleached-blonde hairs.

* * *

I dragged myself into the auditorium at 4:15. Several cast members were talking and standing in small groups on stage. Including *her*. Several more were seated in the house.

As I walked down the aisle, my eyes landed on Public Enemy #1, alone surprisingly enough, and sitting on the stage's edge, his long legs dangling off the side. He seemed focused on his opened copy of *Romeo and Juliet*.

"Hey," Angelina said when I arrived at the first row.

Bree was sitting with her, too.

Mr. Peters stood at Angelina's left as he talked to Liam, our Tybalt.

"That was a long detention. Even for the T-Rex." Bree smiled sympathetically. "And, just so you know, Sloane felt it was necessary to loudly announce to everyone before rehearsal started that you wouldn't be here for awhile because you had detention with him."

Her behavior didn't surprise me, but it didn't stop me from gritting my teeth, then muttering, "Of course she did."

"What did he have you do?"

"Math."

Drew walked to the stage's edge. "O, Juliet, Juliet." He extended his right arm toward me. "Where have you been my beautiful Juliet? O, it's my love. O, that she knew she were."

Everyone but two people, three including me, started laughing. Even Mr. Peters. On a normal day, I'd be laughing. But I wasn't in the mood for Drew's ridiculousness.

"Knock it off, Drew."

Everyone looked at me. Even Public Enemy #1's head had snapped up.

Public Enemy #2 walked to stand beside Drew. "Just because you were stupid enough to challenge Mr. Thatcher doesn't give you the right to take it out on Drew."

"No one asked for your opinion, Sloane," Bree snapped.

"Bree's right." My other enemy shot Sloane a dark look. "Back the fuck off."

"Justin Richardson," Mr. Peters bellowed, "*language!*"

A tense silence blanketed the auditorium.

"Sorry," he said, and almost sounding contrite. "It slipped out."

On a normal day, every part of me would've enjoyed watching Sloane Chaplin get her scrawny butt handed to her. Especially by her boyfriend who rarely swore, and never in front of teachers. Any adult, for that matter.

But today hadn't been a normal day and I said to him, "Don't you dare defend me."

He returned my hostile stare before looking back down at his book.

"Enough." Mr. Peters formed a T with his hands. "Time out." His arms collapsed to his sides. "I warned you this would happen. But some of you are about three weeks ahead of schedule." He looked at me. "I need you to lose the bad attitude since, now that you're here, I want to run through the balcony scene. So, do whatever you need to do to get into character."

I held onto my groan as I dropped my backpack. I then sat in the nearest seat.

"And Mr. Richardson, if I ever hear you use that kind of

language again, you will be serving detention with Mr. Hathaway. Do you understand me?"

Bree and Angelina gave me a "Whoa" look.

Mr. Hathaway was our principal. And Mr. Peters, known as one of the most easygoing teachers, rarely threatened detention.

"Yes," he answered while still focused on his book.

"We'll start the scene in five."

Okay. I could be a professional, like my mom had been, and shake off this lousy day to become an infatuated Juliet for forty-ish minutes.

I closed my eyes and started my deep-breathing exercises.

Chapter Eleven

I stood at the school office copy machine, spitting out copies for Mr. Lowry.

Mrs. Chaplin then breezed in and started talking with Mrs. Oliveri. She sat at the front desk and also managed the office.

Mrs. Chaplin had her concert choir kids during this period. But sometimes her back-up pianist was in the room to work with them. They were talented, too. A different kind of talented than her show choir, which included her "perfect" daughter.

Mrs. Chaplin passed me to go to her mailbox, but on her way out she stopped and faced me. "I heard about your detention with Mr. Thatcher."

I looked over and found myself staring into *her* arctic eyes.

"Did Mr. Peters tell you if you get one more detention, he'll have no choice but to remove you from the play?"

I stared at her and blinked like a total dummy. "No."

"Theater Department policy." She wore a trace of a cold smile that matched her eyes. "I'll have to remind him. But it isn't often we have issues with the students who are, usually, carefully chosen to be in our plays. Because they're also representing the school."

My entire body flushed.

She pierced me with her eyes a few extra seconds before turning and leaving the office.

I chanced a glance at Mrs. Oliveri, watching Mrs. Chaplin disappear from view. She had her nose turned up, then she looked at me and her expression relaxed.

"Don't pay any attention to her," she quietly said. "You'll be fine. Just watch it with Mr. Thatcher. And I can't wait to see the play." She laughed. "It's my favorite Shakespeare play. I was so tickled when I heard Mr. Peters had chosen it. How are rehearsals going?"

I managed a smile and gathered my copies. "It's rough right now, but we'll get there." I headed in the same direction as the Wicked Witch with a Capital B. "Thanks, Mrs. Oliveri."

"Anytime, sweetie."

Just. Perfect.

I'd unintentionally acquired a new, much more powerful enemy.

My mood improved significantly the moment I walked into the club meeting—Meg had been released on probation a day before me—and Natalie gave me a white T-shirt.

"I had these made for us," she proudly stated. "I *never* wear white, but you couldn't see the logo on the black version."

I laughed. Our club's logo was centered at the top of the shirt. A fairly large, bright red heart with a black slash through it. Pacifica Academy was in small black print below the logo.

"Aren't these flippin' awesome?" Meg asked. "Look at the back."

I turned mine over and laughed again. In bold black print was **PRESIDENT**.

"Mine says vice president. Everyone else's says member."

I looked at Natalie. "I can't believe you did this." And the shirts told me there had to be way more to Natalie Carlisle than most students knew—including her close friends.

"I figured since we're doing this, we needed to do it right and really make it official. We can wear them on school-spirit days." She laughed in her maniacal way and silence fell.

We were staring at her. And holding our shirts. Which caused her to roll her eyes.

"All of you need to stop looking at me like I'm a baby animal doing something cute." She sat down and focused on me. "Get us caught up on the *Romeo and Juliet* drama."

I dropped my backpack and, still holding my shirt, sat down. I caught them up and shared my encounter with Mrs. Chaplin. I'd also kept an eye on Ms. Simmons as I talked, though we were at the back of her classroom. But she appeared focused on her computer.

"Well," Lexi began, absently playing with her hair, "I've heard my mom say, many times, 'the apple doesn't fall far from the tree' when she's complaining about my dad and grandma. I guess Sloane can't help being who she is when you think about her mom."

"Lexi, she's an evil—" Natalie glanced at Ms. Simmons, now typing on her computer. "Bitch," she whispered. "Just like Mrs. Chaplin. I don't know why she acts like a queen around here. My friends can't stand her. Or Brandy. And I don't know what J.R. was thinking when he—" She looked at me. "Sorry."

I gave her a tiny smile.

"Mrs. Oliveri was right, though." Meg slipped her arm around my shoulders. She pulled me close for a quick, sideways squeeze. "You're going to have to control yourself."

A complete understatement. *Romeo and Juliet* was too important to me and my future. I needed a letter of recommendation from Mr. Peters for the Youth Summer Drama

Session. But, first, I had to conquer my role as Juliet. Just like my mom had so many years ago.

"Oh!" Warren leaned toward me. "I have something I've been dying to tell you. But it's about him. And her."

I groaned. "I don't want to hear about Monday anymore. Or Bryan's stupid party."

It hadn't taken long for our hallway confrontation to make its way through the school.

"Bryan's party wasn't great," Jade stated. "Except for Brandy throwing up her Jell-O shots in the kitchen." She, Nate, Warren, and Natalie burst into laughter. "The party would've been better if *all* of us had been there. And for the next party we'll have our shirts to wear."

"It's cool you like the shirts. But that's so not happening." Natalie looked at Jade whose smile fell. "And I agree. The party sucked. Most of the boys at this school are Neanderthals. And I *once* thought J.R., Owen, and Gavin were the rare exceptions, but now..." She rolled her eyes.

"Uh, you're sitting with two boys at this school," Nate said, sounding offended.

"I said most. And college boys, including my ex-dick—" Her eyes went to Ms. Simmons, and I wondered how Natalie made it through the school day with such a potty mouth. "College boys are no better. But I like you and Warren. Because you two can have a conversation that has nothing to do with sports and hook ups, and getting trashed at parties."

"Well, I just wasn't ready for a Bryan Costello party," Lexi admitted.

"Most of the juniors and seniors scare me. That's why I didn't go."

"Sweetie, we'll help you get over that," Warren assured Paige. "Can we get back to my story? Please? Kass needs to hear this, because what I heard was very interesting. On Monday—"

"*Warren.*"

"Just listen." He gave me a testy, impatient look. "On Monday, I was heading to the cafeteria for lunch, when I caught J.R. and Sloane in the middle of a hot argument. He was in her face and didn't seem to care who saw it."

I straightened since this story could explain why they'd been noticeably detached at rehearsal. I hadn't heard they'd broken up, but their abrupt union hadn't seemed like big news, either. Not like when he and I started dating. I assumed it was because everyone expected him to "snap out of it" when it came to me and weren't surprised when he moved on.

I shook my head and refocused on Warren.

"You heard everything?" Natalie had been on her phone but put it aside.

"Sort've. I didn't want to be that obvious. But they weren't too far from my locker and I made an unplanned stop." He smiled. "It sounded like he was M-A-D, mad about her" —he raised both hands and did air quotes— "'screwing with his stuff.'"

Paige giggled.

"Not *that* stuff. There was something about a password, too."

Meg and I looked at each other before she asked, "What did she say?"

"She was being quieter than him, so I didn't catch that. But I did hear her ask why he still had your effing phone number."

"He still has your number?" Lexi asked me. "But, maybe, the whole angry, deleting numbers and pictures is a woman-scorned thing."

"No." Nate shrugged. "I got rid of everything Rachel off my phone. And when I found out about her and my ex-friend, I deleted his number and photos I had of us."

"Good for you." Jade smiled at Nate, then looked at Warren. "Did you hear his answer?"

All my club members were leaning forward, with the exception of Nate, and latching onto everything Warren said. Their interest resembled support, and I couldn't help but smile.

"Something about it being none of her business, then he left." His eyes landed on me. "Your turn. What was that all about? Because it had to be connected to your hallway spat."

A part of me wanted to spill the whole story. But a stronger part of me, the part who no longer wanted them inside my head, didn't feel it was worth the breath. Even though I did feel a little more vindicated knowing he'd, and not nicely, confronted her about the picture.

Still, I couldn't help but wonder why he had kept my number.

I looked at my club members and said, "It was an unimportant misunderstanding."

They looked disappointed, but Meg swooped in with, "We need to plan our next club activity, where we can wear our shirts, since Kass and I are done being grounded."

Best, best friend. Ever.

"Meg?"

Her head, and everyone else's, turned in the direction of the familiar voice.

Owen stood just inside the classroom, his backpack hanging off his right shoulder. His light-brown eyes were locked on Meg. I'd always found him to be cute in a jock-meets-outdoorsman way. And great for Meg. Until he'd proven to be another jerk-face.

Meg stood. "What are you doing here?" she asked with not a bit of kindness.

"I'm sick of this." He stepped further into the classroom. "Can we talk?"

All eyes were on them. Even Ms. Simmons was watching over her reading glasses.

"No. I'm busy right now." She crossed her arms. "And if I weren't, the answer would still be no. How did you even know where to find me?"

"The whole school knows about this club."

I couldn't tell, by the way he said it, if that was a good or bad thing. But if most of the Pacifica Academy student body thought of this club as a joke, they were keeping their opinions to themselves. A definite point in our favor.

He glanced nervously at Ms. Simmons and back at Meg. "I miss you," he mumbled.

Her posture relaxed. "You do?"

I willed her to stay strong.

"Can we do this somewhere else? Please?"

Her gaze swept over us and Ms. Simmons, now battling a smile. "No. What do you want, Owen?"

I smiled, and very smugly.

His shoulders wilted, and he walked toward Meg. "That whole thing with Brandy?" He stopped less than a foot away from her and us. "It's not what you think."

Meg remained silent.

"We were walking out of school when she tripped over the door sill."

I wanted to laugh. Brandy Espinosa seemed to be having a bad start to the school year.

"She said it hurt her ankle. I was helping her—"

"Which, I could tell, she greatly appreciated."

"I didn't know she was going to throw her arms around me and kiss me."

I froze and watched Meg's mouth inch open.

Our fellow members seemed as frozen by this information as me and Meg.

"You...kissed? Right there?" Her voice had been soft. And broken.

He frowned. "Why do you sound so surprised?"

"Because I only saw you with your arms around her."

His face paled and reminded me of his friend's reaction to the picture on my phone.

"*That's* all you saw?"

"*That* was enough. Especially since it was Brandy Espinosa. Picturing you kissing—"

"Meg, she kissed *me*. I swear I wasn't expecting it."

"Owen and Meg," Ms. Simmons said in a raised voice, "stop. Right now."

If not for the fact he'd wronged my best friend, I might've felt sorry for him since he looked truly ashamed and apologetic.

Ms. Simmons stood. "Owen, this is a club meeting. Unless you're planning on joining it today, I think it would be best if you left."

He looked at Meg with such longing it caught my breath.

"Meg, I know we can—"

"You heard Ms. Simmons." She leaned forward. "Go. Away."

Frustration replaced the longing. He looked—more like glared—at me, the other members, then gave Meg one final, crushed look before leaving the classroom.

I placed my shirt on the desk, stood, and put my arm around Meg for a sideways hug.

The room remained silent until Natalie muttered, "Awkward."

"And I suppose now wouldn't be the best time," Jade mumbled, "to mention the Falling in Love at First Sight Dance. I'm on the student activities committee."

"Jade, no offense, but I hate school dances." Natalie went back to her phone.

"And I'm not sure I'm really ready for something like that," Lexi quietly admitted.

"But it is coming up pretty fast," Jade finished.

Warren eyed Meg. "You going to be okay?"

She nodded, and we sat back down.

"How come you guys never plan a Halloween dance?" he then almost whined.

"That idea is always rejected by our advisor. Something about teachers and chaperones not wanting to deal with inappropriate costumes. So the committee came up with Falling in Love at First Sight." Jade smiled. "Don't you get it? *Fall*-ing?"

No one spoke. Though I was certain all of us did get it.

"Anyway," she continued, "the theme was also inspired by *Romeo and Juliet*." She folded her hands under her chin. "*Please* promise me you'll think about going—"

"Jade, I don't do school dances," Natalie interjected.

"Because I think it would be a great club activity." Jade dropped her folded hands to her lap and squared her shoulders. "Deal?"

Going to the dance hadn't once crossed my mind. For obvious reasons. But as a club activity, it could be fun. Maybe.

"It's a deal," Warren answered for everyone. "And considering what just happened, I think our next activity should be lunch and a movie date with John Tucker."

"Who's that?" Nate asked. "A new club member?"

"No, silly." Jade smiled. "He's talking about the movie *John Tucker Must Die*."

Most of the girls giggled since Warren had made a great movie choice. Even though it was kind've old.

"And hopefully you won't feel left out during the movie."

Nate frowned at Warren.

"So, if no one has plans Sunday afternoon, and in honor of Kass and Meg no longer being grounded, let's meet up at my place this time. Right at noon. Wear your shirts. I'll get my mom to make food. But bring your own drinks since all we ever have is water and wine."

Warren stood, followed by my other five members.

I smiled since hanging out with them was exactly what I needed after this week. But when I glanced at Meg, unsmiling and staring at her desk, my smile disappeared.

"Meg, don't think about him."

She blinked and straightened. "I'm not."

She stood, and I wanted to hunt down Owen Garrett and give him a hard kick.

Chapter Twelve

Lady Capulet walked toward me. "Thou's hear our counsel. Thou knowest my daughter's of a" —her eyes narrowed as she looked me up and down— "*pretty* age."

I wanted to claw her cold eyes out of her sockets, but held my angelic, rapt expression.

Bree, my nurse, laughed and looked at me. "Faith, I can tell her age unto an hour."

"She's not fourteen."

"I'll lay fourteen of my teeth—and yet, to my teen be it spoken, I have but four—" Bree reached out and gently squeezed my cheeks, and I smiled. "She is not fourteen." She removed her hand and, per Mr. Peters's cutting, went right to, "Peace, I have done. God..."

Her face went blank and we giggled.

"Sorry," she said to Mr. Peters, sitting cross-legged near the stage's edge.

"God mark thee to his grace..." he offered.

She nodded and said, "God mark thee to his grace...thou

was the prettiest babe." She gave me a blinding smile. "I might live to see thee married once, I have my wish."

Public Enemy #2 consulted her copy of the play. And we waited, holding our places.

She looked up, assaulted me with her usual, blistering stare, and I had to concede Mr. Peters had cast the icy Lady Capulet very well.

"Marry, that 'marry' is the very theme I came to talk about. Tell me, *daughter* Juliet, how stands your disposition to be married?"

My smile fell. "It is an honor I dream not of."

She again consulted her copy, and I glanced at Bree whose eyes rolled upward.

How could she not know most of her lines by now? She hardly had any.

"Well, think of marriage now. Younger than you...um...here in Verona, ladies of esteem, are already mothers. For I was your mother much on these years...that you are now a maiden—maid—Thus in brief: The County Paris seeks you for his love."

Bree gave me another blinding smile and laughed. "A man, young lady. Lady, such a man, as all the world—why, he's a man of wax."

Lady Capulet smiled tightly. "Verona's summer have not such a flower."

Bree leaned forward. "He's a flower, in faith—a very flower."

"What say you? Can you love the gentleman? He'll be—I mean, this night you shall behold him at our feast." *She* looked at her copy and back at me. "Speak briefly, can you like of Paris's love?"

"I'll look to like...if looking liking move." I paused for a breath, then added, "But no more deep will I endart mine eye...than your consent gives strength to make it fly."

"Let's stop there," Mr. Peters said. "We need to start the next scene."

"Do I *have* to say pretty in that line?" Lady Capulet whined. "Can't I say marrying?"

He frowned at her, and my patience, that I'd been determined to hold onto, snapped.

"And maybe Lady Capulet should start learning her actual lines before changing them." I returned her sneer. "It's not like she has *that* many."

Silence fell. Until a Montague—the boys waiting in the wings, stage right, for their scene that followed this one—made a high-pitched, angry cat snarl.

Several cast members laughed, myself and Public Enemy #2 not included.

"Thank you for that charming tension breaker." Mr. Peters eased into a standing position. "Kassidy and Sloane, I'd like to talk to you off stage. Montague boys get ready. You need to be laughing and horsing around when you come on stage."

I trailed Mr. Peters down the stage left steps, with Sloane a distant second.

"Ladies," he said when we were standing beside the first row, "whatever this is" —he mimed a circle to encompass us and our animosity— "has to stop. None of us need or want it. From this point on, keep your personal feelings for each other checked at the auditorium doors." He focused on me. "No more comments like that."

I looked away and nodded. Even though *she'd* been nasty first.

"Sloane," he continued, "I know we haven't worked together since *The Bad Seed*, but I have to say, knowing your experience with the musicals, I'm disappointed with your effort."

I tried, really hard, not to smile.

She crossed her arms. "I'm doing the best I can. And why is it she's allowed to wear that shirt when everyone else is still in the uniform?"

I decided as president I would wear my club shirt after school at least once a week. And the giggling I'd received earlier —I'd even caught the jerk-face fighting a smile—hadn't bothered me. There was absolutely nothing wrong with extra advertising.

"I'm not aware of any rule that states theater students can't change their clothes after school. And my advice to you is to try harder."

As he dashed back up to the stage, she faced me, her eyes razor sharp.

"You can lose that smile, DQ." She leaned forward and whispered, "Remember, he's with me. And despite the bitch fit you threw over that stupid picture." She glanced at my T-shirt, then back at me, and smiled. "I think I've changed my mind about that shirt. It's perfect for you." Her smile disappeared. "Because it's pathetic." She stomped away.

A strong part of me wanted to verify with Dad what qualified as justifiable homicide. But I felt certain he wouldn't let me go without answering *his* questions.

The boys ambled onto stage, laughing and jostling each other, and I sat down and started playing with the hem of my shirt.

I didn't care what she thought of my club and the shirt, but I couldn't be sure where her confidence with their relationship was coming from. He'd been keeping his distance from her during rehearsals, though I rarely saw how they were outside of this auditorium.

Totally fine with me, *thankyouverymuch*.

Up until rehearsal, I'd been feeling empowered by our club activity yesterday. We'd laughed our way through the movie about girls getting revenge on heartbreaker John Tucker. Well, not Nate, and I smiled as I remembered his weary "I need to go do something manly. Like drink an entire beer and crush the aluminum can with my forehead" seconds after the movie ended. Our awesome day together had been another reason I'd chosen to wear my shirt.

I heard a burst of laughter on stage, and my eyes landed on Public Enemy #1.

He looked much better than he had this time last week. He'd also been on his best behavior since Mr. Peters's reaming. If something big had been going on in the Richardson home a week ago, the tension must've settled down.

He easily, and arrogantly being Mercutio, said his lines.

I guess Mr. Peters *had* chosen the right boy for Mercutio. Had chosen the right kids for all the important parts. Still, I couldn't shake my irritation and resentment that he'd managed to infiltrate my happy place and *this* play. I also couldn't believe he'd taken to acting so quickly. Like it was some latent talent he'd never been able to express until this school year. If not for the club, I didn't know how I'd get through *Romeo and Juliet*.

I glared at him as he performed his Queen Mab monologue.

I'd wanted my dream role to be effortless. Like I'm sure it had been for my mom when she'd stepped into the role so long ago. And I was embracing Juliet to the best of my ability. But him being here wasn't fair. I didn't care how good he was at playing Mercutio.

I sighed, and was about to stand and head backstage to get ready for my next scene when he faced the house. And his back-to-hypnotizing eyes found mine before he said, "And in this state she gallops night by night...through lovers' brains... and they dream of love."

My breath hitched and I tried to look away as he continued his monologue.

"Over courtiers' knees, that dream on curtsies straight...
over lawyers' fingers, who straight dream on fees...over ladies'
lips, who straight on kisses dream."

He held my gaze for one more beat, then broke our eye
contact to face the boys.

I looked at my lap as I heard his voice become darker. A bit
more frenetic.

Then my entire body started to tremble.

Chapter Thirteen

"Where's Paige?" I dropped my backpack and sat beside Meg on the bottom bleacher. "Did anyone tell her we moved the meeting to out here?"

"I texted her last period," Lexi answered as she played with a lock of her hair.

She was propped against Warren, relaxing against the fence, with her legs stretched out on the highest bleacher. Jade and Nate were lounging beside one another on the next bleacher with their faces angled toward the sun, followed by Natalie, focused on her phone.

Because Ms. Simmons had been absent, I'd received permission from the assistant principal to have a "quick meeting" on the school's rooftop, the closest thing we had to a student quad with it being a big city, private school. It more resembled a school yard with a smaller basketball court and set of bleachers.

"I love living in this city in October," Lexi murmured.

The day being perfect weather at sunny and seventy-five

degrees one of the reasons I'd asked for permission to come up here.

"So, Meg, has Owen tried talking to you since last week?" Jade asked.

"Nope," she said while picking at a deep scratch on the bleacher with her thumb nail. "I just want him to stay away from me." Her strong words didn't match her somber mood.

I scooted closer to her, put my around her shoulders and gave her a quick hug. She responded with a sad, half smile. And I still wanted to kick Owen.

Natalie dropped her phone in her lap. "So is it true she's totally sucking in the play?"

It took me a second to realize she was talking about Public Enemy #2, and I had to laugh. "Pretty much. But how'd you hear about that?"

Natalie, with the exception of me, didn't interact with the theater kids.

"Maddie Harrington told my friend Quinn she's choking during rehearsals."

Maddie had gotten Lady Montague. A really small part considering she, like Lady Capulet, was another musical star, but minus my rival's nastiness.

"Ooh, keep talking." Warren leaned forward. "What else do you know?"

"When did this become the Gossip Club?" Nate peered up at Warren.

"She happens to be the reason our president started this very club. Any news pertaining to her, and J.R., is not sacred. Especially if it helps Kass move on."

"*Any-how,*" Natalie said, "Maddie also told Quinn Junior Mrs. Bitch let it slip the main reason she auditioned was because of J.R. And you."

That unexpected piece of information hung over us. Meg

and I exchanged a brief, shocked look before we turned toward Natalie.

I said, "She told me she was auditioning because it was Juliet Capulet."

"That may have been another reason, but she *so* sounds insecure."

I smiled—a bit like Natalie would—at her words.

Jade giggled. "That's awesome. She needs to be put in her place."

"But maybe she really wanted the part, too?"

"Lexi, if that's true, why is she sucking so bad as Lady Capulet?" I think I saw Natalie's eyes roll behind her sunglasses. "I paid enough attention in freshman English and watched one movie version. It's a small part. And it sounds like she was lucky to get that. But I also heard J.R. is blowing everyone away." She stared at me. "Is that true, Juliet?"

I felt everyone watching me as I softly said, "Pretty much."

I really had no choice but to accept he was talented and let it go. And though he'd, per my threat that Monday morning, been staying away from me, his behavior at rehearsal the other day had rattled me. I couldn't understand why on earth he'd done something so intense.

Warren laughed. "I'm having trouble picturing our soccer star as an artistic performer."

That's because very few kids in school knew the real Justin Richardson. The one who, on my third visit to his house, invited me to sit down beside him at his mom's Steinway grand piano while he played from memory "Let It Be" by The Beatles. He'd even sung the lyrics. Not too terribly, either. After that moment it had become one of my favorite songs.

So. Pathetic.

"Kass," Meg said, "maybe you should consider talking to him?"

Her question, thank goodness, interrupted another trip

down blissful memory lane. "No. Absolutely not. Meg, none of that changes what happened in August." At least I knew Public Enemy #2 wasn't the confident girlfriend she loved to portray.

"Alright. You know what you saw at Owen's party," she snapped, sounding nothing like my best friend.

"I know you're trying to help." She responded with a slight smile, and I then looked at my other club members. "Can we change the subject? Please?"

"I second that." Nate raised his right hand.

"Well, I wholeheartedly agree with Jade, but..." Warren lifted his sunglasses enough to look directly in my eyes. "Meg might have a point, too. He was pretty mad at her last week."

"He was mad at me, too." I shook my head. "What's going on here? This isn't the Get-Back-Together-With-Your-Ex Club."

"Precisely." Jade sat up. "And I have a legit meeting topic. The dance next Saturday?"

My shoulders drooped with relief at her subject change at the same time Natalie groaned.

Jade lifted her chin. "I feel *strongly* we should go together. And not just as an Anti-Love Club, but also as a group of friends enjoying being single."

Going to the dance with them wasn't an awful idea. But what about my enemies?

"I have to say I'm not hating the idea of us going to this dance," Warren said.

Lexi stopped playing with her hair to glance at us. "If we went together, I *think* I could deal."

Jade looked at me. "And you have to go, Kass. You're our school's Juliet."

Perfect. Just what I needed. More pressure on my shoulders.

"Jade, we're an anti-love club." Natalie turned to face her.

"We can't go to a dance with love at first sight as the theme. And I've told you guys I *don't* do school dances."

"The theme is more for decorating purposes."

"Jade's right," Meg said, her voice sounding strong. And more like her. "We can do this. Though there's a huge chance our exes will be there. And with other disgusting people."

"That's the part about all this I'm not loving." Seeing those two together at a dance? With a *Romeo and Juliet* inspired theme? *I'd* never gone to a dance with him. Prom was our last dance of the year, and freshmen and sophomores could only go if invited by upperclassmen.

"Please don't make me go without you." Jade folded her hands under her chin. "I have other friends who are going, but I want *you* guys to be there with me. Because, knowing Gavin, he'll be there. And I thought...maybe...we could wear our shirts?"

Natalie leaned toward Jade. "Have you lost your fucking mind? I didn't get us the shirts so we could wear them to school dances. And isn't there a dress code for these things?"

"Just for prom and Snowflake Formal. Guys, come on. *Please?*"

Jade's arguments were convincing. And I did like the idea of wearing our shirts.

Nate smiled at Jade and shrugged. "I have nothing going on next weekend so I'm in. But do we have to wear the shirts? That might be too obvious. And they're pretty casual."

"Well, I'm in, too," Warren declared. "With or without the shirts."

Natalie moaned. "You guys can't be serious about this."

As Lexi said, "Okay. I'll go," I saw Paige rushing toward us with a girl beside her.

"Hi. Sorry I'm late."

The girl, who had flawless ebony skin, was stifling her sobs and sniffing.

"This is my friend, Alisha. She's also a freshman. And she's here with me to join our club because of Landon Ellsworth. Only this time his jerky response was about the dance."

I would've growled. If Meg and Natalie hadn't beaten me to it.

"What's wrong with him?" I stood and put my arm around the beautiful, heartbroken girl. "Does he think he's a descendant of Zeus?"

"Probably," Paige answered. "He's going with some sophomore."

"Hi, I'm Kassidy."

Alisha gave me a weak smile as she wiped her dark eyes.

Seeing her so distraught over that Landon Ellsworth, and remembering my heartbreak caused by another Pacifica Academy jerk-face, I knew exactly what I needed to do.

I made the rest of the introductions and glanced at Jade. "Count me in for the dance."

I received claps, cheers, and one groan.

"Natalie, you're going." I looked at Paige and Alisha. "We're all going to that dance, together, so don't make any plans. Now we just have to vote on wearing the shirts. Everyone in favor of the shirts raise your hand."

I did a swift count, then nodded.

No matter what, we were a united, immovable force. Nothing, not even seeing exes with their dates or new girl-friends, could bring *us* down.

Chapter Fourteen

I heard munching from the doorway.

I, sitting cross-legged on my bed, looked up to find my sister eating Flamin' Hot Cheetos. I could smell the spicy cheesiness from where I sat and wrinkled my nose.

She came into our room and plopped herself onto my bed. "What'cha doin'?"

"Looking for a super cute way to wear my hair for the dance." I went back to scrolling through all the images on my phone.

"I unloaded the dishwasher. Even though it was your turn."

"Thanks."

"Are there any other chores you want me to do for you?"

I stopped my scrolling to eye her. And based on her syrupy sweet smile she wanted something. So, I put my phone down and said, "I can see right through this. Just tell me what you want."

She released a heavy sigh. "Okay. I was hoping, because you're the bestest big sister, you would let me wear that dress you wore to your birthday dinner to *my* dance this month."

I grabbed my phone and picked up where I'd left off. "You have your own dresses."

"But none of mine are as cute as that one," she whined.

"No."

"You suck."

I ignored her and focused on the images of fancy updos. I wanted to wear my hair up for the dance. A rare hairstyle for me. I preferred my hair hanging loose or in a long wispy braid, a hairstyle *he* really liked, too. He'd told me this not long after we'd started dating while nestling his face between my hair and neck.

"It always smells so good," he'd added before nuzzling the spot below my left ear.

Another display of affection he'd started and swiftly learned drove me the good kind of crazy. Even thinking about him nuzzling *that* spot gave me goosebumps.

I looked at my sister.

Focus.

"I've only worn that dress once and I bought it. Not Dad."

"I promise I won't ruin it. I'm not that irresponsible."

The front door opened and shut, which meant Dad was home from work.

"Did you get *any* homework done today?" I whispered.

"I have tomorrow," she shot back. "Mind your own business, *DQ*."

My temper cracked at the same time Dad appeared in our doorway. And he didn't look completely dead from work.

"Good. You're here." He'd said that to me and seemed oblivious to the tension between Michelle and me. "I need to talk to you girls for a few minutes." He angled his head in the direction of the kitchen. "Meet me in there?"

Michelle heaved herself off my bed and marched from the room.

I couldn't be bothered by her bratty behavior since curiosity had filled my mind.

Our kitchen island counter had become, over the years, our meeting spot. But Dad usually only called these meetings when one or both of us were in trouble, something big was happening at work that would change his hours, or we needed to plan a family vacation.

I perked up at the thought. We normally took a two-week trip during the summer, but we hadn't this past summer because of, well, me. I'd been so caught up in myself and *him* and us, I'd passionately objected to going anywhere for so long. I think I even produced some tears. And Dad, like Meg said, had caved. But, maybe, he'd decided to take us on vacation over the fall break, which fell during the week of Thanksgiving? Or, even better, a longer vacation over winter break? Someplace warm, too. Like Hawaii. We hadn't been there in years. And it's not like I had a reason to be here for the breaks.

I dropped my phone on my bed and practically pranced into the kitchen.

I sat beside my sister at the counter and we stared at Dad. Who looked excited, but also a tad...nervous?

He hesitated, then said, "I have a date. Next Saturday night." He looked at me. "The same night as your dance. And I'm actually" —he laughed— "really excited about it."

Michelle and I exchanged a brief, puzzled glance.

This meeting was about a date?

I masked my disappointment as visions of Hawaii floated from my mind.

"Dad, why are you being soooo dramatic? You've been on dates before."

"But it's been a long time since my last date and, if you remember, it didn't go well."

That date happened over a year ago. He'd met the woman on one of those Internet dating sites. He'd felt the desire to try

Internet dating since it was so popular. But the woman turned out to be married. He'd only found out when the woman's husband followed them to the restaurant and made a scene. She'd thought her husband was out of town.

Not surprisingly, Dad closed his account and hadn't dated anyone since that night.

"Who is she?" I asked.

His dramatics and excitement were a bit unusual.

"She's a new ER doctor at the hospital. Moved here a few weeks ago or so from Sacramento. She's divorced. It happened some time ago."

"Does she have kids?" Michelle asked.

Dad shook his head. "I've gotten the impression it didn't work out."

"Well, does she know about us?"

"Honey, of course she does."

Michelle shrugged. "Is that it?"

"No. Since your sister will be at her dance, and I won't be here either, you'll be spending the evening with your homework. Because you'll still be grounded."

Dad had recently grounded *her* for getting mouthy with the computer teacher at Pacifica Junior Academy who reminded me of the T-Rex.

"But what if I don't have any homework?" Michelle naively challenged.

"Then I suppose I'll have to leave you a list of things you can clean around here. Starting with your bathroom."

She moaned.

"I don't want you on the phone all night, Tweeting or Snapchatting, or doing whatever else it is you do on that thing. And no matter what you choose, I will be checking."

Michelle lapsed into an injured silence.

He transferred his gaze to me. "I won't be able to take you to the dance. Do you think Meg's mom or dad can take you two? And pick you up? In case the date goes..." He finished his sentence with an infectious smile.

I giggled. "Her mom can totally drive us there and back."

"Great." He clapped his hands once. "I feel like cooking tonight. What are you girls in the mood for?"

I giggled again since it seemed Dad was a bit over the moon for this new ER doctor.

He'd always said our mom had been *the one*, her death having been excruciating for many reasons. So seeing him excited over the possibilities made my heart want to sing out loud. This was something we'd never seen in all his years as a single-working dad.

Maybe, just maybe, Cupid's aim was improving.

Chapter Fifteen

Drew and I laughed nervously as we were getting into our places beside each other on the narrow, makeshift bed. The bed would also serve as my "final resting place" during the scene in the Capulet's tomb. But right now, we were beginning scene five in act three, Juliet's Chamber. Also known as the morning after their honeymoon.

Mr. Peters had held off on running through this scene until now, probably because he wanted us to get more comfortable with each other first.

I felt Drew stir, shift away from me, then he was gone and I heard a *thump.* Followed by a burst of laughter from the cast, sitting in the house with Mr. Peters and Angelina.

My eyes flew open, and I sat up and peeked over the side. And I burst into laughter since Drew was flat on his back, because he'd fallen off the bed.

"Mr. Peters," he called out, "I don't think the so-called bed can fit two people."

It really didn't seem longer or wider than a twin bed.

"I would have to agree with you." Mr. Peters sounded

amused and tired. "But now, seeing this scene for the first time, you two aren't in the right places. Not for our matinee audience, anyway."

I had to agree with Mr. Peters on that one.

Drew rolled into an upright position.

"The mansion wall should be up after this weekend," Mr. Peters continued. "Maybe next week we can try this scene with you two on her balcony. But I'm not sure there will be enough room. In the meantime, let's try it again but, Drew, how about you already be up and looking out into the house. As if you're looking out from her balcony?"

Drew nodded and stood.

"Kassidy, I want you sitting on the bed's edge. And we'll see how all that looks. Whenever you two are ready, we'll start with 'Wilt thou be gone?'"

I adjusted my position to let my legs dangle off the side. This bed sat higher than an average bed and with me being on the short side, my feet didn't quite reach the stage floor.

Silence resumed as I tried to become a sleepy, lovesick Juliet. But between everyone in the cast watching us, Drew's fall off the bed, and my stupid nervousness, my giggles were rising from my stomach. I tightened my diaphragm for a few seconds to stop my laughter.

I took a deep breath, then sleepily said, "Wilt thou be gone? It is not yet near day. It was the nightingale, and not the lark, that pierced the fearful hollow of thine ear. Nightly she sings on yond pomegranate tree. Believe me...love...it was" —I battled my giggles now in my throat— "the nightingale," I squeaked.

Hearing my cast mates quietly laughing at my silliness didn't help.

I bit my bottom lip in the hopes pain might snap me out of it. Then Drew looked at me, his eyes wide as he battled a smile. I guess we were all loopy from exhaustion.

"It was the lark...the herald of the morn...no nightingale. Look, love..." Drew, fighting to keep a straight face, glanced at the house. "What envious streaking—" He burst into laughter.

Everyone, including me and Mr. Peters, started laughing with him.

"I'm sorry," Drew said around his laugher. "It's her fault." He pointed at me.

"I tried, really hard, to hold it together, but—" I continued laughing.

Mr. Peters smiled. "It's obvious everyone's tired today so I'm going to call it. Excellent work, though. All of you. It's really starting to come together."

Drew walked toward me. "It's good to see you laughing. You've been kinda serious."

I lifted myself off the bed. "Well, Romeo, all of that was pretty funny."

"It's gotta be tough, though. With those two in the play," he whispered as we headed for the stage right steps. "But J.R.'s been pretty cool. I didn't know him very well until now."

I'd, not surprisingly, heard many of my other theater family members say the same thing about him. Because he'd always been so down-to-earth.

"I've gotten used to seeing them here every day," I admitted.

The fact *they* weren't hanging around each other as much definitely helped. Even now he stood near the front row seats while talking to Cody, Shane, and Liam, his new friends. She stood across the aisle near those seats with Maddie, one of her few other allies. But I knew the two sometimes arrived at and left rehearsal together.

We stopped about a foot away from him and the other boys to collect our backpacks.

"Are you going to the dance this weekend?" Drew asked.

I nodded as I hoisted my insanely heavy backpack onto my shoulder.

"Do you think, maybe, we should go together?"

I halted and looked sharply in his direction.

"You know, because of the whole *Romeo and Juliet* theme?"

Had Drew Chang, one of the few students at Pacifica Academy who could make me laugh out loud, just ask me on a date? To the dance?

My disloyal eyes landed on Public Enemy #1. But he appeared absorbed in his conversation with the three boys. And why did I even care if he'd heard Drew ask me out?

"Well..." My voice faltered since I didn't want to hurt his feelings. I liked Drew—a lot—but in a big brother way. I also didn't feel at all ready to try dating someone new. And he was Warren's unrequited love. "I'm actually going with my club members."

"Right. That club you started." Disappointment settled into his dark eyes. "I get it. But that doesn't mean I won't see you there." He smiled. "And we'll be dancing, my fair Juliet."

"Can't wait." Despite my unromantic feelings for Drew, I really meant it.

Chapter Sixteen

eg and I glanced at each other, I gave her a swift nod, and we walked into the packed gym, the usual location for our dances but prom. That was always held at a hotel downtown.

The designated dance floor, most of the gym but the perimeter, was jammed with students dancing to popular "Like I Do." Jade and the rest of her committee members had decorated the gym using garlands of fall leaves twisted with white twinkle lights. They'd also hung metallic pink and red hearts of varying shapes. Lots of metallic hearts.

It looked like Fall Harvest had mated with Valentine's Day.

Meg went on her tiptoes to scan the gym. The girls, following the almost unanimous vote, decided to wear skinny jeans and heels with our shirts. Meg, after helping me with my updo, had let me flat iron her hair. Her mom's reaction to our outfits had been a raised eyebrow and "I don't think I want to know." But I thought we looked amazing.

"Shit. Kass, everyone's staring," Meg muttered. "I should've voted differently."

Okay. *Some* kids were staring. And pointing as they laughed. But we'd made our choice and come way too far to turn and sprint from the gym like our shirts were on fire.

"Meg, you'll feel better once we find everyone." I removed my phone from my black, crossbody phone case. "I need to text Jade and find out where they are."

I selected Jade from my contacts and Meg said, "We've been spotted."

"By who?" I asked as I tapped out my message of *Where are you guys?*

"The boys." Meg used me as cover as she tried to appear casual while keeping a lowered eye on them. "But don't turn around. It would be too obvious. They're, like, several feet away and diagonal from us. And not looking away. Probably because of the shirts."

I hit send and wanted nothing more than to turn around. "Who's there?"

"It's Owen, J.R., Bryan, and someone else. But his back is to us."

Of course the objects of our scorn, not including Bryan and the other guy, were hanging out at this dance. That's when I realized she hadn't included any girls' names.

"No dates?"

"Not a girl in sight."

Hmm. That was interesting.

"How do *they* look?"

Meg sighed. "Good enough to eat. And kiss for hours and hours. But not in that order."

Now I really wanted to turn around. Thank goodness my phone buzzed.

We're on the dance floor, close to the DJ. Get your asses out here.

"They're dancing. Let's go."

I took a shaky breath, and we walked into the crowd of

dancers. I held my head high since I had a feeling we had an audience. Of *them*. And others who found our shirts hilarious.

We wound our way through dancing students until I spotted the familiar, bright white shirts. Most of our club members were dancing together.

Jade ran up and threw her arms around us. "You two look awesome. We all do."

She grabbed our hands and pulled us toward the dancing circle of Warren, Lexi, Paige, and our newest member, Alisha.

I smiled and watched Warren and Lexi dance with our "baby" members. And not one of my club members, including Jade, seemed to notice the long looks and double takes we kept getting from fellow students.

I looked at Meg.

She cracked a smile as she moved her head in time with the song.

My shoulders relaxed at seeing her relaxing.

"Natalie should be right behind you," Jade said above the music. "And Nate's getting me some lemonade. C'mon!"

Meg and I joined their dancing circle and, within no time, we were smiling as we moved with the music. Then Natalie walked up in really high heels. I had to look up at her.

She'd taken the time to pull her long raven hair into a fancy ponytail. That made my smile grow since she'd been one who'd voted, very strongly, against the shirts.

"So I'm here," she said, "but this is so *not* my kind of music." She leaned closer toward us. "To keep myself from being bored, I decided to hunt down this Landon and shove him off his pedestal. Do you guys know who the little prick is?"

"No," I answered. "But just ask Paige and Alisha."

"Don't do anything to ruin this night because you don't want to be here," Jade whined.

"Jade, relax. I'm just going to play with him for a little while."

As we continued dancing, Natalie walked over to Paige and Alisha. She talked to the girls who angled their heads up and looked around until their eyes brightened. Paige pointed toward the left of us, and Natalie smiled—wickedly—before heading in that direction.

I looked through an opening of kids as Natalie stopped at a blond boy—Landon Ellsworth—who looked not too much taller than me, based on the way he had to look up at her. He also happened to be standing there with a pretty brunette. Probably his date.

I glanced at Meg, also watching Natalie, and we laughed.

Landon Ellsworth would never be able to walk again after Natalie verbally ripped off his male parts. She could be a bit scary. But at this moment her heart was in the right place.

The dance music faded. Seconds later the DJ's voice filtered through the sound system and he said something about "taking it down a notch."

Nate walked up and held two cups of lemonade. "Sorry that took so long." He handed Jade her cup. "I was talking to some guys on the baseball team."

"Did they give you a hard time about the shirt?" she asked.

The opening chords of a slow song filled the gym.

"Yeah. But nothing I couldn't handle."

Definitely a good sign. He'd been the other one who'd voted against the shirts.

Jade returned his huge smile while fanning her face with her free hand. But then she halted at the same time her eyes landed on something behind me. In fact, everyone had stopped to stare at the same spot. A second later I felt two gentle taps on my shoulder.

I whirled from them and became petrified. Literally.

Public Enemy #1 smiled. "Before you open your smart mouth, I swear I come in peace. And to ask you to dance."

My mind went blank, and my eyes blinked rapidly as he stood inches from me and patiently waited for my reply. I tore my gaze from his to look at my club members who were watching us, very closely, their eyes wide with shock. And traces of humor.

I looked back at him. That's when I noticed Meg had been right. He did look good enough to eat, and kiss for hours and hours. And definitely not in that order.

I'd almost forgotten how incredibly yummy he looked in his own clothes.

I lowered my eyes to his lean chest that filled out his blue, untucked button-down shirt *way* too perfectly. He'd rolled the sleeves to his elbows, and I glanced at his defined forearms.

He'd always been so insanely good at being casually hot.

But that didn't stop me from shaking my head and saying, "I don't think that would be a good idea. I'm here with my people tonight." I gestured to my dumbstruck club members.

"DQ, stop being pissed off for five minutes and come dance with me. Please?"

I peeked at Meg. She smiled slightly and shrugged.

Between that, and the fact he'd nicely added the word "please," I said, "Fine."

He held out his hand, and I hesitantly gave him mine.

"We're watching you, Richardson," Warren said in a voice he probably thought sounded threatening.

"I'll try to be gentle with her," he threw over his shoulder as he led me away.

Once we were several feet away from them, he stopped, twirled me once, and I glided toward him. He slipped his left arm around my waist and our hands gently linked.

"So were you the one who decided all of you should wear those shirts?"

I angled my chin up. "No. We voted. Majority won. But I *did* vote to wear them."

He, fighting a smile, said, "Of course you did."

I, not knowing how to respond, stayed silent as we swayed to James Bay's "Us." And I tried, really hard, not to listen to the lyrics that hit too close to home for my comfort level. I also tried, really, really hard, not to notice he'd chosen to wear the cologne I'd helped him pick out. Fresh. Light. And made his neck smell good enough to nuzzle forever.

In a desperate attempt to intercept where my mind went, I asked, "Why are you dancing with me and not what's-her-face?"

His shoulders slumped. "You're determined to be difficult."

"It's a perfectly legitimate question."

"Because I want to. She's not even here tonight." He added something under his breath I couldn't understand before clearly stating, "I rode over here with Owen and Bryan."

That stunned me into more silence.

Had they broken up and it, somehow, hadn't made a dent on the school's gossip mill? Or made it to social media?

"Is it against the rules to say you're looking pretty *wow* tonight for someone who's dressed like her people? And that I've always liked those jeans you're wearing?"

His comment about my snug jeans caused my entire body to heat up. Made worse by the fact he'd said "people" while giving me his crooked smile. Because he knew that smile also drove me the good kind of crazy. Though I wanted to say stop smiling at me like that, I wouldn't give him the satisfaction and chose to focus on his very unexpected compliments.

"Thank you." And I meant it. My T-shirt didn't appear to bother him. He seemed to think it was...cute? But I couldn't be sure if I should be flattered or offended by that. "You look

—" The word scrumptious popped into my mind, but I went with, "Good. Really good."

His mouth fell open in pretend shock. "Dost mine ears deceive me? Did thou just payest me a compliment?"

He'd spoken in a truly awful British accent, and I pressed my lips together to not laugh.

"I know you want to laugh. So, let it out." He placed his head beside mine. "It'll be our secret. I promise I won't tell your people."

My flesh rose at the sound of his voice and his soft breath on my ear.

How could he be so stinkin' adorable and infuriating at the same time?

I needed to take back this conversation. And get my head back on straight in the process. I leaned away from him. "You quoted the Genie from *Aladdin*. Not the play."

"Oh. Right. I watched that movie earlier today with my sister."

The giggles escaped before I could stop them.

His smile grew. "Finally. She does still have a sense of humor."

I quickly composed myself and, still determined to control this conversation, asked, "What's Bethie up to tonight?"

His smile vanished, and I almost felt guilty for my subject change.

"She's with Pearl."

I knew, from seeing it, Pearl the babysitter spent more time with her than their parents.

"The parents are also out tonight. And not together."

I'd never heard him say something like that before and my eyes widened. "Are you...saying what I think you're saying?"

"It's not like they love and respect each other."

"How did you find out?"

"I've suspected it for awhile because of their later than

usual nights and *working* weekends," he muttered. "But when I saw my mom sneaking out the front door one Friday night and into some car waiting for her in our driveway, I knew what she was doing."

That would explain his behavior at the party, as well as his nasty mood and haggard appearance the Monday I'd lashed into him about the picture. That hadn't been his fault.

"I guess I should be relieved Beth's too young to see or understand what's going on."

My heart softened thinking about his adorable, precocious little sister and his unfailing, big-brother protectiveness. Yet another reason I loved—*no*. Nononono.

I, remembering that Monday morning and now knowing what had been going on with him, still felt I needed to say, "Justin, I'm so sorry."

"We need to talk about something else." He shook his head and his smile came back. "How's your dad and sister?"

"Um..." I focused on his abrupt subject change, but normal for him when talking about his parents. "Michelle's grounded for getting mouthy with her computer teacher."

"Huh. Sounds a lot like someone else I know."

I ignored that and added, "And Dad's on a date tonight."

"Really?" He caught my eyes. "How do you feel about that?"

"He deserves to be happy. Michelle and I are pretty independent, too. And soon I'll be at college—" At that moment, my memory presented Stalker-Creep Day, probably because I'd been talking about our independence. "What happened with that creep and the license plate?"

He frowned. "I called my uncle as soon as I left your building, and gave him the asshole's license plate number. He told me he'd take care of it."

Of course. His uncle, his dad's younger brother, was a well-respected SFPD detective.

"Have you had any more trouble since that day?"

"No. And thank you."

He nodded without breaking our eye contact.

We fell silent and the song's lyrics settled around us.

He eased me closer to him and my muddled mind scrambled to find something else to say. But with the song, his mesmerizing eyes and closeness, I couldn't think of one thing.

What on earth was going on here? He'd chosen someone else. And I had no idea why she wasn't here with him tonight.

"Kassidy, I know you're here with your club, but I—" He sighed when the song ended, but he didn't release me when we stopped dancing. Or when the DJ mentioned taking a quick break. "I was wondering—"

Drew bounded up to us. "There she is." But his grin slipped as his eyes fell on my shirt. "And you wore that shirt? To *this* dance?"

I straightened at his comments since it's not like we'd come to this dance together.

"Juliet's a fictional character. She has nothing to do with reality."

I glanced sharply at my dance partner who had quoted me almost exactly. But there had been a slight edge in his voice.

Drew shrugged. "Yeah. True. But do you mind if I steal my Juliet?"

Justin gave Drew an easy smile, but his eyes were dark with...jealousy?

He let me go and stepped back. "She's all yours, Romeo."

Well, if he did feel jealous, I considered it nothing less than poetic justice.

He turned from Drew and me, then headed toward his friends, minus Owen, who were still standing together where they'd been when Meg and I walked into the gym.

"Did I interrupt you guys? I thought maybe you needed

rescuing." Drew followed that up with an apologetic smile. "Sorry about the shirt comment. You do look nice."

"Thanks." I managed a smile. "And you didn't interrupt anything. We were done."

I took his offered arm and the Justin Richardson fog lifted the further we got away from him. But when we reached where I'd left my club members, I didn't see a white shirt anywhere.

Chapter Seventeen

My phone buzzed inside my crossbody case, but I was holding my near-empty cup of lemonade Drew had brought me a while ago. The DJ had chosen another slow song as a way to bring this dance to an end. Kids were leaving in groups, too, so I had a feeling my *best friend* had finally sent me a text.

As I tried to take out my phone while holding my cup, Drew stepped closer to my side.

"I'll take that for you," he said, grinning while he took the cup. "So, who did you come here with? Do you need a ride home?" he asked. And sounding a bit hopeful I would.

I squelched my irritation because Drew hadn't done anything wrong. Except spend the night by my side, along with several of our cast mates, after my club members, including my best friend, deserted me. But his nonstop attention had seemed more like we *were* on a date, and I'd spent the night trying, really hard, not to send the wrong signals. Still, I did appreciate him sort've offering me a ride home and I smiled at him.

"Actually, I think my ride just texted me. Give me a sec." I withdrew my phone and pressed the home button.

Hey. Where are you? Mom's on her way to pick us up.

I frowned at Meg's message.

Where was *I*?

I clenched my teeth and texted *With Drew. Where are you?*

I asked her that in a text I'd sent way earlier. And she'd never replied.

I forced my mouth into a smile and said, "It was Meg. My ride. But thanks for asking."

His dark eyes dimmed, but he nodded.

I dropped my eyes to my phone.

What on earth happened tonight? I leave to dance with *him*, then Drew Chang becomes my unofficial date because the club's dance mojo fizzles. I'd spotted Warren, Natalie, and Lexi here and there, talking to kids in big groups. I'd seen Jade and Nate on the dance floor a couple times. But Paige, Alisha, and my *best friend* had disappeared without a trace.

In the lobby. Meet me here?

I shoved my phone back in the case. "She's waiting in the lobby."

"I'll walk with you." He fell into step beside me, so close our arms touched. "My mom's on her way to get me."

I released a tiny sigh, since I had to stop this before his feelings ended up hurt. I also didn't understand where his interest beyond friendship had come from all of a sudden. Because we got cast as Romeo and Juliet?

"I'm sorry your club members bailed on you," he said as we walked across the gym. "But I had a lot of fun. Hanging out with you like this."

Discomfort surrounded me and I stepped to my left so our arms were no longer touching. I then took a quick breath and said, "Drew, we're friends. Right?"

He didn't respond, and I peeked at him. He was staring at the gym floor while we continued our walk toward the lobby, and guilt joined my discomfort, both pressing my shoulders down. But I couldn't help what I felt.

He raised his head, shrugged, nodded, and said, "Yeah. Of course."

I tried to smile as I said, "Great. And thanks for being such a good friend tonight."

He shot me a tight smile, and I looked away.

Hopefully this wouldn't affect *Romeo and Juliet*. Because Drew was one of my favorite people in theater. I also didn't need tension with my Romeo.

Meg standing just outside the gym's entrance and exit caught my attention. But she dropped her gaze the second our eyes met.

My irritation came back and stirred inside me.

When we reached Meg, still not looking at me, Drew gave her a quick smile and faced me. He then gallantly bowed, like he did as Romeo at the beginning of our first scene together, and straightened. And I returned his normal and familiar friendly smile. Which seemed like a good sign that everything *would* be okay between us on Monday.

I somehow held onto my sigh of relief.

"Till we meet again on the stage, my fair Juliet." He turned, tossed my cup into a nearby trash can, and headed outside with a small group of other kids loudly talking and laughing.

I, now glaring, focused on Meg. "*What* happened to you tonight? I even texted you."

"Nothing," she quickly answered. Without looking at me. "I've been...around. And I didn't see your text until just now."

I didn't believe her, but let it go and asked, "Where were you? I didn't see you."

My snarky tone finally made her look at me. But only for a second.

She was definitely not telling me something.

"I caught up with some of my friends on the cross-country team." She frowned. "And it's not like you were alone all night. What's going on with you and Drew?"

"We're friends." I crossed my arms and leaned forward. "And I hung out with him and my friends in the play because my *other* friends deserted me." Her eyes widened, but I couldn't stop my hurt and irritation from coming out. "We were supposed to be a united front. Then you guys disappeared. And it's something I never expected from my best friend."

She sighed. "Kass, you were dancing with J.R. It looked like you weren't having a horrible time, by the way. And everyone kind of went their own ways. It wasn't personal."

"It didn't feel that way," I snapped. "And I only danced with him for a few minutes."

"I'm sorry if you felt abandoned. Really. It's just..." She turned from me. "We need to go outside," she muttered. "My mom's probably here by now."

She walked outside, and I, after a few seconds, marched in the same direction.

Maybe she wanted to tell me what really happened tonight. But the hurt and irritation burning inside me made me *not* want to ask the right, best friend questions that would make her talk. And as irritated as I was at Meg and my other club members for deserting me, I blamed Public Enemy #1 for wrecking the club's dance mojo.

* * *

"Alright," Mr. Peters said. "I need everyone's attention."

I sat beside Bree in the aisle seat of the first row. Far from Public Enemy #1 who'd dropped into a seat between Cody and Shane at the other end of the second row. But one person was, thankfully, missing. Public Enemy #2 and her mom weren't at school today, which had to explain why she hadn't been at the dance with *him*. She must be somewhere with her family.

"As you can see," Mr. Peters swept his arm in the direction of the stage, "Mr. Lowry and his crew worked very hard on our set this past Saturday."

Seeing the set when I walked into the auditorium had caused my first smile of the day. Because Meg and I weren't speaking. But the corners of my mouth inched into my second smile as I again took in the beginnings of our set that, when finished, would be amazing.

The Capulet's unpainted mansion wall, secured in place by three wide pieces of wood, had been angled toward the house and filled up stage left. The wall also had a massive opening, where I would stand, and a basic—as of right now—balcony attached outside of it that had a narrow platform for Romeo. Mr. Lowry and his crew had turned the spot to the left of the balcony into a climbing wall.

Excitement rose inside me because, as of today, being on stage would feel like I was finally Juliet Capulet. Especially during the oh-so famous balcony scene with my Romeo.

I mentally hugged my excitement. I also couldn't wait to get up there and lose myself in Juliet.

"But before we break in that wall," Mr. Peters continued, "I want to introduce you to my two friends who will be working with many of you a couple times a week, starting today." He pointed to a man and woman sitting in the first row of the house's right side. "Ross brought prop swords and will be working with the boys on the sword fight—"

Most of the boys erupted into enthusiastic applause.

"Thank God," Bree mumbled. "I was getting really tired of them acting *stupid* while using their fists as swords."

She was right, but I giggled, which made her giggle. Those rehearsals had been funny.

"And Vanessa will be working with many of you on the dancing, particularly our Romeo and Juliet." Mr. Peters looked at me and angled his head toward the set. "But I want to spend a moment breaking in Juliet's balcony. There's a rolling cantilever ladder with handrails behind the wall. We're not sure it's going to work very well, because it's a little narrow and steep, but that's what today is for. So, please be careful."

I nodded and stood.

Mr. Peters pointed at Drew, sitting on Bree's left side. "I want you on stage, too, so we can try out that climbing wall."

Drew hopped up and we headed for the stage left stairs.

"That climbing wall is so freakin' cool," Drew said, his smile wide and contagious.

I laughed, but mostly from relief my Romeo seemed back on the friendship page with me. And, thank goodness, without any weirdness. Neither of us needed *that* drama.

He, with a bit of a swagger, veered left, onto the stage.

I veered right to go behind the mansion wall. But when I reached the ladder, I stared up at the platform that seemed a million steps away.

How in the world would I manage this ladder wearing my costume?

I gripped the handrail and carefully took each step. My bubbly excitement doubled in strength the closer I got to the opening. To the point I started shaking. When I reached the platform, I was at the balcony opening. Drew and Mr. Peters were staring up at me. And a round of giggles rippled out of me. Because this would absolutely feel like the balcony scene.

"*There she is,*" Drew sang.

"How're those steps?" Mr. Peters asked. "And do you feel safe up there?"

"A tiny bit scary," I confessed. "But, yeah. I feel safe. I'm just thinking about dealing with those steps in costume."

He nodded. "I agree. I'll talk to Mr. Lowry. Maybe there's something we can do about that." He faced Drew. "The hand and footholds on the climbing wall are in place. You ready?"

Drew folded his hands, then stretched his arms out, and his knuckles cracked.

I laughed, along with Mr. Peters and our audience.

He stretched his neck left, right, and said, "I got this, Mr. Peters." He pounced on the wall as if he were Spider-Man and started climbing like he was the superhero, too.

"Drew, slow down." Mr. Peters watched him closely.

"But in..." he said on a breath, "this scene...I'm in a hurry to get to my Juliet."

I continued laughing as he made it to the point where he could step onto the platform attached to the balcony. He extended his left leg, placed his foot on the platform, and reached for the balcony's railing. Then his foot slipped. His twisted angle pulled him backward.

My eyes widened and I reached for him as he tried to grab the railing. But—as if in slow motion—he fell. Right onto the stage with a *crack!*

Chapter Eighteen

I stared at my laptop's screen and tried to make sense of my English paper due in two weeks. But I couldn't escape the image of Drew toppling backward. Or the crack I'd heard the moment he landed on stage. Mr. Peters had cancelled rehearsal and wasted no time hustling Drew to the nurse's office, with the hopes she hadn't left. I also couldn't escape the murmurings of his right elbow "possibly being broken" because of all the pain Drew felt.

I cringed as I remembered his face contorted in discomfort. The situation hadn't looked or sounded good—at all—when they left. And I tried, really hard, not to envision what a broken elbow for Drew would mean in the play's long run.

He *had* to be okay.

"Hey, stranger."

I spun the desk chair toward the sound of Dad's voice from the doorway.

"Hi," I said. "Is everything okay? At work?"

He slowly shook his head. "We lost a patient involved in the car accident."

I lowered my eyes to my lap as he walked into the room. "I'm sorry," I murmured.

Dad lowered himself to my bed. "Let's talk about you. How was the dance?"

"Fine."

"That's it?"

I nodded. Because that's all I could do. "How was your date?"

"Really...good." He smiled. "I'd forgotten what it was like to be on a date with a woman who can carry on a conversation and listen just as well."

"It sounds like you're going to see each other again?"

"Yes. Definitely." His smile doubled in size. "But I don't know when because of our work schedules."

I wanted to smile since I was happy for him. But I couldn't work up the effort.

"Rough day at the office?" His smile changed to concern.

If he only knew. I didn't feel like going into any of it, though. Especially Drew's accident. Because Dad, being a doctor, would probably squash my hope his injury wasn't bad.

"You could say that."

"Feel like talking about it?"

"Not really."

He sighed, then stood. "Alright." He leaned down and gave my head a quick kiss. "I'll be in the kitchen trying to find something to make for dinner, if you need anything."

He left, and I forced myself to return to my research paper.

I'd barely started yet another body paragraph when my phone started ringing. I snatched it off the desk—maybe news about Drew?—but it was Meg.

I stared at my phone and debated whether to answer. Especially after not speaking to her since she'd walked away Saturday night. But she could be calling because she'd heard about Drew. It had to be all over our school's social media gossip mill by now.

"Hey," I answered.

"I can tell by the sound of your voice you somehow haven't heard the news."

I frowned. "Of course I know. I was there."

There was a long pause on her end before, "You were what?"

"Meg, it happened at rehearsal. Right in front of me and everyone."

"What are you talking about?"

I hesitated, then said, "Drew's accident? He fell off the wall while climbing toward Juliet's balcony. And might've broken his elbow."

My stomach tightened at saying those words out loud.

She gasped. "Oh, shit. Why the hell didn't you text me?"

Okay. Maybe that's not why she'd called me.

"Well, you haven't exactly been my best friend since Saturday night."

Another long pause, then, "Kass, I said I was sorry. I don't know what else to say. No one meant to hurt your feelings."

I remained silent. Hanging out with my theater family at the dance had actually been fun. But I sensed she was hiding something from me.

"I know you have got to be freaking out right now about Drew. But it's gonna be fine."

Points for smooth subject change. And what she'd said was a huge understatement. "You didn't hear the crack."

She gasped again. "There was a crack?"

I heard her shaking her head and pictured her ponytail flipping side-to-side.

"Well, then, maybe what I called to talk to you about will help you right now, since it sounds like there's a really good chance J.R. might—"

"Please don't go there." Because I refused to go there unless absolutely necessary.

"Sloane broke up with J.R."

My eyes widened, and I pitched forward. "When? How? She hasn't even been around." I'd known they'd been distant at our rehearsals, but she'd still been possessive of him.

"It happened at some point after school. Mr. Peters must've cancelled rehearsal, right?"

"Yeah."

"I guess she posted on Snapchat she dumped him. And said something like not wasting her time on a guy with issues and a short attention span."

My back became rigid.

"Do you think she was talking about you? And that you danced the other night?"

"Probably. She's evil enough."

Yes, Justin Richardson was Public Enemy #1, but he didn't deserve that treatment. Not by someone like—and it hit me. He'd chosen someone like her over me. Us. What we'd had for five months. And my brief sympathy for him changed to teen-girl-scorned satisfaction.

"How did you hear about this?"

"Lexi. I think she's friends with everyone in our class. I'm surprised she didn't text you first. But maybe she wanted me to be the one to tell you?"

I let that go and asked, "And what's he saying?" I had long since severed all my social media connections with him.

"Not a thing. But it's not like he's ever been really active on Snapchat."

Because he preferred Instagram. And my memory took me to the day he'd taken a unique picture of our spot at Ocean Beach he'd captioned "Utopia."

"What are you going to do?" Meg asked.

I buried that memory, leaned back, and slouched in my

chair. "Nothing. What can I do?" Except keep a tight grip on my panic.

"What about Drew?"

"Stay positive." And pray to the spirits of Romeos past that Drew would stay my Romeo.

* * *

The cast of *Romeo and Juliet* was silent. We were again occupying the first two rows of the house's center section. Mr. Peters stood in front of the stage and had announced Drew wouldn't be returning as our Romeo. But we'd walked into rehearsal knowing the truth.

His right elbow, due to the way he fell, had hit the stage and taken too much of his weight. He'd broken his elbow and would be in a cast for weeks.

And the show was running in less than a month.

I turned my head and peeked at *him*. He sat with Cody, Shane, and Liam. His wide eyes were locked on Mr. Peters. The fact he and Sloane weren't together anymore not news among the cast. Because we'd lost a fun, hard-working, talented cast member. Our real Romeo.

He turned his head, as if he could feel my eyes, and I looked away.

"Before we get going with the sword fighting and dancing practices," Mr. Peters said, sounding a bit frazzled and not normal for him until full dress and tech rehearsals started, "I need to talk to Kassidy and J.R. Can you join me on stage, please?"

I, shaking, lifted myself from my seat, and Bree gave me a smile that appeared half painful, half encouraging.

We avoided eye contact while we walked onto the stage from opposite sides.

"Okay." Mr. Peters focused on him. "Can you do this?"

"Yeah. I mean—" He ran a hand through his hair. "I think so."

Mr. Peters shook his head. "I need to know you can do this. Because we have less than a month until the show runs. Make a decision. Right now."

I willed him to be honest with Mr. Peters.

He straightened to his full height. "Yes. I *can* do this."

I crossed my arms and looked at the stage floor.

No. He could *not* do this. So he'd nailed Mercutio--a small role compared to Romeo.

"Excellent." Mr. Peters released a quick laugh. "You were making me a little nervous there for a second." He focused on me. "My next question, which is for you both, can you put aside your personal history—no, I'm not blind—and be the Romeo and Juliet this show deserves? And that our audiences will expect to see?"

I flushed at his bluntness.

"I know I can." Public Enemy #1 looked sharply at me. "I don't know if *you* can."

I turned toward him. "What does that mean? I'm the experienced one here. Not you."

"Who around here needs to control their ego?"

"Neither of you are instilling much confidence right now," Mr. Peters said.

We fell silent.

"Can you two get over whatever happened in your past and do this?"

Knowing exactly what my mom would have said if this had happened to her, I looked Mr. Peters square in the eye. "Yes. Absolutely."

"Yes," *he* echoed, and as strongly.

"Perfect. Now I need to go talk to two more understudies." He started to leave but stopped to give us a thoughtful stare. "There's a lot of passion here. My advice is to channel that into your roles. It could end up being something unforgettable when the time comes."

Mr. Peters walked away. My new *Romeo* wasted no time following him.

I, with shaky steps, headed for the stage left stairs.

Had it only been yesterday at this time I'd been excited about the remaining rehearsals? And laughing as I stood at Juliet's balcony, with Drew smiling up at me?

I dropped into my seat beside Bree, and she reached out and squeezed my shaky hand. But all I could do was gently squeeze her hand in return.

Why did he say he could play Romeo? Didn't he understand what that *really* meant?

We'd managed to get along during a nice slow dance on Saturday night. But one, nice slow dance wouldn't fix what happened That Night. And now I'd have to be on stage, with the boy who'd obliterated my heart, and act crazy in love and kiss—my stomach formed a knot.

My heart ached for Drew, but a selfish question appeared in my mind.

What had I done to deserve this?

Chapter Nineteen

Romeo took my left hand without looking in my eyes. "If I profane with my unworthiest hand..." He closed his eyes, then looked at our teacher-director. "Can I have the line please?"

Mr. Peters sat cross-legged in his usual spot near the stage's edge. "This holy shrine, the gentle sin is this..."

Romeo nodded and faced me, again not quite making eye contact. And I wanted nothing more than this scene to be over. Our first rehearsal as Romeo and Juliet.

"This holy shrine, the gentle sin is this: My lips...ready...to smooth that...touch with...a kiss," he added, and too quickly. He also very quickly kissed my hand.

I attempted a shy, yet flirty smile I'd mastered weeks earlier with Drew as my Romeo. "Good pilgrim, you do wrong your hands too much...which mannerly devotion shows in this...for saints have hands that pilgrims' hands do touch—" I yanked my hand from his to hold it out and upright. "And palm to palm is holy palmers' kiss."

He placed his left hand against mine. "Have not saints lips? And...holy palmers too?"

I continued attempting my shy flirtatiousness. But dread hit at what was coming next.

I dropped my hand from his and pressed my hands together, as if in prayer. "Aye pilgrim, lips that they must use in prayer."

I usually giggled after that line. But I couldn't make it come out. And Drew had mastered Romeo's love-struck persistence during this scene. Those actions now nonexistent with *this* Romeo.

"Then let do what hands do. They pray...let faith turn to...despair."

I started to move around him and forced out a giggle. "Saints do not move, though grant for prayers' sake."

He caught my left hand, we faced each other, and the dread consumed me.

"Then move not while my...prayer's...effect...I take. Thus from my lips...by yours...my sin is purged." He ducked his head and gave me a rapid, barely-there kiss.

As if being forced to kiss his mom.

"Stop," Mr. Peters loudly said at the auditorium ceiling.

We backed away from each other as I saw Romeo mouth the F-word.

Mr. Peters stood. "What was that?"

He was, hands down, my favorite teacher. But right now I hated him, Shakespeare, this play, and I especially hated our new Romeo. I still couldn't believe his comment "There's a lot of passion here." Because he must have been sensing our *passionate* dislike for one another.

"I get you're not comfortable with the lines yet, but this scene is legendary, J.R." He walked toward us. "Romeo has just fallen head over feet, crazy in love with Juliet. And, yes, it's their first kiss. But there needs to be some emotion."

I glanced at Romeo. Who looked wrecked. Like a tornado

had sucked him up and spit him back out. The image made the giggles escape before I could stop them.

Mr. Peters's annoyed eyes fell on me. "What? You think this is *funny*?"

I became the focus of everyone in the auditorium.

"I expected more from you, Kassidy," he continued, and I felt about an inch tall. "You weren't wowing me, either. Which is unacceptable, considering how great this scene has gone in previous rehearsals." He angled his head back. "Everyone take five." He brought his head back down. "Except you two."

I stood before him and my face became hot. Because I'd never—not ever—been the cause of his frustration.

Once we were somewhat alone, Mr. Peters shook his head. "I know it's only your first rehearsal together. But I did expect more than what you gave me since you two have been wowing me for the last month. But it was physically painful watching you two."

I wanted to say it had been physically painful doing the scene, but wisely stayed silent.

"We don't have time for rehearsals like this. So, you're going to sit out the rest of the day, together, right up front where I can see you. And your homework is to figure out how to become Romeo and Juliet. You also need to start learning your lines, J.R." He stalked away.

I marched toward the stage left stairs. When I reached the front row I, like Mr. Peters said, dropped into a seat. Romeo copied my actions, but sat, thank goodness, three seats away.

I crossed my right leg over my left and bounced my foot. "Maybe the scene wouldn't have been painful if Romeo knew his lines. Which is an understudy's job, by the way."

He whipped his head in my direction. "Back off, DQ. I've done the best I can learning his lines. And I have just as much homework as everyone else. I also have a life outside of this damn play," he added under his breath.

That remark caught my breath. But only for a few seconds.

I angled myself toward him and leaned forward. "If you weren't caught up in your precious personal life, you'd know what you're doing."

"What do you expect from me?" He angled himself toward me. "This is my first, real rehearsal as Romeo. I haven't had over a month in the role, and I'm not Drew. And what does Mr. Peters expect me to do during that scene? Stick my tongue down your throat?"

I looked at my lap since, for once, I had nothing to throw back at him. And the countless kissing hours we'd logged—though he was a much better kisser than what he'd just said—which led to the afternoon when we'd taken our relationship all the way filled my mind.

"I'm sorry. That didn't come out right. And I'm not mad at you. Even though you've become really good at pissing me off." He gave me a pointed stare, which I returned. "I'm frustrated. I think Mercutio came too easily to me." He sighed. "It's been a fucked up week."

I relaxed, but only a fraction, at his surprising honesty. He did look overwhelmed. And today was his first, real rehearsal as Romeo. Still, the role was too big for him. A newbie. Romeo needed to be played by one of the other boys who'd been active in theater the last few years and *deserved* the part. Like Cody, a senior. Or even Shane or Liam—my eyes widened when a solution landed in my mind. But would I be able to talk Mr. Peters into my idea?

I eyed Romeo as he stared at a spot directly in front of him.

Because he appeared so frustrated, I said, "I'm sorry, too. I know you're trying." My idea grew in strength, though, when he responded with silence.

Surely Mr. Peters would agree to my solution after our rotten rehearsal today.

"I heard about you and Sloane," I politely said since her nastiness could be another reason for his "effed up week." But he could've also been referring to his struggles at home.

He lifted his gaze. "Really." He shifted in his seat and focused on the stage.

I did the same. It looked like they were getting ready for the big sword fight scene. I also tried, really hard, not to analyze his matter-of-fact response.

Throughout Tuesday and Wednesday's dance practices, I'd caught Sloane's withering looks. To the point I'd been tempted to stop and confront her. How was it my fault she'd dumped him over something ridiculous? And Drew falling and breaking his elbow hadn't been my fault. But I absolutely didn't need to make a scene with Sloane Chaplin who would, no doubt, go running to her powerful mommy who could rip Juliet away from me.

Weirdly enough, Sloane seemed more affected by their break-up than him. He didn't seem to care one bit about her or her actions. But then he'd never acted like he cared about our break-up, either. Maybe Sloane had been right about his short attention span.

I'd been nothing more than a spring and summer romance.

"What made you laugh?" he suddenly asked. "I thought Mr. Peters's" —he laughed for a couple seconds— "head would explode."

I hesitated, then said, "Honestly?"

He rolled his head in my direction. "It wouldn't be you if you weren't honest."

"At you. But only because you looked so—"

"Idiotic."

"More like dumbfounded."

He rolled his head forward. "I'm feeling both." He stood, and meeting my questioning look added, "Not all of us were born to do this. I need some air."

My eyes followed him as he walked up the aisle. When he reached the auditorium doors, he jerked the left door open and walked into the lobby.

His statement of "not all of us were born to do this" clung to my mind. I couldn't be sure if that had been a compliment or an accusation. And if it had been an accusation, it also wasn't my fault he'd decided to "try something different" and be an overachiever.

I knew my idea would make me not look my professional best. But if Mr. Peters took me seriously, I'd be saving him and Romeo and me a lot of unnecessary tension and future bad rehearsals.

When Romeo came back, we sat in silence and watched them rehearse the sword fight scene that leads to Mercutio, then Tybalt's death. But as soon as rehearsal ended, and everyone left, I followed Mr. Peters to behind the Capulet's mansion wall where he stopped.

"Mr. Peters, can I talk to you for a minute?"

"I'm not convinced this ladder is our best option, but—" He gave me his full attention. "Did you and J.R. figure out a compromise?"

"That's actually what I wanted to talk to you about." He just *had* to say yes. "I don't think Justin can handle Romeo. He was great as Mercutio—"

"The fact you admitted that means this is about your personal feelings toward him."

I held onto my frustrated sigh. "But he pretty much told me he was overwhelmed by the role of Romeo. Why not let him continue being Mercutio, because he's so good at it, and give Romeo to a boy who really deserves it? Like Cody or Shane, or even Liam."

"Kassidy, that would solve nothing. Except make you feel better."

I straightened at his comment. And the fact this wasn't going the way I'd hoped. But I still said, "It's a perfectly acceptable suggestion. And it's not like he really knows Romeo's lines. How would putting another boy in the role be any worse?"

He gave me an overly patient smile.

My shoulders drooped.

Nonono...*no*.

"J.R.'s our new Romeo. My advice is to accept it and be patient. In fact, we all need to be very patient the next couple weeks. But I know this will come together. I have a feeling you do, too. So, I expect my Juliet back Monday morning and at her one-hundred percent."

He went back to scrutinizing the ladder.

I dragged myself away from him and down the stage left stairs.

Nothing that had happened since Monday afternoon was even close to being fair.

Chapter Twenty

"Kass, maybe Mr. Peters is right. Give him a chance," Meg said as we walked to our club meeting.

All I wanted was to go home, crawl into bed, cover my head with the blankets, and listen to my Visualization Playlist. Especially after this rotten week.

"But he's the one who said 'not everyone was born to do this.' Romeo's too big a part for him. And can you believe he said that to me? Like he resents me for being good at acting."

"Yes, I can believe he said that." She stopped walking, which forced me to stop. "Kass, he was giving you a compliment."

I looked right to avoid her exasperated stare.

Okay. I guess I hadn't thought of his statement as a compliment.

"What exactly did you see at Owen's party?"

I groaned since I didn't even want to relive That Night. "Meg, we've been over this."

"I know that. But you were so upset and crying so hard, all

I really understood was that you'd seen him and Sloane sitting at the hot tub together."

"I also know I said she was practically in his lap. And he wasn't fighting her off."

The images swirled in my mind. Of them. Cozied up together. Sitting on the edge of the Garrett's hot tub, unoccupied at the time. Her laughing and keeping her predatory blue eyes locked on him as she flirtatiously sipped her alcoholic drink through a straw. And the jerk-face had been lapping it up. Like some big dumb dog starved for attention. The only thing missing from that scene had been licking and tail wagging. He'd also, when I walked up, looked unapologetic and even a little irritated.

Because clearly I, the actual girlfriend at the time, had interrupted something.

"I don't want to talk about this," I snapped. "We need to go."

A few minutes later, we walked into Ms. Simmons's classroom. She was busy at her laptop, hooked into the Smart Board. She gave us a distracted smile as we headed toward our club members sitting at the back of her classroom.

I dropped my backpack. "Where are Jade and Nate?"

They responded with silence. Then Warren and Lexi shared a somewhat nervous look and glanced at Meg. Paige and Alisha were watching all of us.

"I told you she wouldn't know," Natalie said to Warren and Lexi. "Kass has been noticeably not around. And obviously caught up in the play and all that bullsh—" She stopped and looked at Ms. Simmons, who didn't appear to be paying any attention to us.

Looking at their almost guilty expressions, I knew something big *had* shifted in the club last Saturday night. "Just tell me."

"I'll tell her since I have much more finesse than you," Warren said to Natalie.

She rolled her eyes, but was not, surprisingly, on her phone.

"It seems the Anti-Love Club created a bit of a love connection for two members."

My mouth fell open.

"Jade and Nate aren't here because they have their first date. Tonight. And though they're not a couple yet by this school's gossip standards, I don't think they'll be at any more meetings."

If it weren't for my shock, I might've laughed at the irony. But as I really thought about it, they had been pretty cozy while we'd watched *John Tucker Must Die*. They'd also been kind of cozy at our last meeting when we were outside. He'd also been getting them drinks at the dance, and I remembered seeing them *slow* dance a couple times.

"I feel totally clueless right now."

It never occurred to me the Anti-Love Club would bring two heartbroken members *together*. And an irrational wave of jealousy surged through me. To the point my vision blurred.

"Kass," Meg quietly began, "there's actually more. I've been wanting to tell you that while you and J.R. were dancing, Owen found me and..." Her voice trailed into silence.

But I knew how her sentence ended.

My vision cleared as I looked at my best friend, her dark eyes wide with uneasiness.

She and Owen had gotten back together at the dance. Which explained why she'd been acting so distant and secretive.

My cluelessness tripled.

Had I really been so caught up in myself and the play this week to miss one love connection and one reconciliation? I had been avoiding people as much as possible and eating—

again—at a table buried in the library, my math book as my companion.

Then, as if the classroom were a stage and the actors had been cued, Owen walked in.

And not alone.

"Owen," Meg said, looking and sounding a little panicked, "what are you doing here?"

"And why's *he* with you?" My already fragile nerves began to simmer at the sight of *him* at my club's meeting. Or what was left of my club.

Ms. Simmons faced all of us, her expression tight with caution and weariness.

Owen looked not-so nicely at me. "I'm here to back him up."

Public Enemy #1 stepped forward. "I really need to talk to you."

I crossed my arms. "Well, I'm busy. And this meeting is for *members* only."

"Fine!" He headed toward my club members. He then dropped his backpack next to an empty desk beside Paige, roughly pulled out the chair, turned it backward, straddled it, and exaggerated making himself comfortable. "Hi," he said to Paige. "I'm Justin Richardson. But almost everyone calls me J.R."

Paige's eyes bounced from him, to me, him, back to me.

"Wow. Someone's been spending way too much time with the drama crowd." Natalie glanced at me. "No offense."

My heart pounded against my chest as I unleashed my most powerful if-looks-could-kill glare on him. "You can't do that," I said through clenched teeth.

He gave Ms. Simmons a phony baloney, angelic smile. "This is a school-sponsored club, right? Meaning anyone can join?"

My arms fell to my sides, and I swung my head in Ms. Simmons's direction.

She released a weary sigh. "Kassidy, he's right."

No. *Nononono*. This could not be happening. Not after this week.

I racked my brain for a logical reason he couldn't join. And then I remembered the reason I'd formed the Anti-Love Club. "But he doesn't have a broken heart."

Okay. That argument sounded better in my head. But the fact remained—

"What, you have x-ray vision now?" he shot back.

"Kassidy," Owen said, "you don't know what you're talking about."

Natalie stood and unleashed her if-looks-could-kill glare that appeared more powerful than mine had felt. "And you need to mind your own business. Why are you even still here?"

"Stop. All of you." Ms. Simmons walked forward. "This is a members-only meeting. And, J.R., unless you're serious about joining today, you and Owen will have to leave."

He crossed his arms and shrugged. "Then consider me a member. What do I have to do to make it official? Burn something?"

My breath stalled in my chest as I faced Meg with my mouth again hanging open.

Oh. My. God. What had she done?

Meg turned cherry red. Just like the night of our Purging.

"I'm sorry," she said, cringing. "I wasn't thinking. But Owen was sworn to secrecy."

I forced my eyes off Meg to focus on Owen, his face the same color as Meg's.

"I thought it was kind've a funny story and I guess I wasn't thinking," he mumbled.

"Meg, what happened to what happens in the club, stays in the club?" Lexi asked, sounding justifiably wounded.

"I think both of you should leave," Natalie snapped. "And take *Romeo* with you."

He shook his head. "I'm not going anywhere."

What on earth had Meg been thinking? And why was he doing this to me? Especially since he didn't have a broken heart—unless...did he join because of *her*?

What little I'd eaten for lunch inched its way up and into my throat. I wanted to run into the nearest bathroom and empty my stomach.

But no. He wouldn't do that to me. Still, why else would he have shot back with that x-ray vision comment? Sloane had been unnecessarily cruel. And he'd held no interest whatsoever in the Anti-Love Club, had even laughed at it, until *this* week.

I took a deep breath to settle my stomach. And to stop myself from clawing his hazel eyes—that I'd once loved staring into like an adoring nitwit—from his sockets. "I'm the president. He's the enemy. He can't join."

"Kassidy, you can't do that."

In that instant hatred for him boiled inside me and my hands formed tight fists.

First the play. Now this.

I had to get out of here before I *did* give him a black eye.

I grabbed my backpack and flung it over my shoulder. "Then I quit." I glared at Meg. "Congratulations on getting back together. But it would be great if you stopped telling Owen about stuff that happened in our club. I'll return my shirt next week." I fled the room.

The betrayal—from him *and* my best friend—mixed with my fury at him for invading something I had started. And loved. The club members, like my theater family, were my people. My friends. Not his. Wasn't being the oh-so popular soccer star enough for him?

I heard rushed footsteps behind me and picked up my pace since it could only be one person. But he managed to snatch my right hand, which I jerked free before whirling on him.

"Would you stop being DQ for five minutes and—"

"Stop calling me that. I hate it!" Because it now sounded like an insult.

He ran his hands through his hair, which caused the dark strands to stick up in several directions. "Fine. Done. But I need to talk you."

"No. After what you just did to me in there? Haven't you humiliated me enough?"

"And, as usual, it's all about you. Instead of getting all the facts and hearing the other person's side, you jump to the wrong conclusions and become *crazy* Kassidy. The victim!"

I took a shaky step toward him. "I am the victim here. You humiliated me at Owen's party by throwing yourself at that viper snake. How could you do that to me after our summer —" Angry tears burned my eyes, but I gave him a Natalie-worthy maniacal smile. "But I got my poetic justice."

Hostility radiated from his eyes.

"You also infiltrate my theater world and now you join my club because of...you're everywhere." I backed away from him. "And I hate you for it." I turned my back on him, my vision blurred by tears, and continued to bolt toward the stairway that would take me downstairs and out of this stupid school.

<h1 style="text-align:center">Chapter Twenty-One</h1>

Dad sat in his other lounger, facing me.

I hugged my legs to my chest. I'd pulled them up and underneath one of his worn UCLA sweatshirts I'd swiped from an old donation pile. I also had on my club shirt.

That I never wanted to give back.

His balcony, right off his bedroom, had become my sanctuary a long time ago. I barely heard the city's traffic noise and felt secluded, meaning nowhere near Michelle.

"Your sister said you've been out here since you got home." He looked up at the sky that had turned to twilight. "Bad night to get stuck at work. I've been waiting for your dam to finally break, because that usually means you'll talk to me."

My dam had broken before I'd escaped school. And had broken on and off since then. I could still feel my last round of tears on my cheeks and taste the saltiness on my lips.

I focused on the sky. "Daddy, I don't even know where to start."

Although their connection surprised me, I knew Jade and Nate deserved to be happy. And they deserved to be happy together. I should've probably felt proud of the fact the Anti-Love Club brought them together. I also knew how much Meg loved Owen. Based on the sad, rejected puppy look he'd given her at that one meeting before he left, I knew he loved her, too. Which meant the whole Brandy Espinosa kissing thing had been nothing. I knew my best friend would never have gone back to him if it had been something else.

I guess I didn't really feel betrayed by Meg. Just hurt because she'd left me out of their reunion. She had been weirdly sneaky about it. Because *we'd* started the Anti-Love Club? But jealousy of them and Jade and Nate had taken a hold of me. Made worse by my ex-jerk-face joining what was my club because of—I shook the thought from my mind.

I also knew I hadn't exactly made myself available this last week. To anyone. His "it's all about you" comment appeared in my head, and I looked at my patient dad.

"I'm sorry. I didn't mean to be so difficult this week."

"Honey, I know you're struggling with the play and him and that girl. Are you and Meg talking again?"

The only information I'd given up throughout this truly foul week.

"Not really. I don't know." I still couldn't believe she'd told Owen about The Purging. But seeing Dad's perplexed face at my vagueness gave me the confidence to start with. "Drew, our Romeo, broke his elbow during Monday's rehearsal and now *he's* Romeo."

After that, I told him everything. I even fessed up to the Anti-Love Club and pulled down the sweatshirt's collar to show him my shirt, which made him smile. I also shared the upsetting turn it took hours earlier. But I didn't tell him about the confrontation in the hallway.

Public Enemy #1's honesty refused to let go of me.

Dad rubbed his eyes, as if trying to comprehend everything I'd been keeping to myself since school started through this past week. "I'm trying to figure out what to respond to first." He sighed. "The club definitely explains your uncharacteristic pyromania."

I shrugged.

"So Justin's now Romeo. That girl broke up with him, you think because you two danced Saturday night. He joined this Anti-Love Club you and Meg formed that brought together two of your friends. And Meg and Owen are back together." He frowned. "I don't remember you mentioning they'd broken up."

"I didn't." Being tied too much to the club, it hadn't felt like a necessary conversation.

"Did I catch everything?"

"Yes." And the heaviness on my shoulders lifted substantially.

He shook his head. "I can't tell you how much I don't miss high school."

I wanted to say it wasn't currently a blissful experience for me right now, either.

"But your club sounds like a good thing if it's helping you work through your hurt."

I frowned. "Really? That's all you have to say about it?"

He gave me an affectionate smile. "Kassi, I know Justin was your first love."

It had felt like so much more than that, though. Like our souls had become one.

"You, not surprisingly, were completely caught up in those feelings this past summer. And his behavior at that party really hurt you."

"But he joined the club."

He nodded. "Which reminds me, you said he showed up at the meeting because he needed to talk to you. Why didn't you give him a chance?"

My forehead dropped to my knees.

Oh...no. Not my dad, too.

"We have absolutely nothing to talk about." It came out sounding muffled since I'd spoken into my legs.

"Because he went to the extremes of joining the club, are you sure about that?"

I lifted my head and said, "Of course I am."

Why was *everyone* on his side? Had he started a Support Justin Richardson campaign?

Dad stood, leaned down, and kissed the top of my head. As he straightened, he said, "Thank you for getting me caught up on your life." He started to leave.

I stared at him. "That's all I get from my Dr. Dad? What about the *Romeo and Juliet* mess going on?"

"You're a professional." He smiled. "I know you'll figure it out."

"Thanks a lot."

"Anytime. I'm going to see what your sister's up to."

"Oh, wait a minute." He stopped, and I asked, "When are you going out again with the doctor?"

"We're working on it." His smile grew. "In the meantime, we're seeing a lot of each other at work." He disappeared into his bedroom.

His smile had actually made me smile, and for the first time all day. I felt stronger. Less weepy. And, like he'd said, I was a professional. Just like my mom had been. I wouldn't let Public Enemy #1 being Romeo affect me anymore. But that didn't mean I would forgive and forget he'd forced me out of my club because of Sloane Chaplin.

* * *

I had just finished my long, wispy braid when the buzzer thundered through the condo.

Dad was at work, so I stepped out of the bathroom and yelled to my sister in the living room, "Are you expecting someone?"

"No!"

I walked to the front door and hit the button on our intercom that would allow me to talk to whoever was at the downstairs door. Probably some annoying solicitor.

"Yes?"

I heard a pause, then, "Hi. It's Justin."

I froze.

What on earth could he be doing here? Was *he* the crazy one? And I now had no choice but to find out why he was downstairs. But I had no intention of being nice about it.

I pressed the button. "What do you want?"

Another pause, then, "I'd like to talk to you if you'll let us in."

Us?

Michelle bounced into the hallway. "Who is it?"

"Um...it's for me." I told him, "I'll be right down." I couldn't let him—them?—into my home. My place away from all the drama at school, namely him.

I opened the front door, slipped into the hallway, and shut the door behind me.

I slowly jogged down the three flights of stairs.

What could he want to talk about? Especially after what happened yesterday. I'd made my feelings crystal clear in the school hallway. What else needed to be said?

As I very slowly cleared the remaining steps, I saw him behind the downstairs door's frosted glass window. He had someone very short with him—Beth. Which meant he was her babysitter for the day. And I remembered what he'd told me about his parents at the dance.

Because of the situation, I would have to play as nice as I possibly could.

I took a deep breath and yanked the door open.

"I swear I come in peace."

He looked, of course, adorable in his soccer shorts, white T-shirt that fit him perfectly, and Nikes. My eyes then fell on his sister standing in front of him and I smiled. She had dressed herself in little girl skinny jeans, a pink shirt, and pink Nikes. She also had on black sunglasses a little too big for her face. And someone—him?—had pulled her long dark hair into a ponytail.

"Hey, cute stuff." I'd given Beth that nickname not too long after we met.

"Thanks, Kassidy. I didn't think I looked that good when we left the house."

My smile vanished as I stared at him while suppressing the urge to roll my eyes.

"Hi. And she was talking to *me*," his little sister declared.

"Thank you, Bethie. And you come in peace? You've said that to me before. What are you doing here, Justin?"

"Wasn't it the truth? And can you at least let us in?" He gestured toward my building.

"Sure. Sorry." It wasn't Beth's fault her brother had become number one on my hit list.

I stepped aside, and he maneuvered Beth and himself into the entryway.

"Why didn't you buzz us in?" he asked once I'd closed the door.

I couldn't go into any of that with Beth here and said, "Just tell me why you're here."

"Okay. Fine." He handed his phone to his sister. "Have fun. But don't buy anything."

"I only did that twice." She sat on the bottom step and went into a game.

He took my left hand and led me away, and we stopped when we were several steps from his sister. He released my hand and his eyes lingered on my long braid.

I tried not to turn pink from his warm scrutiny.

"I'm..." He shook his head. "I'm here for *Romeo and Juliet*."

My eyes locked with his. "I'm listening." Because he definitely had my attention.

"Look, Mr. Peters is right. We need to pull it together. And I know I sucked Thursday. But I know how important this is to everyone. Specifically, you. You still want to get into that program next summer? Right?"

I relaxed at his unexpected thoughtfulness and nodded.

"I don't want to ruin it and I know you don't, either. So I'm here to call a truce until the last show runs." He looked away. "Then you can go back to hating me."

I focused on the floor and concentrated on his unexpected proposal, not his last statement.

We did need to "pull it together." And if temporarily putting aside our drama via a truce made the remaining rehearsals go smoothly, the end goal producing awesome shows, then I couldn't say no. Juliet Capulet and this play were way too important.

I looked up and caught his eyes. "Because this isn't about us, *or* me, alright." I held my hand out. "Truce." He took my hand and we shook.

"What I said to you yesterday. In the hallway? About it always being about you and everything else I said? I was pissed."

"And being honest. It's fine." Not really, because my mind wouldn't let it go. But he certainly couldn't know that. "Is that it?"

"Not exactly." He continued holding my hand. "What would you say to us practicing. Alone. Without the pressure of everyone—Mr. Peters—watching us. I know I could use it since the first show runs in two weeks and six days."

Did he actually look scared?

A twinge of sympathy penetrated my conscience.

"I could also use someone to run lines with for the other scenes," he quietly added.

Justin Richardson was asking for my help. Totally out of character for him, too. Everything, typically, came very easily to him. The role of Mercutio, for example.

How could I say no? Because Mr. Peters had been right about audiences expecting a riveting Romeo and Juliet. I could be a true professional and put aside my feelings for him —it was only three full weeks—and help him and us become the star-crossed lovers everyone wanted to see. And it would mean no more rebukes from Mr. Peters.

I also knew it's exactly what my mom would've done if she'd been in my shoes.

"Okay."

"Really? That was easy—I mean, that's cool." Relief filled his eyes. "Thank you."

We shook again, and I untangled my hand from his. "Is this what you wanted to talk about yesterday?"

"Yep. So are you, maybe, free to start now? Time's not on my side. Our side."

I'd been about to apologize, but then he'd asked me, well, that.

"Please? We can go back to my house. The parents are gone for the day, *working*. And I don't want Michelle, if she's home, to feel like she has to babysit Beth."

I squinted at him as I searched my brain for an answer.

"Are you busy today?"

"Um..." After all his honesty the last few minutes, I couldn't lie to him. And I guess now really was as good a time as ever to start the truce and extra rehearsing. "No."

His face relaxed at my simple answer.

I sighed. "Let me run upstairs and grab a couple things."

I'd made it halfway up the stairs when he said, "You might want shoes, too."

Chapter Twenty-Two

"Let me get a Netflix movie going for her," he said the moment we walked into his house. "I'll be right back."

I'd forced my silly sister to pinky swear she'd tell Dad, if he came home early, I had gone to an extra practice with a cast member. I had every intention of telling him about our temporary truce and helping each other out. But not through a text.

"Do you have any homework?" he asked Beth as they wandered toward the back of the house where the kitchen and family room were located.

"No. I keep telling you I'm *just* a third grader."

"A mouthy third grader."

I smiled and turned right.

My eyes landed on his mom's piano sitting by the living room windows. The piano being one of the few warm items in the Richardson home. The house's neutral paint job, matching furniture, and lack of personal items and photos added to the feeling a real family didn't live here. This part of the house seemed staged. As if it were on sale. The only other rooms I'd been in were his and Beth's rooms, and his dad's home office because it opened to the rooftop level.

I eyed the piano and felt its pull. From "Let It Be" day.

Also known as the day I'd become a goner.

How could I not have fallen—incredibly hard—for him that day?

It hadn't only been the fact he'd blown me away with his playing. Or the fact he'd sung the lyrics, both of us laughing as he struggled with the few higher notes. It was the song. It fit him. His life. If everyone came with their own soundtrack, "Let It Be" would be track one on his.

Sadness, and a little anger, filled me up when I remembered him asking his sister if she had homework. And remembering what he'd told me about his parents at the dance.

I couldn't imagine living in this house with self-absorbed parents like the Richardsons.

I slowly headed for the piano. When I reached the bench, I hesitated, then sat down. I lifted the keyboard's cover and ran my fingers across the keys.

After his spontaneous performance, he'd taught me the second part to "Heart and Soul." We'd reached a point where I stopped getting flustered when he played the first part.

I stared at the keys, then tested a couple to hear the right starting note. When I'd located it, I tapped out the other notes. But then I hit a wrong note and started over.

"You remember. Sort of."

I jumped at the sound of his voice.

He leaned against the piano while watching me and fighting a smile.

I brought the cover down and stood. "Sorry. I couldn't stop myself."

He shrugged. "You rarely can. But I'm used to it."

I frowned and was about to question that comment when

he said, "Relax, D—" He paused, then said, "It wasn't an insult. Truce? Remember?"

I nodded and my defenses lowered.

"Ready? Beth's all set and I thought we'd go to the rooftop. Since it's a nice day."

He silently followed me toward the stairs, and I suddenly became aware of my snug skinny jeans and black T-shirt.

I hurried toward the second floor.

"I need to grab *Romeo and Juliet*." He veered right, toward his bedroom.

I tried, really hard, not to think about the times we'd spent in there. Particularly That Afternoon. And other random afternoons that followed. But only on days Beth had been off with friends or Pearl, because we were supposed to be off together. It had always started out that way. Until, sometimes, our mouths and busy hands took us to the brink of explosion—

He emerged from his room with his copy of the play.

"Your face is red." He gestured toward the stairs leading to his dad's office and out to the rooftop. "Is everything okay?"

"Yes. Why wouldn't it be?" I jogged up the steps and went for the French doors.

I needed to get a grip. This was business. I wouldn't be here if not for the play.

Unlike my dad's balcony, the Richardson's rooftop had good views, especially on clear days like today. I caught a glimpse of the bay and top of the Golden Gate Bridge as I headed right for the double lounger. I also smelled the jasmine coming from one of their flower pots.

I sat down and blocked the memories of all the time we'd spent out here throughout the summer. Specifically, a special conversation we'd shared in this very spot. I then reached into my crossbody bag and withdrew the two DVD's I'd had the foresight to grab.

He sat in a chair across from me.

"Here." I handed him the movies. "One is the best movie version of *Romeo and Juliet*. I'd watch that one first since it's like the play. The other is a weird modern version, but with the Shakespearean language. Maybe the movies will help you find your inner Romeo."

"Thanks. I may have seen this one."

He was, not surprisingly, shaking the Leonardo/Claire version.

"Do you know where you want to start?" My phone had vibrated and chirped while I asked my question, and I removed it from my bag.

Meg had texted, *Hi. Are you okay? I miss you.*

My emotions almost got the better of me as I stared at her message.

"Who is it?" he asked. "Someone from the play?"

"It's Meg." I wanted to reply but didn't know what to say. Though I missed her, too.

"Are you really mad at her for getting back together with Owen? It was a stupid misunderstanding that wasn't *his* fault."

I gave him a scorching stare since I didn't appreciate his snarky tone. "No. I'm not mad about that. I'm happy for them."

"Okay. If you're not mad at her about that, what are you mad about?"

"I'm mad she told Owen about The Purging who then blabbed to you."

I could tell he wanted to roll his eyes. At me and the club. That, as of yesterday afternoon before I quickly left, he joined. A part of me wanted to ask if he'd actually stuck around, but I didn't want to give him any satisfaction whatsoever.

I narrowed my eyes.

Could this truce realistically work without us suffering the same fate as Romeo and Juliet? But at the hands of each other?

"So, what did you burn?"

I halted, then yanked my eyes from his to stare at my lap.

Guilt wound its way through me as I remembered dropping my favorite picture of him—that really represented That Afternoon—into the bucket and soaking the photo with lighter fluid. But it had been good therapy, despite everything that followed The Purging. And what I had burned was between the club and me.

"You know what," he muttered, "your expression is all the answer I need. Forget I asked. It's none of my business anyway."

I lifted my head at his now nasty tone and said, "You're right. It isn't."

He nearly ripped open his book. "I think I want to start with something easy. Like when Romeo enters act one, scene one."

I frowned. "Why are you upset? I'm not the one who decided to *throw* myself at—"

"Stop saying that! It's not even—"

"This is so not going to work." I stood.

He exhaled—loudly—through his teeth. "Kassidy, stop. Please."

We exchanged a long stare until he leaned back in his chair.

After a few additional tense seconds, he said, "We shook on our truce and I'm committed to seeing it through. I'm committed to all of this."

"Even if it means we may kill each other before the play runs?"

He, surprisingly, started laughing, and I slowly sat back down.

"Wouldn't that be a twist. Romeo and Juliet killing each other instead of themselves."

I had to smile at that, especially since I'd just been thinking the same thing.

He stood and dropped his book on the chair. "Now that we're past all that and back on the same page, let's try the scene at the Capulet's Ball."

I didn't know if I wanted to practice that scene after our highly tense moment. And after how awful the scene had gone on Thursday.

I stayed seated as he walked to the open spot on the rooftop. Where we'd slow danced for the first time. We'd agreed to dance to the first song that came on Pandora's "Love Song" station, if it wasn't sad, which turned out to be Ed Sheeran's "Thinking Out Loud."

"Get your cute butt over here, D—sorry. That's going to take some getting used to."

I dropped my bag and phone on the lounger—Meg would have to wait—and cautiously joined him at our dancing spot.

We got into our positions, as if we were on the school's stage.

"Why did you say that?" I asked. "And you don't need the book?"

"Why did I say what? And not for this scene. I learned the lines after Mr. Peters ripped into us."

"You're *infuriating* because you know exactly what I'm asking about."

"And I think you're stalling."

I transitioned into a besotted Juliet. He then gave me a smile that caught me off guard, took my left hand, and gazed straight into my eyes.

"If I profane with my unworthiest hand...this holy shrine, the gentle sin is this. My lips...two blushing pilgrims, ready to stand...to smooth that rough touch with a tender kiss." He gently pressed his lips to my fingers, straightened, and met my eyes once more.

I gave him my shy, yet flirty smile that felt authentic this time. "Good pilgrim, you do wrong your hands too much... which mannerly devotion shows in this...for saints have hands that pilgrims' hands do touch." He released my hand so I could hold it out and upright. "And palm to palm is holy palmers' kiss."

He placed his hand barely against mine. Only our fingertips were touching.

"Have not saints lips? And holy palmers too?" He flattened his hand against mine as he spoke, never once breaking our eye contact.

I brought my hands together in prayer. "Aye, pilgrim, lips they must use in prayer."

Would he actually kiss me?

He covered my hands with his and stepped to the point our bodies almost touched. "Dear saint...let lips do what hands do. They pray: grant thou, lest faith turn to despair."

I was supposed to giggle and move around him. That's how I'd always rehearsed this scene. But he brought me closer and lowered his head, which made my heart rate accelerate.

"Saints...do not move, though grant for prayers' sake."

"Then move not while my prayer's effect I take. Thus from my lips...by yours...my sin is purged." He pressed his mouth against mine.

I remembered our very first kiss. And the fact he was *such* a good kisser.

He lifted his head, and we stared at each other. Until I remembered I spoke next.

"Then..." I smiled. "Have my lips the sin they have took."

He returned my smile. "Sin from my lips? O trespass sweetly urged." He cupped my face. "Give me my sin again."

Our mouths fused, and I remembered our head-spinning second kiss. But, unlike that kiss, he brought this one to a swift end, released me, and stepped back.

"Was that better?"

I wanted to shake my head. To clear the fog he created without trying. But I couldn't let him see his kisses had affected me. Kisses that *hadn't* affected him.

"You kiss by the book."

He gave me his crooked smile. "Clever. And, I'll be honest, I've hardly looked at that scene Romeo has with Friar Laurence. Act two, scene three? Can we do that next?"

"Sure." I walked ahead of him and sat back on the lounger.

I could be a professional, like my mom, and do this with him for the next few weeks. Especially if I visualized our success as Romeo and Juliet.

Chapter Twenty-Three

"Hi."

Meg didn't respond or look at me, but she did stop digging in her locker. The school, thank goodness, was still pretty quiet, which meant we could talk without interruptions.

"I'm sorry I never responded to your message." I had no excuse for my behavior, but I continued with, "It was a very strange weekend. But I know that's not a reason for ignoring you. And I'm here to tell you, in person, I miss you, too."

She turned toward me and smiled faintly. "I know you and the other club members are mad at me about what I did. Owen and I were talking one afternoon. Just getting caught up. He asked about the club and it came out. *I'm* sorry."

I leaned forward and put my arms around her. She readily returned my hug.

"I know you didn't do it on purpose." I pulled away from her. "And I'm sure everyone, even Natalie, knows that. Or will eventually."

She went back into her locker and produced a package of pencils. "They seemed pretty upset on Friday. I'm not sure

Natalie will ever speak to me again. But you know Lexi and Warren. And Paige seems like a forgiving person, too." She unzipped her backpack, shoved the pencils inside and closed her locker door. "Are you okay?"

I actually did feel better than when I left this place Friday afternoon. "I'm fine." But before I went into the truce he and I made, I had to say something. "I'm sorry if I always make it about me. I don't mean to."

She zipped up her backpack and leaned against her locker. "Kass, you don't do that. You just get really caught up in your feelings." She frowned. "Did J.R. say that to you?"

"He was angry when he said it, but it doesn't make him wrong. I promise I'll try, really hard, to work on that."

She smiled. "It's who you are. And, most of the time, it's pretty entertaining. But I mean that in the most loving, supportive way."

I laughed. "What happened? After I left Friday?"

"Nothing. Ms. Simmons, who I think was having a shitty day and didn't want to deal with us anymore, ended the meeting."

I couldn't blame Ms. Simmons. The tension in her classroom had been at boiling point.

"Meg, I am happy you and Owen worked everything out." I smiled. "Have you two officially reconnected?"

She grinned. "We're kind of easing back into that. But we did go out Saturday night and it ended pretty well."

We giggled.

"I didn't mean to keep it from you." Her smile slipped. "But you were having such a crappy week with the play and fell off the map. And knowing about Jade and Nate, and that we started the club. It was easier to wait. But Friday didn't go the way I thought it would."

"Meggie, it's fine. All is forgiven." I paused, then said, "So Justin showed up at my place Saturday morning. To call a

Romeo and Juliet truce to get us through the next few weeks. We also spent a good part of Saturday rehearsing at his house."

Her mouth inched open.

"We're going to keep doing that until he's feeling more comfortable in the role."

She shook her head.

"Stop looking at me like that and say something."

"Whoa. And you clearly didn't kill each other—well, I haven't seen *him* yet today."

"It started off rough, but we got through it. I promise he was fine when he dropped me back off at my building." After an emotionally calmer, uneventful afternoon of running lines.

"Kass, I'm proud of you."

"Thanks. But I'd do anything to salvage *Romeo and Juliet*. Mr. Peters wasn't too happy with either of us last week. I need this play to be extraordinary. And not just because I need a letter of recommendation from him for the Youth Summer Drama Session."

If I, like my mom, could successfully do a Shakespeare play, I could do anything.

"Does this truce mean you might sit with us today? At lunch?"

"No. I mean—I would love to sit with you. But Drew's back today and I was going to sit with him and Bree and whoever else is there from the cast. You understand, right?"

Yes, Saturday had gone well after we, like professionals, put aside our emotions. But that didn't make us friends.

"I get it," she said, but disappointment filled her eyes.

We started walking toward our first periods.

"What did Dr. McDreamy say about your truce?"

I smiled as I remembered Dad's initial bewildered expression after I'd, very indifferently, told him how I'd spent my Saturday and the reasons why. "He was surprised. For about ten seconds. Then he said he knew I'd *'figure it out.'*"

Parents could be so smug.

"Have you met that doctor he likes so much?"

We reached her classroom first and stopped steps from the doorway.

"No. They haven't even been on date two yet. Because of their schedules."

She nodded. "So, what are we going to do about the club? It's below eight members."

I paused. In the strangeness of Saturday and being lost in homework on Sunday, the club really hadn't crossed my mind.

"I don't know. We'll...talk about it later." I scurried down the busier hallway.

When I pictured *him* being a member, my anger from Friday reignited. But I doused the flame before a raging fire started, because our truce and the play were too important.

I also wasn't at all ready to give up my shirt and face the *what now?* with the club.

* * *

I walked into the crowded cafeteria for the first time in over a week. I instantly found Meg, cozied up to Owen. They were sitting, and chatting and laughing with other jocks, including *him*. Not too far from them I spotted Sloane and Brandy sitting close together and talking. I could only imagine who and what the evil twosome were talking about.

Meg caught my gaze and raised her arm ever-so slightly to give me a friendly wave. But I noticed a sadness in her wave that, well, stung. Because I couldn't sit with her anymore.

Owen looked my way and tried smiling. *He*, however, kept talking to his friends.

I waved sadly back and forced myself to find my cast mates. Who I saw on the far right side of the cafeteria.

I headed their way, and spotted Warren and Lexi sitting

with some other kids. They gave me the same friendly but sad wave that I returned. I didn't notice anyone else from the club on this side of the cafeteria, specifically Jade and Nate. I did want to know how their first date went.

When I reached my cast mates, the first thing I noticed was Drew's turquoise cast, which already had several signatures on it. I knew, through Snapchat, he'd missed last week due to the constant discomfort and refusing to take "the serious S-word."

"Hey, you," Bree said as I dropped my lunch on the table beside Drew.

He looked up at me and smiled. "There's my Juliet."

I sat down and the stinging subsided a bit at their warm welcome. I'd missed being in the cafeteria for lunchtime. Missed talking to my friends. No matter what happened, I'd always have my theater family. "Hey, Spider-Man. How are you feeling?"

"I'm okay. And, yeah, that was pretty stupid. I don't know what I was thinking."

"You were being a cocky ass wipe," Shane said before taking a huge bite of his equally huge ham-and-cheese-and-potato-chip sandwich.

I wrinkled my nose and looked back at Drew.

"Kass, I'm really sorry. I put you in a rough spot."

"It'll be fine." Though at this point I couldn't be certain about it being fine.

"That's not what I've been hearing," Drew mumbled.

We hadn't sworn our truce and extra practices to secrecy, but I knew him well enough that he wouldn't want it broad-casted to the cast of *Romeo and Juliet*. I didn't want everyone to know, either. It would mean unnecessary and additional drama, and I pictured the Queen of Peroxide's bleached-blonde head bursting, even though she'd dumped him.

I opened my lunch bag. "Rehearsals should be much better this week." I hoped.

"You sound pretty sure of that," Bree replied. "Do you know something we don't?"

I opened my Sprite and took a quick sip, all while avoiding her probing eyes.

Shane shrugged. "J.R. nailed Mercutio. No reason he can't nail Romeo, too."

We all looked at him.

He smiled at his choice of words. "You know what I mean."

I smiled at Drew. "We definitely miss you." Without question. "I miss you, *O Romeo, Romeo*." I batted my eyelashes..

He laughed. "Sign my cast before you start eating, my fair Juliet."

I picked up the black Sharpie in front of him and paused to think about what to write. When I had it, I removed the cap and wrote: **You'll always be my #1 Romeo! Your Juliet**

Chapter Twenty-Four

I frowned as I watched Justin on stage with David. They stood a couple feet from our four Verona street pillars that were slowly but surely being constructed. They were rehearsing act two, scene three, and he was floundering. Not too much with the lines we'd gone through twice on Saturday, but with the emotion.

He was *not* acting like a boy in love who wanted to marry the girl of his dreams.

His struggles were confusing, too. We'd surprised everyone yesterday, including Mr. Peters, by our strong performance during our scene at the Capulet's Ball.

"Riddling confession finds but riddling shrift." Our Friar Laurence guided Romeo closer to the stage's edge and they stopped.

"Then plainly know my heart's...dear love is set on the fair daughter of rich Capulet."

"Okay. Stop there."

He'd said the line with almost no emotion and it didn't surprise me Mr. Peters stopped the scene.

He freed a heavy sigh. "J.R., you're supposed to be a boy in love who is desperate to marry the girl."

Romeo seemed as exasperated with him as he said, "I know that."

I cringed at his very irritable reply.

"What's wrong with him today?" Bree whispered. "He was pretty good yesterday."

We were sitting together in the front row.

"I don't know," I whispered back while I kept my eyes on him.

"If you know that," Mr. Peters replied, "why am I not seeing it?"

Justin, uncharacteristically, shoved his hands into his pockets and stayed silent.

My frown deepened.

What had changed between yesterday and being back today? More problems in the Richardson home?

I tried, really hard, not to care, but something was affecting his performance today.

Mr. Peters held up his hands. "Take a break. Get some water. Get some air. And come back when your head is clearer. In the meantime—" He lowered his hands and faced us. "Kassidy and Bree let's do act two, scene five."

Also known as our favorite scene together because of the silly moment between us.

We stood, and I watched as he walked off stage with David, who had put a reassuring hand on his shoulder while quietly talking to him.

As we walked on stage, I caught sight of Sloane off stage left. She mumbled something to Maddie and rolled her eyes.

I almost couldn't stop the urge to march up to her, grab a handful of her hair, drag her to the stage's edge and throw her off. Especially since she still didn't really know *her* lines.

"Can someone please carry out the Nurse's chair and footrest?"

We waited for some of the extras—those doubling as backstage crew—to bring out the furniture, and I saw him far off stage right. He was still talking with David, but now Cody and Shane were standing with them. It looked serious, too. Then, like he could feel me watching him, he turned his head and our eyes snapped together. And he looked at me as though all of his problems today were my fault. Which didn't make any sense. We had yet to do a scene together and our paths, as usual, hadn't crossed during the school day.

"Kassidy and Bree, places, please."

He broke our heated look first, and I took my place near the chair.

Bree entered following my dialogue Mr. Peters had cut down to seven lines. And I realized, because of his nasty look, I felt exactly like Juliet in this scene. Anxious and impatient.

* * *

I drummed my nails on the lobby bench while I waited for Justin to leave the auditorium.

Mr. Peters had asked him to stay behind following rehearsal that hadn't included any of his, or our scenes, after his petulant behavior. Everyone else had left.

He was acting like a total ass today. Still talking to Mr. Peters?

I re-read Meg's text and figured something *must've* happened at home last night. Something I had to ask him about, though none of it was my business anymore.

Yeah. Text you after I talk to him.

I put my phone back in my sweater pocket and the door to my left burst open.

He came out and I jumped up, which caught his attention.

He stopped and *smirked* at me. "Oh, my Juliet waited for me. I'm touched."

What was with the antagonistic attitude?

He turned and headed into the main building.

I followed him. "Hey. You're the one who wanted the truce. What's your problem?"

"Yeah, well, maybe I made a mistake," he answered as I caught up to him. "And I'm not in the mood for this—" He gestured harshly at the space between us. "So, do you think you could control yourself and not say anything? I got an earful from Mr. Peters."

"Can you really blame him? You were being a complete jerk."

I saw a muscle in his jaw twitch as we continued our speed walking toward the school's main entrance and exit.

I reached deep into my soul for my compassionate side. "Did something happen at home last night? With your parents?"

The problems with his parents, more often than not, were the reason behind this side of him. A side he, typically, controlled by feeling the anger or hurt or frustration, then letting it go.

"Everything's as usual on the Richardson front. But I sure do appreciate your concern."

My temper snapped, and I stopped walking. "You're a phony, Justin Richardson."

That caused him to stop and he faced me.

"You show up at my place, without warning, and make this big deal about calling a truce. And how important the play is and that you don't want to ruin it. Then I give up my Saturday to rehearse with you and everything's fine on Monday. Then you, for apparently no reason, act like this the next day?" I started walking again and shook my head while I rushed by him. "Forget the truce. Forget everything. I have better things to do then—"

"You're right. You do. And I'm sorry."

Now I stopped and faced him. Defeat had replaced all of his antagonism.

"Mr. Peters said I have until Thursday to get my act together. Or he's booting me."

I pressed my lips together.

Mr. Peters had *never* done such a thing. And being so close to the show's run?

"I can't be Drew." He again shoved his hands into his pockets.

This was about replacing Drew?

"Justin, Mr. Peters doesn't expect you to be him."

"That's what he said when I told him the same thing."

Where on earth was his insecurity coming from? He'd seemed so confident yesterday. And definitely on Saturday.

"What else did he say?"

"That instead of trying to be like Drew, I should be focusing on making Romeo my own." He released an almost sad laugh. "But that's a little hard when Juliet despises you."

Oh. I guess we did have that problem. Still, we had our truce. And I didn't exactly despise him. Even though I had told him I hated him not even a week ago. "I don't despise you. And I promise I'm committed to our agreement."

"I know. But, in the end, will it really be enough to pull this off?"

"It'll have to be." I straightened. "We can do this. I've been visualizing it."

He cracked a smile, then walked toward me. "Okay. I won't walk away."

I stared at him. "You were actually going to quit?" I hadn't been able to hide my amazement. Because Justin Richardson wasn't a quitter.

"I was thinking about it when I left the auditorium."

We started walking, and at a normal pace, toward the doors.

"This whole acting thing. It's not me. But here I am. Because of—" He glanced at me. "Because it seemed like a good idea. And I wanted twenty, stupid extra-credit points."

I sighed. "You're being too hard on yourself. You were fantastic as Mercutio—" I fought a cringe at my slip, though I'd said the truth. I also prepared myself for his reaction to my honesty.

He stopped us at the doors. "*Fantastic*?"

It was a little scary how well I knew him. And there came the crooked smile.

"Fantastic. That's a pretty strong word."

"I can see your head getting bigger. Will you be able to fit it through the doors?"

He laughed as I pushed—more like shoved—one, then the second door, open.

His mom had parked her white Range Rover in the school's pick-up zone.

I saw her through the tinted windows, in the driver's seat, and talking on her phone. Beth, in the backseat, looked focused on something in her lap. Probably her iPad.

"I know you love walking home, but can we give you a ride?" he asked while we jogged down the steps.

My steps faltered.

Where had *that* come from?

But I recovered with a quick smile and picked up my pace. "No. But thank you. I'll soon be losing these walks for a little while." Daylight Saving Time ended the week we started full dress and tech rehearsals, which meant Dad would start picking me up from school.

Justin stopped at the passenger-side door. "You still haven't had any trouble since that one day? Right?"

I nodded and my heart softened a bit at his continued concern over Stalker-Creep.

Maybe that's why he'd offered me a ride home?

He opened the door. "See you tomorrow."

"And you'll be a much more recognizable Justin Richardson?"

"I can guarantee it." He removed his backpack, slid into the SUV, closed his door and they drove off.

The corner of my mouth curved into a tiny smile. Because I believed him.

Chapter Twenty-Five

As I sat in the Theater Department's outer office and worked at their round table, I heard Mr. Lowry moving around in his office. He hadn't given me any work today, but Mr. Peters had left me a laundry list of things to do, which included organizing his *Romeo and Juliet* binder.

I was hole punching several papers when Sloane walked in. As if she were the department's queen. She flounced toward the table, then held out a piece of paper.

We hadn't interacted with one another, outside of rehearsing on stage, since we'd gotten in trouble with Mr. Peters. I'd been staying as far away from her as humanly possible.

"This is for my mom, from me. Make sure she gets it."

I went back to my hole punching. "Put it in her office yourself."

She lowered her hand. "Ooh, someone's in a mood today," she said quietly, but with clear venom in her voice. "Could it be because our new Romeo can't handle the pressure?" She made a *tsking* sound. "I guess he's not leading-man material."

I took a deep breath, looked up at her, and whispered, "Our Lady Capulet isn't doing too well, either. Considering she's had weeks to learn her very few lines. He's only been Romeo a week. What's your excuse?"

Her icy blue eyes sharpened to a point. "You think you're something so special," she whispered back. "Mr. Peters's little pet."

This coming from Mrs. Chaplin's daughter?

"No one cares about the fall shows anyway. Because they're boring."

She couldn't really be standing there, insulting William Shakespeare and *Romeo and Juliet*. Then I remembered Natalie telling us about Sloane's slip to Maddie. That she'd auditioned mainly because of him. And, strangely enough, me.

"If Shakespeare and *Romeo and Juliet* aren't good enough for the oh-so wonderful Sloane Chaplin, why did you even audition?" That, as I hoped, shut her up. And, since Mr. Lowry had yet to hear us, I decided to free my irritation. "What's your problem? He chose you. And then, after all the bragging you did, *you* dumped *him*?"

"Only because of you. He can't, and for reasons I'll never get, seem to stay away from you. It's too weird."

I heard the jealousy in her voice, but it didn't make me feel victorious. Because disgust had been laced with the jealousy. That's what made me stand up.

"We danced once," I snapped in a lowered voice. "And you weren't even there."

Her glare pierced me to my soul. "That's the other part of this that makes me sick. I heard about what you wore and he still danced with you."

I started shaking. At her all-over nastiness.

"And I'm not just talking about that night," she said, without whispering.

I leaned forward. "Then what are you talking about? He joined the Anti-Love Club Friday because of you."

Oh...no.

I really did need to get better at controlling my mouth. Especially in situations like this. But based on her expression, she hadn't expected to hear that.

"He actually joined your pathetic club?"

I straightened, because I was wasting my breath and energy on Sloane Chaplin. She didn't get it and probably never would. A teeny-weeny part of me felt sorry for her.

"What's going on out here?" Mr. Lowry asked from his doorway. He had his arms crossed as he gave us that unhappy-with-student-behavior look. "Sloane, where are you supposed to be right now?"

She flashed him her one-hundred percent fake, innocent smile. "Ms. Simmons told me I could drop off this note for my mom."

"Then drop it off and get back to class. Now."

She stalked into her mom's office. Two seconds later she stalked out and, without a second glance in my direction, left the outer office.

Mr. Lowry shook his head, then pointed at the table. "It looks like Mr. Peters gave you enough work to keep you busy for two periods. You need to get back to it."

I sat down and stared at the papers on the table.

I had ended up in another biting verbal battle with Mrs. Chaplin's daughter. And our latest battle had happened with Mr. Lowry nearby.

All I could do was hope—beg the universe—it didn't turn into a big, ugly mess.

* * *

"Kass, don't worry about it."

Meg stood with me at my locker as I replaced my morning books with those I would need for my afternoon classes.

"Almost no one around here likes Mrs. Chaplin. Or her Queen of Peroxide," she quietly continued since we were surrounded by other students doing the same thing as me. "Mr. Lowry is super cool, too. He won't say anything."

I finished loading up my backpack and closed my locker door. "That doesn't mean she won't go running to her mom about it."

"I don't think she's as powerful as you think. It's not like she's the principal." She smiled tentatively. "Let's talk about something else. Like Kimi's big Halloween party this weekend? I want you to go with us."

Kimi being Meg's cross-country teammate, who was throwing her first big party.

"You and Owen just got back together. Talk about three's a crowd."

"I promise it won't be like that."

"Meg, I'm really not feeling the spirit of Halloween. And even if I wanted to go, I don't have a costume."

"Wear Michelle's cute flapper costume she wore last year. It'll fit you."

I hesitated.

"Pretty please? I swear we'll be on our best behavior. And, in case you're hesitating because of a certain Romeo, he's not going."

Though it surprised me he wouldn't be going to the party, he wasn't the reason behind my hesitation. Because I'd walked away yesterday feeling as though something had shifted between us after our spat in the school. It was a subtle shift. But I somehow felt the tension between us had settled down. I wouldn't, however, be sure of that until today's rehearsal.

"It's not that. I'm just not feeling it."

"Well, would you think about it before saying no? I think

it'll be good for you. Get you away from *Romeo and Juliet* for a night."

I smiled. "Okay, Meggie. But if I decide to go, I'll have to ask Dad."

"Dr. McDreamy won't say no. Now, we have to talk about the club."

I sighed since I couldn't even deal with the club right now. "We'll talk about it—"

"Later. You keep saying that, but you're in full avoidance."

"And enjoying every minute of it. I have the T-Rex next and can't be late."

The rest of the school day went by as I weighed going to the Halloween party. And what to do about the Anti-Love Club.

Maybe Meg and I could hand it over to Warren and Natalie?

If Justin really had joined the club, I could never—not ever—go back. Which still hurt my heart. But I had to do everything in my power to keep *Romeo and Juliet* from falling apart.

Mr. Peters wasted no time breaking us into our choreography groups with Ross and Vanessa when everyone showed up at rehearsal.

I threw myself into the practices. But, during a brief stop while Vanessa went over the steps with students who had two left feet, my eyes wandered to the back of the stage. The boys were practicing their sword fighting while carefully avoiding the set construction area. They were having a great time, too, since sporadic bursts of laughter filled the stage area.

My eyes found him, and I couldn't stop my soft smile.

He, like he said, was in a much better mood. Even now he stood with Shane. Both of them were laughing, pretty hard, as Liam, our Tybalt, dramatically flourished his sword and poked

Cody, our new Mercutio, who as dramatically clutched his chest and fell to his knees.

Hopefully, they'd get over their silliness, and soon.

When rehearsal ended, that had been nothing but practicing all the choreography and rehearsing those scenes, I went to pick up my backpack, but heard, "Hey."

I turned.

He gave me *his* smile. "You looked good up there. During the dancing. Mr. Peters told me I'll be with your group tomorrow."

Mr. Peters's vision was Romeo, wearing his mask, swooping in, dancing Juliet away from Count Paris and into their scene. Drew and I had it almost mastered before his fall.

"Thanks." I smiled and my cheeks warmed at his surprising compliment. And my mind tried taking me back to earthworm day, but I stopped it with, "You guys are still acting a little silly with those swords."

He laughed. "We'll get over it. Well, maybe not Cody and Liam."

We shared a quick laugh.

"So," he walked closer to me, "are you free Saturday? To practice?"

If I did go to the party, it wouldn't be until nighttime. "Sure. Your house again?"

His smile slipped. "Can it be your place? The parents are throwing their Halloween Masquerade for their stupid rich friends this Saturday. The house will be a zoo because of it."

That must be the reason he wasn't going to Kimi's party. But it didn't seem like his style to stick around for anything family related.

"Meg said you're not going to Kimi's party this weekend. Is that why?"

"Twice a year, around Halloween and on New Year's Eve, they like to show us off."

Yikes.

Because we didn't start going out until late March, this was new information. And, in spite of our recent, turbulent history, his matter-of-fact statement sliced through my core.

His smile came back. "You and Meg were talking about me?"

My face became warm again and his smile grew. And earthworm day did fill my mind.

"We were just talking about the party." I shrugged and picked up my backpack.

I didn't know any other way out of this.

"So are you going to her party?" he asked.

I adjusted my backpack onto my right shoulder, and he took another step closer. He then reached out and helped me gently pull strands of my long hair out from underneath my backpack's strap. He'd started doing that right before our first-kiss day in my bedroom.

Our eyes collided, and I couldn't look away as I said, "I don't know if I'm going to her party. Meg's hoping I will. It could be fun. I guess."

He blinked, breaking our eye contact. "About Saturday? Practicing at your place?"

I released a tiny breath and took a step back. "It should be fine. Dad's working. Maybe Michelle can go to a friend's house."

Where on earth had all that come from?

"Same time?" he asked.

Because we were acting like, well, us? At least the us *before* we became a couple.

I brought my attention back to our conversation. "What time did you show up?"

"It was almost eleven." He laughed. "I know you're not an early riser when you don't have to be."

I laughed, too, since he happened to be right. And was the

total opposite of him. He rarely missed a morning run at some ungodly hour to stay in shape for soccer season.

"Kassidy?"

I met his gaze that had turned serious again, but held warmth instead of bitterness.

"Thanks for yesterday. I really needed to hear all that."

I grinned. "Yes. You did. And you do seem much better today."

He stepped back. "It's only going to get better, too."

Something about the way he said that, combined with our...moment...caused excitement to flutter within my tummy.

Chapter Twenty-Six

"It is, it is. Hie hence, be gone, away." I approached him. "It is the lark that sings so out of tune...straining harsh discords and unpleasing sharps. Some say the lark makes sweet division. This doth not so, for she divide—*divideth*—us."

My slip caused his longing but desperate expression to splinter somewhat as he turned and headed for Dad's balcony railing.

"O now be gone...more light and light it grows—" I shoved him. And he pitched forward, right into the railing. My hands flew to my mouth. "I'm sorry."

He shook with laughter as he righted himself. "Easy, Wonder Woman."

I joined his laughter and lowered my hands. And I tried, for the billionth time since he'd arrived, not to notice how irresistible he looked in his shorts, a T-shirt, and a baseball hat he had on backward. He also had morning stubble that only added to his casually hot look.

I really was totally pathetic.

"Okay," he said, his laughter subsiding. "Let's take this to when I leave."

I nodded and joined him at the railing.

He cleared his throat and became a desperate, yet sad Romeo again.

"More light and light...more dark and dark our woes."

"Then Bree has her line and Juliet says 'Nurse?' and Bree has her lines. Then I say...then, window, let day in, and let life out."

"Farewell..." He cupped my face and gazed into my eyes. "One kiss, and I'll descend."

This kiss had a sweetness to it. But he ended the kiss after a breath and let me go.

I took two steps back and tried to ignore the fog he still managed to cause. That I needed to get over since I was determined to be a professional. And the kiss had merely been that of a true Romeo, having been banished from Verona and not knowing when he'll see Juliet again.

"It's getting there. What do you think?"

"That was good." I gave him my back. "You're a lot more confident with the lines, too." I sat down on the lounger and hugged my legs to my chest. "I'm not even sure we need to keep doing this. You're really starting to get it."

"Because this is obviously helping me."

He unexpectedly sat by my feet on the lounger. The closeness felt nice. Familiar.

I smiled at my knees.

"Can we keep doing this until dress and tech rehearsals start?"

I shrugged since it was only one more week. "If you think you need it."

"Oh, by the way, I watched those movies you loaned me. But I forgot to grab them before I left." He grinned. "It was helpful. And you're right. The older version is better."

In that moment, he vaguely reminded me of the actor who played Romeo in that movie. A taller, currently scruffier version of him, and with a modern boy's short haircut hiding under his baseball hat.

"I'm glad the movies helped. What else do you want to run through?"

We'd spent significant time rehearsing the balcony scene, minus any embracing and kissing because Shakespeare hadn't specifically written it in his play. Like their other kisses were. Mr. Peters had never requested those actions of Drew and me, either.

He looked at his watch. "I need to head home." He glanced at me. "I need to get some homework done before I have to become *presentable* for the party. But I was hoping we could, maybe, do this again tomorrow?"

I stared at him. "Won't you be up late because of the party?"

He frowned. "I'll be asleep before midnight. Their stupid parties are boring. That reminds me, did you decide about Kimi's party?"

"Yes. And I'm going. But only at Meg's endless persistence this week."

"You don't let anyone force you into doing stuff, D—" He sighed. "Not calling you that has been harder than I thought it would be." He paused, then said, "Why didn't you ever tell me you hated that nickname? It's not like you to keep something like that to yourself."

I picked at the lounger cushion. "I didn't hate it...until August."

He fell silent, and I continued picking at the cushion. I hoped, for the sake of our comfort level we'd finally achieved and *Romeo and Juliet*, he'd let my honest answer go.

"So, do you think you'll be up for doing this again tomorrow?"

Thank goodness.

"My curfew is back to eleven on weekends."

He laughed because I, unlike many of my classmates, had a strict weekend curfew. But after begging, Dad had extended my curfew, and all week long, to midnight this past summer.

"Where would we rehearse? Dad's off tomorrow and Michelle, even if he was working, has homework that she couldn't do today because I made her go to a friend's house."

"My house isn't an option, either. The parents won't be in the mood for company."

I didn't respond since I caught his meaning.

"But I have an idea on where we could go. Are you in?"

I smiled again. At the familiar, playful tone I really liked hearing. I was also curious about what he had in mind. "Yeah. I'm in."

He held his hand out. "Tomorrow, Juliet."

I grasped his hand and we shared a firm handshake. "Tomorrow, Romeo."

* * *

Kimi's Victorian home reminded me of Meg's house. Old on the outside, completely remodeled inside. The house's main level was packed with students, mostly juniors and seniors, dressed in every costume imaginable. There were, funnily, a few girls dressed as Wonder Woman, and I smiled as I remembered Justin's response to my shove. My smile faded, though, when I pictured him at his parents' stuffy Halloween party and, most likely, keeping an eye on Bethie.

I refocused on my beverage choices—I couldn't allow myself to go there—spread out on the oversized island counter in Kimi's deluxe kitchen. Several partiers had brought alcohol, and among the soda and juice choices were bottles of vodka and rum and whiskey.

The whiskey bottle had its top off and the strong, bitter smell filled my nose. To the point I could taste it and my stomach flipped.

I moved to another counter where I saw lemonade.

I reached for the carton and poured myself a cup as Michael Jackson's "Thriller" started playing for the second time since we'd arrived.

"Kass?"

I set the lemonade down and turned at the sound of Jade's raised voice.

She'd adjusted and pinned a mermaid blanket around her waist and had on a pink bikini top. She'd curled her red hair enough to create thick waves, and sparkly eyeshadow and lip gloss completed her Princess Ariel costume.

She looked gorgeous, but I wondered how she could walk while wearing the blanket.

"Hi," I said, looking for, I assumed, her Prince Eric. "Where's Nate?"

She giggled. "Talking with some of his baseball buddies." She inched toward me because of her tail. "Are you okay? About me and Nate?"

This was the first time I'd really seen her since the dance. Our paths had crossed in the school's hallways, but we'd only exchanged smiles.

I grinned. "I'll admit I was surprised when they told me about you two. But I think it's pretty awesome, Jade."

She threw her arms around me. "Thank you. It's all because of you, too."

I laughed. "What do you mean?"

She released me. "We never would've gotten together if not for the Anti-Love Club. I mean, we've known each other forever, but never spent any time together since high school started. I was caught up in Gavin." She made a sour face. "And he was caught up in Rachel."

"Are either of them here? I haven't seen them, but that doesn't mean anything."

"I don't know and don't care." She gave me a smile that matched her sparkly face. "I feel differently about Nate. Like this is how it's supposed to be. *Us*. You know?"

Yes. I definitely understood that.

"And Meg and Owen are back together...happily...based on what I saw in the living room." She giggled. "I don't think a crowbar could pry those two apart."

Something else I fully understood.

Warren, or Phantom of the Opera, walked up behind Jade with Lexi, dressed as a "naughty" Dorothy.

They pulled me into a hug. And I tightly embraced them.

"You're rockin' the flapper girl tonight, Juliet," Warren said once we'd separated.

"Thanks. Are you going to burst into 'The Music of the Night' before this is over?"

He smiled. "You know, I was actually thinking about that. I'm not too bad. Maybe I should try out for the spring musical this year. If J.R. can blow people's minds performing Shakespeare—" He stopped and almost looked guilty for mentioning him. As did Lexi.

And I knew, right then, what was happening. "He really did join the club. Didn't he?"

They nodded, and I suppressed the frustration.

Lexi giggled. "If it makes you feel better, he didn't say much to us on Friday. Natalie made it clear, by the looks she was giving him, she was plotting ways to kill him. And I don't think he really appreciated Warren playing our club song."

I giggled, too. At the same time, I didn't understand his behavior. He wasn't acting like a boy with a broken heart. Or that he'd been dumped the way he had by Sloane. Who also hadn't come to this party, *thankyouverymuch*. But what did I know about how brokenhearted boys acted. Nate and Rachel broke up in February. Though his wounds were apparent at the club's beginning, he'd also had months to recover from the initial heartache and humiliation. Still, Justin's break-up with Sloane was none of my business. We also had our now working truce and it couldn't be jeopardized this close to the show's run. I had to let it go.

But the bratty part of me still didn't want to give up my club T-shirt. That I had earned.

"Madam President, we're down two members," Warren said. "Some freshman showed up at the meeting on Friday and really only talked to J.R. That kid was the other reason I played our song." He laughed, and it sounded a bit like a Natalie laugh. "But we need two more members." He glanced at Lexi. "We, the remaining original members, even Natalie, want to keep the club going."

Hearing those words touched me, and to the point emotion filled my eyes. Until Meg timidly appeared at my side while holding up the sides of her bright yellow, Belle from *Beauty and the Beast* dress. But her face was glowing more than Jade's.

"Please tell me you guys have forgiven me."

Warren and Lexi gave Meg a long, severe stare. Then, when it seemed she might timidly retreat, they pulled her into their arms for a hug. Nate—or Prince Eric—then walked up behind Jade and slid his arms around her waist. And her glow became blinding.

"Is this an unofficial Anti-Love Club meeting?" Nate asked.

"Yes," Warren replied. "We're trying to figure out what to do next since we've lost you two lust birds and our founding members. But we've gained a Romeo and a freshman."

Another awkward silence fell and I, determined to show I

could move past all that drama, said, "Warren, I think you'd make a great new president."

There were approving nods and Jade said, "Yes. That's perfect."

Warren straightened. "I was thinking that myself."

Meg looked at Lexi. "Any interest in being vice president?"

She shook her head. "I think Natalie would be much better. Warren's gotten pretty good at dealing with her feisty side."

"I'll blow up her phone with texts about it tomorrow until she can't stand it and agrees to do it just to shut me up. She's at some party tonight at San Francisco State with her friends." Warren looked at me. "Do we have to do anything else? To make it official?"

"We'll probably have to submit the changes to student council," I said. "But I can do that this week and let you know by Friday?"

Warren nodded. "What about getting the two new members?"

Nate laughed. "You're pretty good at eavesdropping. Keep doing that. I'm sure you'll hear other couples fighting in the school's hallways."

"Stalk people on Snapchat, too," Meg added.

"Okay. We'll carry on but, so sadly, without you four."

Before the mood turned too serious, Jade glanced at Nate over her shoulder. "Grab my phone for me?" He reached into his pants pocket and withdrew her cell. "Everybody get around me. I want to take a picture of the original Anti-Love Club members. I just wish Natalie and Paige were here. And Alisha. Where are those two?"

"I don't think Kimi extended the party invites to freshmen," Meg replied.

I stood against Jade with Meg hugging my right side. Nate,

Warren, and Lexi stood behind us. When we were set, Jade tapped the camera app and held her phone out and up.

"Everyone smile!"

A second later she snapped the picture. And it occurred to me I was the only one in the group who'd actually *lost* the club.

Chapter Twenty-Seven

I flopped down beside Dad on the couch. His bare feet were propped up and crossed on the ottoman, and he had his laptop in his lap.

"Is Detective Atwater getting close to catching the perp?"

"Yes. But the killer committed another heinous crime. I'll spare you the details."

"Thanks," I mumbled, and I wondered if the "heinous crime" had been inspired by one of the many *pret-ty* intense crime documentaries he recorded off *Investigation Discovery*.

"I'm reading over what I wrote last night before I start for the day." He looked at me and smiled. "You look nice. Are you sure today is only a rehearsal?"

I scanned my outfit of crop skinny jeans and a loose, sleeveless gray top. I'd also chosen my black sandals. Because he'd said to wear shoes like that in his text he'd sent as he left his house several minutes earlier. And the oh-so familiar spark I had always felt when getting a text from him returned and heated my insides.

"I'm totally casual. And this is strictly business." Something I really needed to remember since we *were* professionals. Staying focused on that helped me to not dwell on silly sparks and the fact I'd lost my club because of him.

"Where are you going?"

"I don't know." I shrugged, though I was very curious about where we were going. "It has to be some place quiet, though, and secluded if we're—why are you laughing?"

"Because it sounds like a date to me. But I'm not a twenty-first century teenager."

I stood. "Dad, you have absolutely no idea what you're talking about."

"I know I don't." He laughed a couple more seconds, then said, "But this funny conversation is reminding me Lauren and I going on our second date Wednesday night."

He hadn't said her name before and curiosity replaced my outrage at his insistence the rehearsal was a date.

"It won't be a late night because it's a school night for everyone."

"Are we going to get to meet her?"

His smile grew. "Yes. She definitely wants to meet you two, but there's no rush. We're getting along great at work. And keeping it professional as you would say. But we're just now at date number two. Let's see how that goes, first."

I knew he was being cautious not only to protect himself, but us. I could count on one hand how many women, in the years he'd been single, he'd introduced to us. And only a couple of those women had turned into his girlfriend.

"I get not rushing. But you know you turn into a grinning fool when you talk about her."

He laughed. "No. But thank you for your honesty."

"Anytime," I threw back at him. "He should be here any minute. I'm going to wait downstairs so he doesn't have to find parking."

He returned to his computer. "Tell Romeo I said hi. Then tell him I said to keep you away from lighter fluid and matches."

Would he *ever* let that go?

I glared at him. "Ha, ha."

He smiled. "He shoots"—he mimed throwing a basketball into the hoop— "he scores!"

I battled a smile as I said, "So lame."

"And ask him if he knows anything about guns."

"*Dad.*"

His shoulders shook with laughter as I turned and stomped toward the door.

* * *

Justin and I walked across the warm sand. And as we passed the volleyball nets I tried, really hard, to squelch my shock he'd brought us to Ocean Beach. Because this place, specifically our spot at the sand dunes, located at the opposite end of where we were, held so many, well, amazing memories. One in particular on my sixteenth birthday. That I blocked before it took over my mind.

My question of why he'd chosen to bring us here was on the verge of escaping my mouth. But I somehow forced myself to swallow the question since I *needed* to stay focused on why we were here today.

When we were about halfway between the water and the volleyball nets, he stopped and spread out the oversized towel he'd brought.

I dropped to the towel and sat cross-legged, and he sat across from me. He then opened his copy of the play. As he focused on, I had to assume, his lines, I scanned the beach.

Despite the beautiful October weather, the beach wasn't

too crowded. For some reason, Ocean Beach didn't attract huge amounts of locals or tourists. Another reason we'd been able to find our spot at the sand dunes. There were a few groups of girls sunbathing nearby. I could even smell their suntan lotion. There were also some kids playing in the shore and several people walking their dogs. One guy was playing fetch with his Golden Retriever, drenched from running in and out of the water to get its ball.

"Is it even so?" he said, and I brought my eyes back to him. "Then I *defy* you, stars." He groaned. "That sounded way too dramatic."

He, like me, had his sunglasses on, but I could see, based on the angle of the sun, his frustration while he stared at his book as if searching for inspiration.

"Is it even *so*? Then I defy you, stars." He tossed the book onto the towel. "That was even worse. I really hate those two lines," he muttered. "And Drew delivered them without even thinking about it."

I tried to catch his eyes as I said, "But this isn't about his version of Romeo."

He looked at me. "You two had pretty good chemistry. And not only on stage." He picked his book back up and fanned the pages. "Are you two...going out?"

My eyes darted left.

Had he somehow found out about Drew's interest in me? Surely Drew hadn't said anything to him. And then I remembered Justin's kind of jealous reaction when Drew walked up at the end of our dance. But why did he care if we were dating? He'd made his choices.

I forced my eyes back to him and said, "Not that it's any of your business, but no. He's always been more like a big brother."

I didn't really understand where he'd seen the chemistry

thing. Drew and I had been comfortable playing off each other in our scenes, but kissing him had felt odd. Unnatural. Another reason my feelings for Drew were nothing more than friendly.

"I was just asking. You've been sitting with him at lunch."

Wait, he'd noticed that?

"I also saw what you wrote on his cast. With all that and the dance—" He shrugged.

What did I write on his cast? Something about Drew being—oh. Wow.

Had that been the reason behind his insecurities last week?

"Justin, I was being—"

"You. Honest."

I crossed my arms. "You used to like that about me."

He lifted his shoulders, shook his head, and said, "I never said I didn't still like that about you."

I leaned forward. "Then why are you upset? It was nothing. A silly cast comment."

"Yeah, well, you wrote it and I saw it at the wrong time."

"What does that mean?"

He also leaned forward. "I heard you talking to Mr. Peters about replacing me."

I froze.

How had he even heard us? I'd made sure we were alone.

"I know exactly what you're thinking, too. I forgot my sweater. I left it on the back of a front row seat. You two weren't talking quietly. Because you thought you were alone."

He looked away, and I felt my face, already warm from the sun, become red hot.

I'd been so focused on my mission, I'd never heard the door. Not that we would've heard it opening and closing from that far away. Being auditorium doors, they weren't noisy.

The guilt shrouded me. Because that hadn't been my finest

hour as a young actress. And the pieces of his insecurity puzzle last week snapped right into place.

I'd—and unintentionally—ripped the stage right out from underneath him.

"Justin..." I sighed. "I was angry. At you. The situation. The terrible rehearsal. It seemed like a good idea at the time."

Silence, with the exception of the ocean's rumbling and the seagulls squawking, settled around us. Two things then crossed my mind and I said the first one.

"That's why you called the truce and wanted these extra rehearsals."

He nodded. "And because what you said was the truth. Which I didn't like hearing. Especially that day. But after I was done being pissed at you..." He looked back at me. "I remembered what you and Mr. Peters said about me being Mercutio. I knew I could do the same thing with Romeo. But I also know *you* and that if we didn't get on the same page, we wouldn't get through this. Then, on Tuesday, I saw what you wrote on Drew's cast and..." He gave me a hint of a smile. "I meant what I said to you Wednesday. After rehearsal?"

"I know you did. Justin, I really am so sorry." And every part of me meant it. Especially since he'd been working so hard.

"It's fine. It was two wake-up calls I needed."

I decided to ask my second question—because I had to know—and took a quick breath. "Is all that why you joined the club? Payback? For what you overheard me saying?"

He slowly shook his head, but it didn't appear out of denial. More like...frustration?

He stood and stepped off the towel. "I can't focus on *Romeo and Juliet* right now. I'm going to grab the ball from the car. Meet me at the empty volleyball net over there?"

I squinted up at him. "You brought a volleyball? And you want to play? Now?"

"Why not?"

I gestured at the space between us. "We're in the middle of something here."

"Are you nervous? Because the last time we played it was a blow out."

"You drive me *crazy*."

He simply smiled and headed toward where he'd parked the SUV.

Two wins—him—and one win—me—later, we were in the middle of our longest volley yet. Until I, going for the ball, lost my footing and practically nose-dived into the sand.

Just. Perfect.

I heard him not bothering to hide his laughter as I rolled onto my back. I stayed like that as I brushed sand off my face and mouth. And it struck me—this rehearsal day had turned into something more resembling a date.

I frowned.

It's not like I had to share this part of the day with Dad.

Justin, still laughing, appeared above me.

"I hate you."

He held out his left hand, which I grasped.

"That's not what you said on Tuesday," he said while helping me up.

"What happened to letting the girl win *once* in a while?" I brushed off the sand.

"That doesn't sound like the Kassidy Pashen I know and —" He tilted his head right and made it clear he was staring at my butt. "You missed a spot. And how do you know I didn't let you win that one game? But I did win this last one."

I answered by giving my backside several swipes.

He walked over to where the volleyball had landed after my spectacular wipeout and plucked it off the sand. "Okay. I have to get that scene and those lines right before we leave."

I knew he was a perfectionist when it came to his piano playing. I'd gone to most of his soccer games in the spring and saw the perfectionism there. But seeing his perfectionist side this up close and very personal caused exhilaration to shoot through me.

Chapter Twenty-Eight

I peeked at him as he rested his head against the headrest. Between his tousled hair, sun-kissed face, and sunglasses, he looked better than good.

I knew I looked pink, even though I had put on a *teensy* bit of makeup this morning. That I'd probably sweated off during our volleyball games. I'd also pulled my hair up into a tight ponytail after game one.

I suddenly wanted to check my appearance in the passenger-side visor mirror.

"You're staring," he said, his eyes straight ahead. "But I know you still think I'm hot."

I released my best disgusted groan. "You're so obnoxious. I don't know how you and your ego fit in this SUV."

"Said the girl who can have a pretty healthy ego of her own."

I faced him. "I'm not the one who struts around school like I'm hotter than coffee."

That hadn't sounded ridiculous in my head. And he laughed for several seconds.

"Being with you is like riding the Space Mountain roller

coaster." He tore his eyes from the road and flashed *his* smile. "I never know what you're going to do or say next."

I couldn't be certain, but his comments had sounded like compliments.

"Speaking of egos, on Tuesday before we left school, you already knew what I thought about you as Mercutio."

"Yeah, but 'fantastic' is like you were saying I was out of this world."

"And there goes your big balloon head."

"I'm only trying to get you to see the word from my point of view."

My mind went to earthworm day. When he'd complimented me and given me my nickname. The official start of it all, though it took us months to cross the "friendship line."

Had he said it that way on purpose? Because if he had, his facial expression didn't show it one bit.

"So," I began and because I'd had yet to ask him, "how was the party last night?"

"Entertaining."

I knew he didn't mean that in a positive way. "What happened?"

He stayed silent, and I started to doubt he would answer me. Maybe he didn't feel comfortable talking with me about his parents anymore since we were now nothing more than cast mates with a personal history.

"It's incredible to me," he finally said, and with that trace of bitterness, "those two act like the happily married power couple who has it all, including the two *perfect* kids, in front of their asshole friends. But when the show's over, they're nothing. That house is nothing."

His hands tightened on the steering wheel, and I placed my hand on his right wrist. I'd started doing this during moments like these about a month into our relationship.

He released the steering wheel and our two hands joined.

He gave mine a quick squeeze and we rested our arms on the center console.

My mind drifted to a day in June, about a week before That Afternoon, when we'd been lying back on the double lounger and watching the sky transition to twilight.

I'd rolled my head right to look at him. "What does *the* Justin Richardson see himself doing in...hmm...ten years? Blowing people away with your piano playing?"

He'd laughed and rolled his head left. "I don't know. I'm not like you. I haven't known what I wanted to do since I was eleven." He'd then clasped my hand and, more seriously, added, "I think I'm still trying to figure out who I am." His eyes had narrowed. "But I do know I'll be better than my parents. At least when it comes to having a family."

Maybe that alone was why he appeared to be everything his parents weren't the handful of times I'd been around them.

My building came into view and snapped me out of my thoughts.

He swiftly released my hand, and I shifted forward in my seat.

"This was a great day. Thanks for all your help. Yesterday and today."

He pulled up and stopped alongside a car parked right in of my building but left me enough room to comfortably get out.

"You're welcome. And it was a great day." I honestly meant that, too. "Your Romeo's getting there. We still have two more weeks. But Mr. Peters will get demanding this week and definitely next."

"Thanks for the heads up."

I reached for the door handle but paused to look across my shoulder at him. He was watching me, but I couldn't pinpoint his *look*.

"Justin, I think it'll be a much better week."

"I know it will."

I returned his grin and slid from the SUV.

I could feel his eyes as I walked up the front stoop and let myself into the building. When I closed the door behind me, he drove away.

He seemed so much like the *real* Justin Richardson now. The boy from before That Night. And our banter, comfort with each other, and chemistry was the *real* us.

I turned and headed up the stairs as a question burned bright inside my head.

Why—outside of our bickering which started before That Night—had he chosen her? At the same time, I had a feeling I'd never know the answer to my burning question.

* * *

I walked up to Ms. Simmons's desk after class.

"Hi." She paper clipped our grade sheets for the research paper together. "You submitted your paper and I have your grade sheet?"

"Yes," I answered, and stopped myself from adding the word gratefully. "I also just wanted to say I'm sorry. For how I acted that Friday. It was a really awful week."

She looked at me and surprise filled her eyes.

I'm sure she rarely heard students apologize for bad behavior.

"Thank you, Kassidy." She laughed softly. "There never seems to be a dull moment in those meetings."

I gave her a half smile. "I also wanted you to know I won't be coming back to the club. Meg and I are handing it over to Warren and Natalie...I think." I needed to follow up with him about Natalie being the new vice president before I submitted the changes to student council.

"I figured. But, since you and Meg did start this club, I

think it would be a nice gesture if you two came to this week's meeting and announced it to the entire club."

Panic gripped my breath for a few seconds, then I said, "But they already know."

I'd been doing so incredibly well separating *Romeo and Juliet* from him joining the club. Yes, our extra rehearsals were going extremely well. But seeing him in this classroom with my people would be a visual reminder of what I lost the moment he'd stubbornly sat down and said, "Consider me a member." And for reasons I still didn't understand.

"That may be true," she continued, "but I think they should all hear it from you, being the club's founder?" She smiled. "Tell Meg she's required to come, too. You'll be fine."

I nodded and turned away from her desk.

Was I being punished for an evil version of myself in a former life?

Now I had to find Meg in the cafeteria and tell her Ms. Simmons's request. But she wouldn't care. Owen hadn't joined our club and they were enjoying their happily ever after.

She, as usual since they'd reunited, was sitting with Owen and other jocks and him.

I straightened my shoulders and headed for their table. Sometimes we didn't see each other after lunch, or after school because of rehearsals, and I wanted this over with.

When I arrived at their table everyone, including him, stopped talking and looked at me. Two soccer players, the same two who'd been sitting with him and Owen the day the cast list went up, watched me closely. Probably wondering if I would cause another scene.

Justin caught my eyes, smiled, and I looked at Meg. Her smile seemed hopeful, because I knew she wanted me to sit with them.

"Can I talk to you for a minute?"

Her smile changed to surprise before she nodded and stood.

I wasted no time walking away. Once we were in the hallway, I told her what Ms.

Simmons had said to me. And, like I thought, she replied with a flippant shrug.

"I know this isn't a big deal for you."

"Kass, we'll be in there for, like, five minutes." She frowned. "Why are you still acting like this? You said you two have been getting along great during your extra rehearsals."

"That's a completely different situation." Apparently, not even my best friend would ever see this from my point of view. "And what I'm trying, really hard, not to be mad about is that I think he joined to irritate me. How is any of this fair? It's my club. Our club. Or it was."

"Kass, that doesn't make any sense. Have you thought about asking him?"

"I did, sort of, ask him. But his answer was needing to play volleyball."

Her mouth dropped open. "You didn't tell me you two played volleyball yesterday."

"Meg, that's not the point."

"Going to the meeting for a few minutes isn't a big deal. So let it go. It's not as if you don't have more important things to think about right now." She smiled. "Please, please, *please* sit with us today. I feel like I never see you anymore."

I felt the same way, but I didn't feel comfortable enough with him to sit with them at lunch. "Meg, being friendly with each other doesn't make us friends. I'm sorry."

After we shared a mutual sad smile, she veered left and I veered right, toward where I'd been sitting with my cast mates.

My lingering frustration went away, though, the moment I walked into the auditorium and saw the set. My eyes widened.

Mr. Lowry and his crew must have worked long and hard on Saturday morning.

The four pillars, that would be as tall as the Capulet's wall, were almost complete. The small section of steps placed between each one were finished. Though that part of the set still needed to be painted, the Capulet's wall and Juliet's balcony were done. The opening had paneled-window doors, which opened out. Between that, the rustic paint job and the fake vines wrapped around the balcony, as well as the vines they'd secured to Romeo's climbing wall, it looked like an authentic fourteenth century mansion wall.

I smiled, and anticipation simmered inside my tummy as I approached the stage.

The simmering only multiplied when Mr. Peters immediately divided the girls and boys for costuming. The girls went to the stage left dressing room; the boys went stage right.

"Kassidy, you have four costumes." Angelina smiled. "One for the ball, a *regular* dress for a couple scenes, one for your wedding, and a burial gown."

I giggled. I'd been hoping I'd have at least three. But four costume changes also meant spending a lot of time getting in and out of the elaborate clothing.

"Mr. Peters wanted me to stress to please be very, very careful with these costumes since they're on loan from a few different places," Angelina continued. "He also wanted me to tell you they're probably not going to fit you perfectly. But that's what today is for. If your dress is just too big or too small, he'll have to trade it in for something that fits you better."

We nodded, and Angelina reached for the first dress on rack one. A gorgeous, square neckline, flowing red Elizabethan gown with red and gold material down the very front. And I knew, before she handed it to me, it was my ball gown.

I, falling in love at first sight with the gown, scarcely heard her say, "Help each other out with changing. But quickly. He wants to get through acts four and five."

Bree and I raced behind the first of two dressing screens. The dressing room also had two makeup stations, two full-length mirrors, and a single bathroom.

Sloane and Maddie went behind the farthest screen. The other girls were still getting their costumes from Angelina.

Several minutes later, Bree carefully zipped me up in the heavy gown and my breath caught since the dress was a little snug.

"Wow." Bree turned me toward the nearest full-length mirror. "You look great."

My breath caught again, but only because I looked how I envisioned myself on the first day of school when I saw the poster for auditions. The only difference being I had styled my hair in my long wispy braid today.

As I continued admiring myself in the mirror, I wondered if my mom had looked and felt like this the first time *she* put on Juliet's ball gown. Dad didn't have pictures of her as Juliet. He'd once told us he regretted not taking more pictures of her in her shows before she became sick and had to stop performing.

Angelina, when she saw me, smiled, which I returned. And brought my mind back to here. I then felt the other girls' eyes. Knowing I had to be getting a nasty stare from Sloane, I did feel the very unprofessional urge to turn and stick my tongue out at her. But I knew my mom never would've acted like that. And I could totally control myself.

"Mr. Peters wants to see you when you're ready. He's doing the same thing to J.R. Something about his vision." Angelina shook her head.

I grabbed a handful of both sides of the gown and lifted it enough so I could comfortably walk without the bottom dragging. Angelina opened the door for me and I scooted past her.

Mr. Peters stood near the Capulet's wall while holding the binder I'd organized.

I approached him and spotted Justin with Cody and Shane—they were already finished?—walking from the direction of their dressing room and onto the stage. He barely glanced my way, but then stopped and did a double take. Which caused the other two boys to stop and also look my way. And his mouth curved into a mischievous smile, which reminded me of our first-kiss day in my bedroom.

"Excellent," Mr. Peters said while we continued our long stare that lasted until he, walking again, disappeared behind the Capulet's wall.

My body suddenly felt hot. But I didn't know if it was the warm heavy gown or our long stare making me feel that way.

Chapter Twenty-Nine

I, feeling quite proud of myself, put the Smart Board pen back in its place and stepped away from the board. Until I looked at the T-Rex.

"You missed two steps." He pointed to where I'd left out the easy step that gave me the final answers for both x's.

"That's because I did it in my head."

"That isn't what I asked you to do."

"But I reached the right answers. And everyone in here knows how to do that step."

His face became red as some of my peers started, of course, snickering.

I hadn't meant for all that to come out. But why did he have to be so unreasonable?

"Fix it."

I picked the pen back up. And, as I subtly rolled my eyes, hastily added changing, first, the -13 to a positive and bringing it to the other side, then did the exact same thing with the -5.

"I did catch that. You're not that sneaky. Am I going to have trouble with you today?"

I put the pen down again, faced him, and gave him my best angelic smile. "No."

"Sit down."

I headed back to my desk and avoided everyone's eyes, specifically *hers*. Because I'm sure she'd enjoyed every second of my tense moment with the T-Rex.

He started going through another problem, and my eyes drifted around the classroom.

Today was Halloween and one of the few days we were allowed to be out of uniform. We could wear costumes, but with all the "appropriate costume rules," almost everyone wore jeans and various shirts. I'd, like almost every other girl, chosen skinny jeans. Not being a huge fan of Halloween, I chose to wear my snug, San Francisco Shakespeare Festival T-shirt.

There was nothing wrong with generating as much good karma as possible.

I glanced at the clock.

A little less than two hours until our first day of running through the play, from beginning to end, as much as possible. And the normal, genuine excitement of being part of something spectacular bubbled inside me, lasted through my remaining afternoon classes, and right into rehearsal. Where Justin and I nailed our scene at the Capulet's Ball. And the electricity between us intensified the further we got into the balcony scene.

I leaned against the railing as he reached the spot on the climbing wall where he could step onto the somewhat narrow platform that now looked like the balcony's outer ledge.

"Thou knows the mask of night is on my face...else would a maiden blush bepaint my cheek" —I smiled— "for which thou has heard me speak." I reached for his free hand and our fingers locked. "Fair Montague, I am too fond...and thou may think my behavior light."

He released my hand and stepped onto the ledge. He walked carefully to where he wouldn't block me from the house and kneeled, also carefully, which made us eye level.

"But trust me, gentleman, I'll prove more true, than those that have more cunning to be strange." I placed my hands on his shoulders and gazed into his eyes. "Dost thou love me? I know thou will say 'Aye,' and I will take thy word. Yet...if thou swears...thou may prove false." I giggled. "O gentle Romeo, if thou does love me, pronounce it faithfully."

He cupped my face and kissed me. Which caught me off guard since we'd never rehearsed it this way. But I went with it by hooking my arms behind his neck.

We ended the dizzying kiss and he said, "Lady, by yonder blessed moon I swear—"

"Stop!"

We looked at each other, then at Mr. Peters, sitting in the front row with Angelina. They were staring at us with wide eyes. And in that pause I noticed many of our cast mates standing in the wings, stage right, also watching us. Their expressions resembled amusement.

"Where did all that come from?" Mr. Peters stood and walked toward the stage as Justin and I slowly broke apart.

I could tell he was thinking the same thing—what had we done wrong *now*?

"Incredible." Mr. Peters shook his head, but now he looked...impressed? "I think you two have officially found your Romeo and Juliet."

We exchanged swift, tiny smiles.

"Please. Whatever you do, don't lose what you're doing here today. And we'll pick it up at Romeo's last line."

Justin nodded, and we, grinning, went back to our embrace that wasn't as tight.

But we were close enough he discreetly placed his lips near my left ear and whispered, "This spot still smells good."

Chapter Thirty

My phone buzzed and chirped with a text message as I tried, not really hard, to read Nathaniel Hawthorne's *The Scarlet Letter*, our new project in Ms. Simmons's class.

I picked my phone up off my bed and smiled.

Meg had written, *How was rehearsal? 10 days and counting...*

Our best one yet.

Actually, it had been beyond better than that. But what had it been about today that caused everything to click? And to the point I know I would've made my mom proud.

For the first time, I had felt like Juliet Capulet.

Was it the extra rehearsing? And getting along? Combined with being out of uniform?

He'd looked pretty—the word scrumptious again popped into my head—in his jeans that fit him perfect back *there*. And in his dark gray T-shirt with the word IMAGINE printed on the front. A T-shirt I'd seen him in before and that also fit him perfectly.

Fabulous! Owen's on his way over. We're going to watch the original Halloween.

I laughed and typed, *Yeah, right, you're going to watch the movie.*

I was about to drop my phone when another text came in and my eyes widened.

Hey. What are you doing?

This was the first time Justin had sent me a text not related to our extra rehearsals. And a pretty big spark ignited inside my chest as I smiled at my phone.

I hesitated, glanced at my book, and responded, *Not reading The Scarlet Letter. What are you doing?*

As soon as I hit send, Meg's message came through.

My parents are home. But at least we don't have to hand out candy.

How romantic. You, Owen, your parents, and Michael Myers.

I waited for their replies and his came first.

Waiting to take Beth trick-or-treating. And watching the Romeo and Juliet version we like. Again.

Hmm...we?

My smile doubled in size.

We killed it today.

I read his messages a second time and two things occurred to me. He'd watched the movie at least twice and was thinking about our rehearsal today, too. And his flirty comment "This spot still smells good" appeared in my mind for the hundredth time.

The spark inside my chest was replaced with a lightning strike.

Don't forget about the trick-or-treaters. xx

xx

To him I said, *Again? So that explains you finding your inner Romeo.*

Michelle came into our room. She'd long since exchanged this year's pirate costume for her pajamas. She finished doing something on her phone, then sat down on my bed. I scooted closer to the wall and she stretched out beside me.

No. Today wouldn't have been the same with a different Juliet.

"Who are you texting?" she asked while trying to look at my phone.

I shielded the screen, and she rolled her eyes and went back to her phone.

My face, my whole body, warmed at his compliment. That I had no idea how to respond to since "Thanks" didn't seem good enough. Another response, though, was on the tip of my fingertips: Today wouldn't have been the same with a different Romeo.

But I went with, *We did kill it today.*

Drew and I had never achieved that kind of genuine passion all the times we'd rehearsed the balcony scene. Remembering specific parts of today's rehearsal—the kissing —made my head a little woozy and reminded me of our *passionate* summer together.

Michelle started laughing. "I've been watching your face. And it keeps turning more and more red. Which means you have to be texting *Justin.*"

I elbowed her and added, *Michelle's right here. And acting totally ridiculous.*

"What's he saying?"

"None of your business. Did you need something?"

Dad always worked pretty late on Halloween night, and we were always told to be at home on Halloween night. Maybe that's why I'd never been too crazy about the "holiday."

"I want you to come watch scary movies with me. We don't hang out anymore."

Her last statement, the second time I'd heard something

like that in two days. But I wasn't trying to be self-absorbed. Just staying focused. On the big final picture.

Nosy little sister. I get it.

I paused, debating my next message, but decided it would simply be me, being honest. And he did say on Sunday he still liked that about me.

I think it's sweet you're taking Bethie trick-or-treating.

But my smile dipped when I pictured what Beth's life would be like if she didn't have him. She'd probably have to rely on a babysitter or nanny to take her trick-or-treating. To take care of her in general.

"It'll be fun," my sister enthusiastically said. "We'll pop some popcorn—please? You're not doing anything important. Except texting your Romeo ex-boyfriend."

I blinked and focused on her. "Michelle, you know I hate scary movies. And we're texting about our rehearsal today." Not at all a lie...sort of.

Thanks. I'll let you get back to the nosy sister and not reading The Scarlet Letter.

My smile returned as I tapped out, *Tomorrow, Romeo?*

"You're awfully smiley and red for just talking about *Romeo and Juliet.*"

"If I say yes to the movies, will you stop being so nosy?"

She sprang from my bed. "I'll go pop the popcorn. And they're doing a *Halloween* marathon on AMC."

I groaned since *The Scarlet Letter* sounded like a much better option.

Tomorrow, Juliet.

* * *

I dropped my backpack and sat in the aisle seat beside Bree and right behind him. He sat in the first row and was talking with Cody, Shane, and Liam.

I'd never sat with him before rehearsal, but I'd found myself being pulled toward him when I walked into the auditorium. And Bree happened to be sitting here, too.

She leaned close to me and angled her head away from the boys. "So I meant to tell you yesterday," she whispered, "that you and J.R. were on *fire* during rehearsal." She laughed. "Are you two back together?"

I smiled and, keeping my eyes on him as he laughed at something they were talking about, whispered, "No. We're just being professionals."

She slowly nodded, but her narrowed eyes told me she didn't believe me.

And even I wasn't sure I believed me.

He, smiling, suddenly angled himself toward me, then hooked his right arm over the seat's back. "How'd it go not reading last night?"

I felt Bree watching us as she started talking with the other boys.

"Michelle talked me into watching a *Halloween* marathon."

He released an exaggerated gasp. "You watched horror movies last night?"

I laughed. "She pulled the I-miss-you card. I couldn't say no. How did your night go?"

He shrugged. "Not bad. She has enough candy to last until Christmas. But I did steal all of her Snickers. And ate most of them."

I giggled. Because he loved that candy bar. And he could, in the typical gross, teen-boy way, eat a king-sized Snickers in two bites.

"Ooh," I heard Bree mumble. "What's *she* doing here?"

I dragged my eyes away from him and froze when I saw Mrs. Chaplin marching down the aisle parallel to where we were sitting.

"She doesn't look happy, either."

She headed straight for Mr. Peters, standing on stage and talking with the backstage and tech crews.

All the anticipation and excitement I'd been feeling about today's rehearsal became consumed by panic, and I glanced at Sloane. Sitting at the very end of our row with Maddie.

And her snide smile said it all.

Oh, no. *Nononono*.

But our confrontation in the Theater Department office had been a week ago.

Mrs. Chaplin pulled Mr. Peters away from the crew and they started quietly talking.

"What do you think this is all about?" Bree asked.

"She's probably bitching about something that's none of her business," Shane muttered.

Justin caught my eyes and he frowned.

Then Mr. Peters called out, "Kassidy?"

I felt everyone's eyes as he motioned with his left hand for me to join them on stage.

I slowly stood.

What had the viper snake done?

As I started walking toward the stage right steps, I saw Justin's face harden as he looked directly at Sloane?

Focus.

I tried, really hard, to hold my head high as I cleared the last step and followed them off the stage and into the wings.

Mrs. Chaplin punished me with her notorious ice-cold stare. "I've been hearing teachers complaining about you. Again."

My eyes widened and I leaned away from her. As if her words had actually bit me.

"Who exactly?" Mr. Peters calmly, and a bit condescendingly, asked. "Because I haven't heard a thing."

"Mr. Lowry said there was a problem last week while she was working in the office."

Outrage replaced my shock. "There was no problem. Until Sloane walked in."

Totally the truth, and I didn't care one bit I'd just blamed her precious, "perfect" daughter. And Mr. Lowry had seemed way more annoyed with her than me.

"He never said a word about it to me."

Mrs. Chaplin arched her right eyebrow. "And there was another incident with Mr. Thatcher yesterday."

I looked at Mr. Peters. "I didn't do anything wrong. And he hates me."

Okay. Very childish. But I could never do anything right in his class. Ever. And how had Mrs. Chaplin found out about what happened yesterday? It hadn't seemed like that big a deal. Unless...Sloane had told her and lied about what really happened.

"Of course it's all Mr. Thatcher's fault." She straightened and kept her ice-cold stare on

Mr. Peters. "Kassidy was warned about her behavior weeks ago and there's been no change. As chair of this department, I'm removing her from this play. Immediately."

I lost my breath as her coldly spoken words filled my head. Then the stage, the set, my dreams started to collapse around me.

She couldn't be doing this. Not this close to the show's run. Not after yesterday.

My heart began pounding. So hard my chest hurt. Then Mr. Peters, surprisingly, started laughing. But when her stare turned into a glare and she crossed her arms, he stopped.

"Oh, you were being serious?"

"Perfectly."

That's when the realization hit. She could've had this conversation alone with us at any point today. But she'd chosen now to show off her power while making an example out of me.

In front of the entire cast.

Humiliation merged with my panic, and I struggled to catch my breath.

Mr. Peters crossed his arms. "I don't appreciate this decision being made without any knowledge." He now sounded irritated. "And this is my show, Mrs. Chaplin. We're nine-and-a-half days away from our first performance. Kassidy's not going anywhere."

Relief eased my racing heart.

Until she said, "You don't have authority over my decisions. And Bree's her understudy. She's a talented, *well-behaved* young woman. I know she's prepared to step up."

I pictured Mrs. Chaplin and her equally rotten daughter being pitched into hell.

Mr. Peters's back became stiff. "I'm sure she is, too. But I will be taking this to Mr. Hathaway before this day is over."

Mrs. Chaplin shrugged and eyed me. "You're excused and can go home."

I, with my mouth open, stared at her as she marched away.

This could *not* be happening.

I had never—not ever—been in trouble like this. Being removed from a play for my behavior? But, up until having the T-Rex, teachers had never taken me as a disrespectful student. If anything, they'd, like my friends and classmates, found me entertaining. I also didn't know if the T-Rex had even been the one who talked to Mrs. Chaplin about me.

I looked urgently at Mr. Peters. "I swear I didn't *do* anything. Especially to Mr. Thatcher. And Sloane really did start it that day—"

"Kassidy, calm down," he quietly said. "We'll get this straightened out."

I wanted to believe him and knew he wouldn't let horrible

Mrs. Chaplin come in and mess with his show. But he wasn't the chair of the department or the principal. Who would most likely have the final say. And I started to tremble when I remembered her indifferent response to Mr. Peters saying he'd be taking this to Mr. Hathaway.

Her reaction couldn't have been a good sign.

"We're not losing the incredible progress we made yesterday over this. Okay?"

I forced myself to nod. "Do I have to leave?" My voice had sounded close to shrill.

Mr. Peters wouldn't make me leave rehearsal. Would he?

He watched me closely as he said, "It would be best if we listen to her until I can talk to Mr. Hathaway after rehearsal."

I pressed my lips together and the stabbing pain in my heart stole my breath. The same pain from nearly three months ago. Also because of Sloane Chaplin and her evilness. She had to be behind this. But I couldn't understand why.

If this was really about Justin and she still wanted him, why had she broken up with him in the first place? I hadn't been a threat. We'd only shared one slow dance. None of this made sense. And now I had no choice but to face my cast mates and walk out of this auditorium without shedding a single tear.

I also had to walk out of here without going straight for Sloane and her scrawny neck.

I took a deep but shaky breath, turned from Mr. Peters, and headed for the stairs.

I kept my eyes down since I knew everyone—*Sloane*—had to be watching me. I quickly jogged down the steps and went right for my backpack.

"What's going on?" Justin asked.

I answered by picking up my backpack and shrugging into the straps.

He stood. "What are you doing?"

I forced myself to look at him and my four other *former* cast mates. Their confused and worried expressions matched his. Then Bree jumped up and closed the small gap between us.

"She got rid of you. Didn't she."

I gave her a quick nod and said, "You're Juliet as of right now."

Justin stood close beside me, too. "What the fuck happened?"

I took two steps backward as Mr. Peters walked up to us. I had to get out of here before my dam shattered. I couldn't stand the way all of them were looking at me. And I could never look at her. Or I would do something awful and I'd get expelled.

"No." Bree glanced at Mr. Peters. "This isn't right and I won't do it. I'll quit."

"Me, too," Justin said, and as strongly.

Now I really had to get out of here since I hadn't expected this much support.

"Everyone needs to calm down," Mr. Peters slowly said before concentrating on me.

I turned before he could say anything and sprinted to the auditorium doors.

"Kassidy, wait a minute," Justin called out.

But I kept up my fast pace through the auditorium doors and out of the school.

Once outside, I pulled my phone out of my backpack's front pocket.

I stopped walking and texted Meg, *Sloane won. I just lost Juliet.*

I then went into my contacts and chose the only other person I needed to talk to right now. Hopefully he wasn't in the middle of an emergency. Or with a patient.

As I waited for him to answer, I realized I also wanted my

mom. And to the point the ache inside my heart spread to every single part of me.

Meg's reply hit my phone as Dad's voicemail picked up. But I tried him again.

I started walking home. And when I thought I'd get his voicemail again he answered.

"Kassi, what is it? Why aren't you at rehearsal?"

I paused for a second before the tears exploded from my eyes.

Chapter Thirty-One

Please answer your phone.

I moaned and handed my phone to Meg. "I can't talk to him," I said around my tears that wouldn't stop flowing for more than a few minutes.

Michelle's arm tightened around me as I rested my head back on her shoulder. We were on my bed, our backs against the wall, and Meg had settled herself on my right side. She also kept handing me fresh tissues.

"Kass, he's called twice. He's obviously worried about you. Just talk to him."

"But Sloane...did all this...because of him." For reasons I still didn't understand.

And I couldn't stop myself from thinking if he'd stayed away from her at Owen's birthday party *none* of this would be happening.

"You need to give him a chance. You even said he was ready to quit."

"Yeah," Michelle murmured. "It doesn't feel right calling him a jerk-face anymore."

My phone started vibrating, then ringing.

Meg looked right at me as she answered, "Hey. It's Meg. She's right here."

I lifted and frantically shook my head.

I didn't even know what I would say. Yes, he'd been willing to walk away, but I couldn't shake my irritation with him, her, them. Even myself. Because...maybe...if I hadn't been mouthy with the T-Rex yesterday, Sloane wouldn't have walked away with more ammunition.

Meg forced me to take my phone, then scooted off my bed and stood. She motioned for my sister to follow her, which she did, and they left and closed the door behind them.

I tried to sniff away my tears as I wiped my wet cheeks with my left hand. Once my eyes were somewhat clear, I filled my lungs with air, and slowly released it.

I placed my phone against my ear and mumbled, "Hi."

"Hi," he answered. "Kassidy, tell me what happened. All Mr. Peters told us—after he *wouldn't* let me go with you—is that we wouldn't be rehearsing your scenes."

He'd wanted to leave with me? And Mr. Peters hadn't rehearsed Juliet's scenes?

I relaxed against the wall at hearing all of this, paused for a couple more seconds, then told Justin everything that happened between me, Mr. Peters, and the Wicked Witch with a capital B. I also told him about my meeting tomorrow with them, Mr. Hathaway, and Dad. Who'd rescheduled his second date with Dr. Lauren because of all this. And I couldn't escape the guilt mingling with my heartache, even though he'd said she "completely understood."

"I'm sorry," I said. "I don't know what happened yesterday in math."

"Why are you apologizing?" He sounded a tad on the angry side. "It's obvious this is all Sloane." He paused, then said, "I think this is my fault, too."

I knew he had to be connected to Sloane's nastier than

usual self, but also wondered if her behavior stemmed from something deeper. She seemed to be the only one in the cast out of her comfort zone, and in spite of her musical experience. Even Justin, with zero acting experience, had connected with the play, his characters, and most of the cast. Without him, Sloane really only had Maddie.

But I had no interest in reliving our drama in August. The official start of all *this*.

"Justin, I can't talk or think about any of that right now."

"I'm not talking about all that crap."

"Then what are you talking about?" I snapped. Then I sighed and said, "I'm sorry. I didn't mean to snap at you. I know you're trying to help."

"What day did you and Sloane get into it in the office?"

"Wednesday. Another day of me giving her ammunition." I released a sad laugh. "I really need to start controlling my mouth."

"No. You don't," he answered, and still sounding angry. "That's not who you are. You know the T-Rex is an asshole who has no sense of humor. And don't let what happened with Mrs. Chaplin—who stupidly believes everything Sloane tells her—get to you like this. She hasn't won—"

"But what if she does?"

"She won't. And this isn't who you are."

The corner of my mouth lifted in a tiny smile. Because he knew me so incredibly well. He was also right.

"What time's your meeting tomorrow?"

"Lunchtime."

"I'll meet you at your locker and walk you down there."

My tiny smile inched into a bigger one. "Thanks. And I'm really glad Meg answered my phone." Every part of me meant it, too, as I heard him softly laugh.

He'd reminded me I was stronger than the weepy girl I'd been since I left school.

"I am, too." I heard the smile in his voice. "Kass, I...I'll see you tomorrow."

It sounded like he'd started to say something else, and all I could think to say was, "Okay."

I dropped my phone on my bed, and went to my Vision Board where I focused on the special picture of me with my mom and dad.

Like Justin said, Mrs. Chaplin hadn't won and she wouldn't win, either. I had to believe that. And as I stared at my beautiful mom dressed as Eliza Doolittle, I lifted my head and squared my shoulders.

Though I wanted her to be actually standing beside me, I still could feel her with me.

* * *

I closed my locker door and found myself looking at my only public enemy.

"I hope you enjoyed your last rehearsal on Tuesday, DQ," Sloane said, and in a phony, pleasant voice. "But I wonder what Mr. Peters and Romeo will do without their mousy little Juliet Capulet."

I, determined to show her she hadn't beaten me, leaned forward and said, "Don't. Call. Me. DQ. That nickname has nothing to do with you. And if you're so *magnificent*, how come you didn't even get the Juliet understudy?"

"Good point, Kass," Meg said from behind me.

I looked over my shoulder. And smiled. Warren, Natalie, and Lexi stood with her.

"I didn't know an umbilical cord reached this far," Natalie said in her biting, maniacal way. "And I'm shocked you're able to do your dirty work without Brandy beside you."

Sloane's eyes narrowed into slits. "Screw you, Natalie. You're such a bitch."

"It takes one to know one, Sloane."

Wow. Had Lexi said that?

"You guys are so pathetic. But at least I don't have to deal with you anymore."

She'd thrown her insult right at me. She then turned and marched through a group of students and reminded me of her mother yesterday as she approached the stage.

"We heard Junior Chaplin posted on Snapchat last night that her mom" —Warren did air quotes— "'pulled you out of the show.'"

I knew I'd made the right decision to throw myself into homework and continue to avoid all things phone-related after Meg left.

"So is that really it?" Natalie asked. "And can she even do that?"

"She told Mr. Peters she can and I don't know. My dad and I are meeting with her, Mr. Peters, and Mr. Hathaway at lunch."

"Well, we came by to let you know we've got your back."

I smiled at Warren, at all of them, and their much-needed and appreciated support filled me up.

"We also wanted to bring you some good news." Warren put his arm around Natalie. "I convinced her to be the club's new vice president."

Oh. Right.

In the excitement of our awesome rehearsal on Halloween, and the rotten drama that followed yesterday, I'd completely forgotten to check in with Warren about Natalie being the club's new VP.

She rolled her eyes. "If you can call stalking me on Snapchat and blowing up my phone with texts about it *convincing me*, then, yes. But I agreed under strong protests."

"Thank you, Natalie," Meg said, smiling.

"I'm not sure I'm talking to you yet."

Meg's smile disappeared and her face became pink.

"So do you think you can get those changes submitted to student council?" Warren interjected. "But after today."

"And send us a text after your meeting?" Lexi asked.

I nodded, and they, even Natalie, came forward and we shared a group hug.

"I'm definitely not into all that drama shit," Natalie said when our hug ended. She looked at me, her normally razor-sharp dark eyes softening. "But I know you don't deserve what Chaplin and her Junior Bitch are doing. They need to be taken down a hundred notches."

"Thanks," I murmured.

As Meg and I walked to our classes, I searched for Justin. But I didn't see him anywhere, which meant he must already be in his first period.

"Keep doing your deep breathing," Meg said. "Text if you need me. And if you can."

"Okay." But I also planned on praying to the spirits of my mom and William Shakespeare I would be at rehearsal this afternoon. As if none of this had ever happened.

Chapter Thirty-Two

I started shaking as Justin and I cleared the last step. So much so I had to stop and begin my deep-breathing exercises.

"I don't see your dad in the office." Justin then took my hands, angled me toward him, and jiggled my arms. "Kassidy, look at me."

I did, but while taking a huge breath and soundly releasing the air. I then said, "Justin, I can't lose Juliet."

"You *won't*," he replied, his eyes locked on mine. "It'll be fine. Between you, your dad and Mr. Peters, Mrs. Chaplin doesn't have a chance. But watch that smart mouth of yours."

He was trying to make me smile, but I could only keep deep breathing.

He let my hands go to look at his watch. "I need to tell you something really quick."

I continued breathing, but it had slowed a fraction.

Why did he look and still sound guilty? Because of what happened in August? Which now seemed like a million months ago.

"I pissed Sloane off last week. On Wednesday, actually."

My deep breathing ceased since he had my full attention.

"She caught me on my way to lunch and was acting stupid. She said she'd heard I joined your club because of her." He frowned. "I asked her where the hell she'd heard that, then laughed in her face, and walked away before she could answer."

I stared at him as disbelief replaced my shaking.

"Because of that and *Romeo and Juliet* now, finally, going so well—"

"Wait—you didn't join the club because of her?"

Now he stared at me. "Were you the one who told her that?"

I lifted my shoulders. "It may have slipped out in the heat of the moment."

His head fell back on his shoulders and he took a deep breath. After another breath, he looked at me. "Your mouth drives *me* crazy. But life would be boring without it."

I stayed silent, not entirely certain how to respond.

"And no. I didn't join the club because of her. Why would you even think that?"

"Because of the way she broke up with you," I snapped, my fragile nerves on the brink of blowing apart. Then stupidity hit. At my clear overreaction to why he'd joined the club.

But if not because of her, why *had* he joined?

He sighed and said, "We can talk about this later. But will you—"

"J.R., shouldn't you be at lunch?"

Mr. Peters's voice and appearance made us look up and over at him.

He strolled by us, then stopped outside the school office. "I think it's continued, remarkable progress you're here to support your Juliet. But she needs to come with me and you need to get to lunch."

Justin took a step back. But as I turned to follow Mr. Peters, I caught him point at me, mime texting, then point at himself.

I nodded and, holding my head high, walked into the office.

The reason Justin hadn't seen Dad in the main office was because he happened to already be in Mr. Hathaway's office. With Mrs. Chaplin.

I'd been completely honest with Dad about *everything*, and at his insistence, after he got home from work and before he called Mr. Hathaway. So the tension rippling in the space between Dad and Mrs. Chaplin nearly sucked the oxygen from the office.

I tried to continue my deep breathing as I, after dropping my backpack, slowly sat beside Dad. Mr. Peters sat in the seat to my left and on Mrs. Chaplin's right side.

We became the barrier between Dad and the Wicked Witch of Pacifica Academy.

Mr. Hathaway, seated behind his desk, more resembled a retired football player than a private high school principal. The *big* football players who, according to Meg, played defense.

"I appreciate everyone agreeing to this meeting and hopefully it won't take long." Mr. Hathaway looked at Dad. "We all respect your profession and that you must have patients waiting for you."

Dad nodded, but I could sense his tension. I could also feel Mrs. Chaplin's animosity from her seat on the other side of Mr. Peters.

I'd never done anything to this teacher, so what could Sloane be saying about me that would cause all her hostility?

Like Justin said yesterday afternoon, I usually didn't care one bit what people thought of me. Especially people like Mrs. Chaplin and her Queen of Peroxide. But their intense dislike for me had, at this point, cost me Juliet Capulet. And I cared immensely about that.

"I've had a chance to talk to everyone about what happened at rehearsal after it was brought to my attention yesterday afternoon," Mr. Hathaway continued, and his way of saying Dad had gotten to him before Mr. Peters since he'd still been at rehearsal. "As I understand it, Mrs. Chaplin was under the impression Kassidy's recent behavior with two other teachers had broken strict Theater Department rules. And is why she was removed from the play. Is that correct?" He focused on Mrs. Chaplin, but something about the look he gave her didn't seem to support his supportive comments.

A little fire called hope lit within me.

"Yes," Mrs. Chaplin answered, and without emotion. "It seems Kassidy has very little self-control, more often than not."

"And if her actual teachers feel that way," Dad countered, but with an edge to his voice, "why haven't they contacted me? My phone is always on and with me twenty-four hours a day, seven days a week."

Score one for Dad.

And maybe Mrs. Chaplin had a point. But I never meant it as disrespect and I know Mr. Lowry knew Sloane had started that argument in the office. Mrs. Chaplin just didn't care how her daughter acted around here. Then again, Mrs. Chaplin didn't care how *she* acted.

"I did talk to the two other teachers," Mr. Hathaway smoothly said. "Mr. Lowry, the teacher she reports to during her theater elective, did recall an incident not too long ago. But he insisted Kassidy hadn't been the problem." His eyes went to Mrs. Chaplin and back to Dad.

I, somehow, stopped myself from smiling.

"But Mr. Thatcher, her math teacher, admitted Kassidy

can be quite outspoken in his class. She received a detention several weeks ago because of it."

Mr. Hathaway's eyes went to me and my face burned.

Thank goodness I'd remembered to tell Dad about *that* horrible day, too. He hadn't been happy about the detention. But, being the best dad ever, he'd let it go. Probably because I'd been such a hot, almost hysterical mess yesterday while we were talking.

"She told me about the detention and we dealt with it." Dad turned his unhappy stare on me, and I looked at my lap.

"Please know Mr. Thatcher added her behavior isn't anything he hasn't dealt with before, being a long-time teacher. It's why he didn't contact you."

Hmm...maybe my math teacher didn't hate me after all.

"And this would be a good time for me to add," Mr. Peters calmly said, "this is my third year working with Kassidy. I've never had any problems with her. With the exception of my colleague, I've never received any complaints from other teachers about her, including Mr. Thatcher. And I know if Mr. Lowry had been upset with her about what happened that day in the office, he would have mentioned it to me. As I'm sure you can guess, we've been spending a lot of time together because we're preparing for the show."

I caught Mrs. Chaplin stiffen in her seat as Mr. Hathaway nodded.

Score three for Mr. Peters.

I peeked at Dad and saw his face had relaxed. But only a fraction.

"Then after hearing my daughter's actual teachers really aren't having problems with her, I want to know why she was pulled from the play. And why it happened the way it did. In front of the entire cast."

I cringed at Dad's sudden hostility. He almost never became hostile. With anyone.

"I'd like to address that, as well," Mr. Peters said, and not sounding happy, either. "We weren't expecting it, and most of the students were extremely confused and upset by what happened. Yesterday was their worst rehearsal since we started blocking in September."

For some reason, what he said surprised me. Even though I'd seen how confused and shocked Shane, Cody, and Liam had looked before I fled the auditorium. And Justin and Bree had made their feelings perfectly clear. But, at the same time, I allowed the warmth from all the support I'd received and kept receiving surround me.

In that instant, I knew we, and my mom and Shakespeare, had won.

"I'm only eight days away from our first show. We can't afford rehearsals like that."

"I understand. I'm also terribly sorry" —Mr. Hathaway glanced at me, Mr. Peters, and Dad— "about everything that happened yesterday. I can assure you it won't happen again." His eyes then settled on Mrs. Chaplin, who had become disturbingly silent. "It appears this was all a huge misunderstanding. Because of that, I'm putting Kassidy back in the show."

I mentally did Snoopy's happy dance while thanking my mom, the universe, and William Shakespeare.

"But," he firmly added and now focused on me, "I expect you to watch your behavior in Mr. Thatcher's class from this point moving forward."

Snoopy slowly stopped his happy dance.

I still nodded, very cooperatively, and said, "Thank you, Mr. Hathaway."

He smiled. "Alright. We're done." He stood, followed by Dad and Mr. Peters.

As Mr. Hathaway and Dad shook hands, I stood. Mrs. Chaplin, on the other hand, stayed seated, her face an emotionless mask. Apparently, she and Mr. Hathaway *weren't* done.

Snoopy picked up where he'd left off with his happy dance.

"Thank you again for coming in." Mr. Hathaway then turned his smile on me and Mr. Peters. "And please know I'm looking forward to seeing the show next week. As is my wife. She's read everything Shakespeare wrote."

I returned his smile before I followed Mr. Peters from Mr. Hathaway's office. Dad was right behind me.

When we reached the main office, Dad and Mr. Peters stopped and they shook hands.

"Thank *you*, Mr. Peters," Dad said as he released his hand.

He smiled. "Not a problem. I meant everything I said in there." He looked at me. "I'll see you at rehearsal and fully expect to see what you and J.R. gave me on Halloween."

He sauntered out of the office.

Dad, after a quick goodbye wave to Mrs. Oliveri, guided me from the office. We walked to the main doors where he paused and faced me. But he didn't look happy.

"Kassi, I know most of this wasn't your fault," he said. "But between your behavior in Mr. Thatcher's class, a detention, and what happened at Meg's house...not a banner start to the school year."

I started playing with the hem of my sweater. The last time he'd looked at me with such disappointment had been when he picked me up after The Purging, and my Snoopy-dancing high vanished. But because he was the best dad ever, I said, "Thank you."

He gave me an affectionate smile and left.

I dug out my phone. I chose Meg, Warren, Natalie, Lexi and, of course, Justin and texted, *We won! Tell you about it later. But my dad and Mr. Peters were so awesome.*

The hundred-pound weight lifted off my shoulders the second I hit send.

I knew Justin and Meg were sitting together in the cafeteria, and I pictured my text hitting their phones at the same time. But I headed for the library. I needed to triple check my math homework since I was, especially now, going to be a perfect student in the T-Rex's class.

YES! But I knew they wouldn't let that bitch win. xx

I laughed at Meg's text and his message hit.

So that means you can be your irresistible Juliet at rehearsal.

I, now wearing a gigantic and goofy smile, typed, *Better than irresistible.*

Chapter Thirty-Three

I rushed onto the stage.

David, or Friar Laurence, said, "Here comes the lady."

Romeo, giving me *his* smile, rushed toward me and our arms went around each other. Then he lifted me off the stage and we kissed. Like we'd done as a real couple a million times before. And my tummy fluttered. Even though *this* embrace and kiss were written in the play. It also lasted until we heard Friar Laurence quietly clear his throat.

Romeo gently lowered me and his face looked as warm as mine felt.

Friar Laurence walked up and placed himself between us, all while fighting a smile.

Romeo's playful grin that reached his eyes, which stayed connected with mine, kept me mesmerized and a little breathless as we rehearsed our short scene. To the point that when Friar Laurence grasped my upper arm, I jolted and broke eye contact with my Romeo.

"Come," Friar Laurence said, grasping Romeo's upper arm. "Come with me and we shall make short work...for, by your leaves, you shall not stay alone 'til Holy Church incorporate two in one."

I took a moment to catch my breath and shake my head back into the present, then headed off stage beside Justin. Who clasped my right hand, gave it a squeeze, and let go. Too quickly. But a thrill shot through me and ended at my heart. And warmth reached every part of me. Including my face. That began to burn as we approached Shane, Cody, and Liam, standing in the stage left wings and smiling at us like David had been trying *not* to during our scene.

"Excellent," Mr. Peters said from where he stood in front of the stage. "Mercutio, Benvolio, Tybalt, and extras better be ready. But some of you boys still need to settle down with your sword fighting."

Justin, Shane, and David looked at Cody and Liam. Then the boys burst into laughter.

I giggled as I walked around them.

My Romeo and I had beyond nailed yet another scene, and I, like my mom, was exactly where I belonged.

I all but floated backstage to find Bree, so I could give her the highlights of what happened during my meeting since Mrs. Chaplin's daughter was sitting with Maddie—her only ally—in the house. But I did plan on telling my Romeo *everything* after rehearsal.

* * *

Justin laughed. "Your dad really said *actual* teachers? Twice?"

I laughed with him and nodded.

We stood outside school while he waited for his mom to pick him up. We were also the last two remaining from the cast.

"That's so fucking awesome. I wish I would've been

there." He laughed again. "A lot of us wish we would've been there."

My smile faded when I remembered Dad's "not a banner start to the school year." "Yeah, but my dad wasn't happy about the detention. Or hearing I can be *outspoken* in the T-Rex's class."

"Has he met the T-Rex?"

"No. And I don't want him to." I frowned. "I have to be on my best behavior in his class from now until the last day of school."

I'd temporarily lost everything once. I could never let it happen again.

His mom pulled up, and I stepped back. But he captured my right hand and gave me *his* smile.

"We'll give you a ride home. And don't even try arguing. Because you *won't* win this."

His smile, of course, made me smile. Then made my tummy somersault. And I honestly didn't want to argue as he led me to the rear passenger-side door.

"Is it okay if we give Kassidy a ride home?" he asked his mom.

She looked her as-usual glamorous self with her dark hair pulled up in a fancy updo, designer sunglasses, and designer outfit. And I pictured beautiful and rich Natalie Carlisle looking like this in thirty years.

"Of course." She smiled, but it held little warmth. Something I'd learned very quickly not to take personally when Justin and I had been together. "How are you?"

I shrugged out of my backpack, slid into the seat, and noticed Bethie wasn't in the backseat. He then closed my door.

"I'm good, Mrs. Richardson," I said as Justin climbed into the front seat and shut his door.

"You'll have to turn around and head toward Clay," he told her.

She nodded and we pulled away from the school.

"Where's Beth?" he asked.

"Pearl's bringing her home. I was detained after rehearsal. Which is why I was late picking you up."

I watched his jaw, his entire face, harden before he faced his window.

His mood changed so immediately my breath stalled in my chest. And I knew the change *had* to be related to what he'd told me at the dance.

My stomach flipped at a different reason she'd been late picking him up.

"How's my son doing during your rehearsals? He said he's Romeo now?"

Her question snapped me out of the sickening thought. But I frowned at her confusion. He'd been Romeo for over two weeks. Still, knowing Justin and their absenteeism, he probably hadn't rushed to share that information with them.

I leaned forward, unleashed my brightest smile, and said, "He's doing *fantastic*." I glanced at him and could tell he was fighting a smile.

"I never knew you were interested in acting. When did that start?"

His smile faded. "It's a new interest. But don't go out of your way concerning yourself. It's for fun."

I sat back.

She went for her cell, charging in the center console, when we reached a stoplight.

I'd witnessed a few interactions between him and his mom, and she'd always been good at ignoring his defiant attitude. That only came out when he interacted with his parents.

"You and Mr. Richardson will be going to a show? Right?"

Her head snapped up at my question. Then the light

turned green and she hit the gas pedal. "Oh…well, we'd like to. But we're both terribly busy with work right now."

He looked at his window and before I saw his face. But her indifferent response filled my heart and soul since he'd been working so hard and really was incredibly fantastic.

I wanted nothing more than to reach for him.

The car became silent, except for his directions, until we reached my building.

"Thank you for the ride," I said as he got out and I opened my door.

She tapped something on her phone and held it up to her ear. "It was nice seeing you."

I didn't respond while hauling myself and my backpack from the backseat.

He pushed the door shut behind me, a little hard.

"I'm sorry," I murmured while we walked toward my building's stoop. "I shouldn't have asked her that." I sighed. "I am trying to control what comes out of my mouth."

He stopped at the first step. "Kassidy, she didn't say anything I didn't already know." His eyes met mine. "Stop worrying about that. Unless you're in the T-Rex's class."

I nodded, and as he headed for the SUV, I said, "Justin?"

He turned and our eyes locked.

"Thanks for being pretty awesome yesterday and today."

We smiled at each other. Genuine, warm smiles, too.

"So we're still on for Saturday. Right, Juliet?"

His question made me tingle all over as I said, "We're still on for Saturday, Romeo."

I then turned and headed up the steps with a bit of a bounce.

Chapter Thirty-Four

"**Y**ou're smiling again," Meg teased me. "Which is surprising because of where we're going next."

We were headed to our final Anti-Love Club meeting, but my smile grew.

I finished loading up my backpack. "We had a fantastic rehearsal yesterday, Sloane stayed away and couldn't even look at me—" I closed my locker door. "I feel...lighter."

And Justin and I were more than getting along.

"Speaking of Queen Peroxide," Meg began as we linked our arms, "I've been meaning to tell you about something very interesting that happened at lunch yesterday. When you were in your meeting."

I glanced at her.

"J.R. came into the cafeteria. He dropped his lunch on our table and went right to Sloane. He got her, and not happily, to go out in the hall with him. They weren't gone long. But when she came back in, it looked like she wanted to commit cold-blooded murder."

My curiosity burned as I asked, "What did he say? When he came back to the table?"

"Owen asked him what that was all about, but he shrugged and said something about it being unfinished business. And he looked pissed. But also satisfied."

Hmm. That did sound very interesting. Maybe, someday, I'd ask him about it. If the moment ever presented itself. But right now, I loved not caring about Mrs. and Junior Chaplin.

Meg smiled. "Kass, you should've seen his face when he got your text. And I know you're tired of hearing this, but I really think you should talk to him."

I knew we still had *a lot* of chemistry and that it really, really showed during rehearsals. And I still experienced a warm buzz when I thought about him being willing to walk away from the play if I had lost Juliet. But it could just be the truce and our professionalism and our dedication to *Romeo and Juliet* fueling our chemistry now. It seemed like we were *us* again, but at the same time not. If anything, and when we weren't on stage, we were right back where we were a year ago —at friendly, sometimes flirty, banter.

"I don't know, Meg. What happened in August doesn't seem important anymore. Maybe, when the show's over, he and I can go back to...I have no idea." Because after our emotionally and physically passionate relationship, friendship would be impossible.

"Okay. I'm just saying..." Her voice trailed off as we reached Ms. Simmons's room.

We needed to focus on the club and saying goodbye. That, for some reason, wasn't bothering me like I thought it would. Even knowing he would be in there. Or at least I thought he would—my eyes widened when I registered there were *ten* students at the meeting.

Wow. Warren was a bloodhound when it came to sniffing out heartbreak.

"There they are," he said when we walked further into the classroom.

Ms. Simmons looked up from her computer long enough to give us a satisfied smile.

Warren and Natalie were sitting on desks in the middle of the classroom and facing the eight members. The only members I recognized were Warren, Natalie, Lexi, and Alisha. And, without Justin, Warren and a very awkward freshman kid were the only boys.

"You're missing two members," I said the moment we reached the two now in charge.

"Alisha said Paige is now in love with some other kid in her math class who's helping her out," Natalie said while scrolling through her phone. "I guess they have some study date planned for this weekend. And I don't give a sh—" She glanced over her shoulder at Ms. Simmons, who seemed to have mastered tuning us out. "I don't know or care where Mr. Romeo is today. But I so loved hearing you beat those two evil bit—well, you know."

I smiled. "Thanks. I feel free of them." And I meant every word.

Lexi walked up. "Isn't this so cool?" She gestured to the members, but then caught herself and her smile fell. "I mean, there's serious drama going on in here. I think some stuff happened at Kimi's party last weekend."

"A little booze," Warren mumbled, "combined with girls experimenting with their naughty sides via naughty costumes equals this." He held his hands out toward the members.

I had to laugh. But I straightened a bit as my soul burst with pride.

The club wasn't at all about being anti-love. The club was about members owning their heartache and bonding with other heartbroken kids before moving onto, at least in Jade's and Paige's situations, a better someone. Meg had been the only one to get back together with the boy who'd temporarily broken her heart.

A jealous pang came out of nowhere, despite what I'd just told Meg. But I immediately let the pang go. I couldn't and wouldn't begrudge my best friend any happiness.

"I submitted the paperwork to student council this morning." I refocused on why we were here. "You and Natalie are officially in charge of the Anti-Love Club." I leaned toward them. "But maybe you guys should consider changing the club's name? Anti-Love Club doesn't seem to fit anymore."

Warren, Natalie, and Lexi looked at each other, then nodded.

"*Fabulous* idea. The three of us have been talking, too." Warren pointed at Natalie and Lexi. "And we've decided, as much as we all loved The Purging—even Natalie—to make that optional and something new members can do by themselves. Strictly for safety purposes."

I flinched.

Not one of my better, brilliant ideas.

"But we're going to continue our club activities. We're going to Snowflake Formal together next month and I can't wait." Lexi bounced up and down.

"I told you guys I'm not going to another school dance." Natalie dragged her eyes from her phone. "But don't tell Jade I said that."

"Anyway," Warren said, looking at me, "we're also keeping 'You Give Love a Bad Name' as our song. It's good therapy for new members. And it really was an inspired choice."

A much better, brilliant idea.

"We're going to continue what you started. That reminds me—" His gaze shifted to the members, talking together. "Everyone? Look at me, please. The meeting's starting." Once Warren had everyone's attention, he held his left hand out toward us. "These two are this club's founders. But, sadly, will no longer be continuing their leadership or membership in the club. And they *will* be greatly missed."

We stared blankly at their blank faces. Until one girl's face lit up with recognition?

"You're Juliet. And J.R. is Romeo." She gave me a sappy smile. "You're soooo lucky to be in the play with him." She had freshman-crushing-hard-on-a-popular-super-cute upperclassman written all over her freckled face.

I caught Natalie rolling her eyes and I narrowed mine.

"Where is he?" the other boy asked. "He's supposed to help me work on my game today." His face turned beet red. "Girls run away from me when I walk up to them."

Natalie eyed him. "No matter what J.R. thinks of himself, he's not a Greek god. Or a miracle worker," she added under her breath.

Score one for Natalie. Still, it was pretty sweet of him to take the kid under his wing. He could be, when he really wanted, dizzyingly charming. And this awkward freshman might learn something from him. I still didn't know why Justin had joined the club, but I guess his motives for staying weren't as snarky as I'd assumed.

"You ready? Owen's waiting for me."

"Sure." I only had one more thing to take care of. "About my shirt—"

"Don't even think about giving it back." Natalie smiled wickedly. "This club isn't going anywhere. And you might need it and us again. But minus Mr. *Romeo*."

I smiled and threw my arms around her. She, surprisingly, responded with an equally big hug. Then all five of us were hugging.

Maybe I hadn't lost anything after all.

Chapter Thirty-Five

"So where were you yesterday?" I asked Justin. "It seems some of the new club members like you." I'd been waiting for the right time to ask about his absence from the club yesterday. Especially when I remembered the girl's silliness over him and what that kid said.

We were on his rooftop, and he glanced at me from where he was stretched out on the single lounger, but I couldn't see his eyes since they were shielded by his sunglasses. "I was talking to some guys on the soccer team. And you were there?"

"Meg and I had some final club business. Before you got there."

"Kassidy, you didn't have to leave your club. It's not what you—"

"It's fine. Really." And I honestly meant that. But it didn't stop me from unleashing my best smirk. "The future Romeo in there said you're helping him work on his *game?*"

"Hey," he said, rolling his head forward, "when you got it, why not share it."

I groaned. "How do you manage to stay upright with such

an enormous head? And how did I never notice this about you before?"

"Because you thought it was cute." He looked at me again, then lowered his sunglasses enough to reveal his eyes. "And you still do." He pushed them back on his nose and went back to his sunbathing.

I threw his copy of *Romeo and Juliet* at his head.

"Ow." He fixed his sunglasses. "Watch it. I don't think Mr. Peters would appreciate Juliet battering Romeo less than a week before the play's first show."

I smiled, and very satisfyingly at my perfect aim.

He rolled onto his left side. "Kass, can I be honest with you about something?"

I was stretched out on the double lounger and rolled onto my right side. "Sure."

Hmm. What was this about?

He hesitated, then, smiling, said, "Being in this play... being a part of all you guys...has been the best time I've ever had at school."

I gasped, and from honest shock. "This coming from our soccer star?"

But, maybe, the acting had tapped into the piano-playing-performer side of him?

"I love soccer, but *Romeo and Juliet* has challenged me in ways I never expected."

"Shakespeare has a way of doing that."

"That's definitely part of it, but it was also you."

I halted, not sure I'd heard him correctly.

"I already knew you were a force of nature. But being in your world, with you, the last several weeks, I wanted to be better than great. Especially as Romeo." He laughed. "I've made some really cool, new friends. And I feel like I've found a part of myself that has nothing to do with my parents. I only know how to play the piano because of my mom."

His surprising honesty kept me frozen and mute. Emotions, from feeling flattered and shocked and confused, filled my head.

Where was all this coming from? Our awesome rehearsal week?

I shook my head. "I'm flattered. And thank you. Really."

He appeared to be squinting at me. "Is your head getting bigger right now?"

I ignored that and said, "I appreciate what you said, but it's not me making you fantastic. You seem to have a gift for acting." A thought occurred to me and I playfully asked, "Does all this mean you'll be summoning your musician-singer side and auditioning for the spring musical?"

He laughed. "Hell, no. That was between you and me. And even if I wanted to, I couldn't because of soccer."

That was true. But I giggled at what else he'd said as the flattery tripled in strength. Because it meant our "Let It Be" moment back in April had been just as special to him.

"That reminds me, are you working on anything right now? I know you've been busy with the play and home-work..." My voice faded while he slowly nodded.

"Yeah. I've started working on a John Legend song." He abruptly sat up and threw his legs over the lounger's side. "Let's run through the beginning of act five one more time. Then I have to take you home and get Beth to a slumber party."

He gently tossed the book back to me and I caught it with both hands. I quickly found the start of act five and attempted to focus.

What on earth happened here?

He took a deep breath and started with, "I dreamt my lady came and found me dead."

* * *

The buzzer shattered the quietness in our condo, to the point I jumped.

Dad, in the kitchen and taking a break from his writing, grabbed a bottle of water. "Are you expecting someone?" he asked, closing the fridge door.

"No. But I'll go see who it is." I'd just changed into my pajamas and had been heading into the living room to binge watch something on Netflix with my sister, but I changed direction and went for the intercom. It couldn't be a solicitor at this hour.

I pressed the button. "Hello?"

A second later I heard, "Hi. It's me. I really need to see you."

I stared at the speaker as if it had turned into Justin.

I heard Dad's approaching footsteps. "Who is it?'

"It's Justin. I'm going to buzz him in."

He, and not happily, looked at his watch. "It's after eight."

"Daddy, I know that. I don't know why he's here."

I opened the front door and stood in the entryway as he walked up the stairs. He hadn't sounded happy and his "I really need to see you" caused warning alarms to go off in my head. Which only became louder the moment I saw him.

He looked horrible. Like he had that Monday morning, but minus the stubble. And he had a distinct...wildness?...in his eyes. That were not quite focused on Dad. Probably because of the way my dad was looking at him.

"Hi, Dr. Pashen," he mumbled. "I was wondering if I could...maybe...take Kassidy out. For a while."

My mouth inched open. Then Michelle walked up, but didn't say a word. The tension was a bit intense.

"Do you know what time it is?"

"Dad, you're making it sound like it's the middle of the night."

"I'm sorry. I know it's kind've late. And I should've texted first. Or called. But I—" His eyes darted to me, and I knew something *big* had happened at home.

I faced my dad. "Can I go? Please?"

Dad's face remained set in unhappiness. But after several, very long tense seconds, he gave me a curt nod.

I dashed into my bedroom and changed.

In the five months we'd been together, Justin had never done anything like this. And in spite of all the constant strain with his parents.

"Do you know anything about guns?" I heard Dad ask as I approached them.

He cautiously shook his head.

"*Dad*!"

"Well, I'm thinking about getting one. Research purposes for my book?"

I released a little moan as he cautiously nodded.

Dad looked at me. "I want you back here at ten."

"But it's Saturday night."

"Ten. Not a second later."

"That's fine," Justin said, very cooperatively.

I held my tongue at Dad's total unfairness as I backed Justin into the hallway. But I did soundly close the front door behind me.

*　*　*

He took my hand and pulled me to his side when our bare feet touched the cool sand.

We were at Ocean Beach, but this time he'd parked near our spot. It was dark, and a little foggy and eerie, but I felt beyond safe by his side and with our fingers tightly linked.

"Justin, what are we doing here? And why do we need a towel?"

This was the first time I'd spoken since we left. The

tension radiating from him kept our drive silent. Because it seemed like one sound might cause him to blow apart.

"I need Utopia right now."

I stayed silent as we trekked through the sand and headed for the place that held so many special memories. The best memory had happened on my birthday back in June.

We'd spent the day together since Dad had worked until six. Justin had been willing to take me anywhere I wanted and that wasn't too far away, but I'd chosen Utopia. After a couple of fairly modest kisses—there had been people around—I'd settled between his legs to face the ocean. His arms had been tight around my waist and he'd rested his chin on my left shoulder, his lips oh-so close to *that* spot. He'd then, after nuzzling my neck, whispered in my ear, "I'm crazy in love with you" and sealed it with a long, Romeo-and-Juliet-worthy kiss.

I'd never even said the words back to him, and he hadn't expected them. My eager response to his kiss the only answer he needed.

I glanced at him now and wondered if he, despite being so upset, was thinking about that special moment, too. Because I still couldn't understand, this moment aside, where that Justin Richardson had gone. And in one night. Then we were there. A slightly sheltered spot at the base of the sand dunes, a few long steps from the ocean's shore.

The sound of the ocean waves, that matched his mood, prompted me to pull away from him and ask, "What's going on? What happened tonight?"

He kept his eyes on the water. "My mom's boyfriend showed up at the house. Picking her up for some bullshit, *work* thing. He's a violinist."

My hands flew to my mouth.

This violinist probably *had* been the reason she'd been late picking him up the day they took me home.

Oh. My. God.

"But how do you know he's the guy?"

He dropped the towel he'd been holding in his left hand and shoved his hands into his soccer team hoodie's front pocket. The sweatshirt and his actions the only thing about him right now that showed he was a sixteen-year-old boy.

"She looked way too good for a work thing and was acting stupid. Like…" He looked at me. "Like a sixteen-year-old girl, but I don't mean that as an insult."

I lowered my hands. "I understand."

"When I asked the asshole, who was also at the party last Saturday, what the hell he was doing there, she actually got embarrassed and snapped at me for being rude to him."

I reached for his left arm, gently tugged his hand from the pocket and gave it a tight squeeze. "And your dad?"

"Gone. As usual. I think he's messing around with one of his clients. And I know she's screwing around with that guy because of my dad." He let go of my hand to run his hands through his hair. "Do they—does *she*—think I'm stupid?"

I stepped toward him and lifted my arms to slide them around his waist. But caught myself and quickly lowered them. I sighed and said, "Justin, they're not thinking about anything or anyone but themselves." I wanted to add "as usual," but kept that part to myself.

He faced the water. "I feel like I'm going to burst into flames. Or a million pieces."

I watched, wide-eyed, as he yanked his sweatshirt over his head and off, followed by his T-shirt. Then I was reminded of how insanely good he looked in just a pair of jeans.

"Can you hold these for me?"

I took his clothing. "What are you doing?"

"I'll be right back."

I continued my wide-eyed stare as he marched toward the shore and, unbelievably, allowed the waves to tackle him. And

I wanted nothing more than to follow him, regardless of the water's frigid temperature and the cool, night air.

I also wanted him to be all mine again. So I could do more than simply stand there and watch him battle the anger and hurt.

I wanted, like I'd done so many times when we were together, *to* wrap my arms around his waist and hug him until I heard his breathless laugh. Then I wanted to hook my arms behind his neck, pull his head down to mine and kiss him to the point he forgot about everything but us. Something else I'd done so many times.

But I couldn't. Because he wasn't mine. And we still had a wall between us.

It had thinned a lot, especially this past week. And tonight I'd been, like when we were together, the first person he'd turned to because of his parents' selfishness. None of it changed the fact we had a distance between us. That might never go away.

He trudged out of the surf, his jeans spewing water and clinging to his legs.

When he reached me, he bent down, grabbed the towel, and started drying his soaking hair and body. He then wrapped the towel around his shoulders, keeping it closed with his hands, and stepped so close to me his bare toes just touched mine.

I could smell the sand and salty ocean all over him. He wasn't even shivering.

"I'm sorry," he barely said over the ocean waves pounding the shore. "But you're the one person I can talk to about this shit. And I didn't want to come here by myself." He gave me a swift, half smile. "I didn't scare you? Did I?"

I stared up at him. "No, I'm worried about you. And don't apologize. I've seen you like this before."

He shook his head. "This feels different. Kass, I don't

know how much more I can let go." His voice sounded hard and bitter and sad. "I can't wait to get the hell out of that house. And if not for my sister, I'd go to the other side of this country for college. Maybe the other side of this world."

I hugged his clothes to me since I couldn't hug him.

We'd talked about this before, during the summer. And I clearly remembered the...longing in his expression when I'd mentioned I was considering a couple of schools on the East Coast because of their top-rated theater departments.

"What kind of mother lets her piece-of-shit boyfriend pick her up at the door, knowing her son is going to answer it? At least my dad keeps his girlfriend away from the house."

Something about him throwing around the words "boyfriend" and "girlfriend" while talking about his married parents made me want to hunt them down and unleash the vicious side of my personality. And tongue.

We continued staring at each other, the ocean feeling like it was roaring in my ears.

If I leaned forward and angled my head up, and he leaned down, we'd be able to kiss.

Was he thinking the same thing?

He slowly lowered his head and took a step back. "Thanks for listening."

I released a breath I'd been holding onto. I tried, really hard, to release my disappointment, too. Because I wanted him to kiss *me*. Not me as Juliet.

The look he gave me reminded me of our first moment on earthworm day. "I've never done anything like that." He glanced at his soaking jeans. "I think your crazy is rubbing off on me, too."

"*I've* never done anything like that." But I'd wanted to be out there with him.

"I'm actually getting cold."

I heard myself say, "Well, you did strip down to your jeans and act like you were sacrificing yourself to Poseidon."

His mouth curved into a small smile seconds before he laughed quietly. "Kassidy, I've really..." His lowered voice faded into a deep sigh. "I need to dry off before we go."

Chapter Thirty-Six

The moment I stepped into the auditorium I looked for Justin, but I didn't see him—just like I hadn't seen him all day.

As I approached the stage, I did notice our completed set. Mr. Lowry and his crew worked hard to finish everything over the weekend. They'd even added a single, yet massive set backdrop positioned behind our street pillars. A picture of a classic Italian village that looked like it could be fourteenth century Verona.

Today happened to be day one of full dress and tech rehearsals.

Excitement bubbled within my tummy that matched the energy in the auditorium. There were people buzzing around all over and *this* energy was why I considered the auditorium my happiest place in the school. But still no Justin.

When I later came out of the dressing room, wearing my flowing red gown, I finally saw my Romeo. And I stopped and did a double take.

He stood behind the Verona backdrop with David,

wearing his Friar Laurence robe, and with Cody and Shane, who were dressed similarly to Justin, being Team Montague.

I'd never seen him in his costume before. The three had on black, snug jeans, black shoes, and fitted blue jackets with high collars in the style of hipster. Cody and Shane had on white shirts under their jackets. But Mr. Peters had costumed Romeo differently up top. His shirt looked sage green and his jacket was a bit more elaborate, with black trim and simple black embellishments along the jacket's opening. The sleeves had black, more detailed designs that started at the cuffs and stopped at the elbows.

I knew, without being close to him, his costume would bring out the green in his eyes. And my tummy did about ten somersaults when I pictured what he would look like during the Capulet's Ball before he took off his mask and our first big scene together really started. Where we kissed. Twice. A scene we'd rehearsed so many times it no longer felt like acting.

Justin laughed at something they were talking about, but the moment he saw me approaching his smile grew. He wasted no time leaving his buddies and met me at the slight opening between the backdrop and the Capulet mansion wall.

"I meant to tell you last week you look pretty *whoa* in that dress." His eyes, that were in fact hypnotizing because of his costume, widened. "That dress was made for you."

"Thanks." I giggled, feeling the silly need to curtsy. "You look pretty *whoa*, too."

"Yeah." He adjusted his jacket's flaps and collar. "I look good."

I rolled my eyes, even though he really did look that good.

I suddenly felt hot. From his closeness. And the heavy gown. I gathered my hair and held it on top of my head, then started fanning my face with my free hand.

"This dress is beautiful. But it's heavy. With the lights, and the makeup I'll be wearing, I think I'll feel like a Himalayan red bear stuck in the Mojave Desert in the middle of July."

He laughed while shaking his head.

"How are you doing?"

His laughter and smile gradually disappeared. "Much better than Saturday night. But I'm sore. Working on the Garrett's house yesterday had felt great. But climbing that wall today might kill me."

He'd told me, before dropping me off, he'd be spending Sunday in Stinson Beach with Owen and his brother and dad to help them work on the beach house they were remodeling.

"What time did you get to school? I didn't see you at lunch."

His smile came back. "You were looking for me?"

I returned his smile. "I was worried about you." And *really* wanted to see him.

"Thanks. And Owen's mom picked me up and dropped us off after lunch."

"And the parents?"

He shrugged. "I haven't seen them since Saturday. Which is normal. And I really don't give a crap, either. I'm not going to let that bullshit get to me. Especially this week."

This was the Justin I knew when it came to the way he dealt with his parents.

We heard a mic come on, followed by, "Those of you getting mics," Angelina said, "need to get on stage. As soon as everyone's hooked up, we'll start."

Panic flashed across Justin's face.

"Are you nervous?" I asked, and deliberately quoting him from our rehearsal/volleyball day. "It's just a dress and tech rehearsal."

"I know, but with the mics and the costumes and the set being done, it feels like more than that." He took a shaky breath. "I can't believe this week is here."

"I get it." I freed my hair and took his hand. "Getting mics is painless and super fun."

Rehearsal flew by, despite the pauses due to the normal tech challenges.

And Justin and I were in it. I was so in it, authentic tears streamed from my eyes while I watched Friar Laurence at his little table, gathering my vial as he delivered his monologue that explained how the drink worked and his plan. He then handed me the vial.

"Love give me strength, and strength shall help afford." I stood. "Farewell, dear father." And that ended act four, scene one, which meant the sound crew muted our head mics.

David, smiling, put his arm around my shoulder. "Are you alright, young padawan?"

"Excellent work," Mr. Peters said. "But off the stage, please. The crew needs to switch those beds."

I wiped my eyes as we headed stage right. "Yeah. Just got caught up in the moment."

My Romeo met us right off stage. He stared at me, his face an odd combination of concern, probably because my eyes were still a bit wet, and...admiration?

David wandered right, and we stepped out of the way to allow the crew to bring out Juliet's bed. The scene where I drank the potion was next.

"That scene was awesome." His blinding smile caught me a little off guard. "You know you're some kind of amazing out there. Right?"

The crew flew back by us with the cot. Which meant I had no choice but to get back on stage, and not respond to his head-spinning compliment beyond my own blinding smile.

Chapter Thirty-Seven

When Meg and I reached the auditorium doors, I stopped and faced her. "Thanks for walking me here. And doing my hair at lunch."

She, being the best, best friend imaginable, had pried herself from Owen to sit with me and some of the cast, including Drew still wearing a cast, to lend support and her hairstyling skills. She'd pulled the sides of my hair, that I had taken time in the morning to softly curl, into a fancy braid since *Romeo and Juliet's* first show, the matinee, started in thirty minutes.

I'd eaten little at lunch. Because my stomach wouldn't stop gurgling and rolling.

Meg came in for a hug, but I held up my hands. "No hugs. Hair and makeup?"

"Right." She smiled. "Kass, you look perfect. Just don't think about anything but being Juliet."

I nodded, filled my lungs with a deep breath and slowly released the air. Which sort've helped my queasy stomach.

I couldn't think about my Romeo keeping his distance all

week, outside of rehearsals. Or that our truce was nearing its end. Or that I was still crazy in love with him.

But I *could* follow Mr. Peters's advice and channel my emotions into Juliet Capulet.

"And keep doing your deep-breathing exercises." Meg opened the auditorium door. "You're late. I'll see you later."

I forced myself not to look for him while I headed for the dressing room.

Bree and I exchanged quick smiles as I dropped my backpack. I then took my gown and went behind the dressing screen with her. And I kept breathing slowly and deeply. But the tight dress squeezing my sides amplified my stomach's queasiness and my head turned fuzzy.

"You're pale." Bree gave me her back so I could zip her up. "They brought water in."

"I think I need to sit down." I zipped her beige and brown nurse's costume and made a beeline for the stool in front of the first makeup table. "I'll meet you out there in a minute."

She nodded and followed the extras out of the dressing room. Sloane and Maddie followed a minute later, but I caught Maddie giving me an encouraging smile before she left.

At least Sloane's nasty opinion of me hadn't rubbed off on Maddie.

Because the dress was so tight, I couldn't put my head between my knees. All I could do was focus on each slow, deep inhale and exhale. But the pressure of this all-too important show going perfectly, it being the only one we did for the students, became too much for me.

I stood, dashed into the bathroom stall, and shut the door. I took big swallows to settle the nausea, which slowly worked. I leaned against the door, closed my eyes, and went back to deep breathing. I also took some comfort from the fact Dad once told me my mom had always gone through this same thing.

"Kassidy?"

My eyes flew open at hearing Justin's voice. But why was he here instead of Bree?

"What are you doing in here?" I called out. "You're not a girl."

"Not since I last checked," he called back, and I heard the smile in his voice. "Bree told me what was going on. I offered to come get you. I also have a little present for you."

I opened the bathroom door about an inch. I saw, through the crack, him standing barely inside the dressing room and holding the door slightly open.

He tilted his head right to catch my eyes and frowned. "I've never seen you like this."

"It's normal, first-show jitters."

"Kass, you're hiding in a bathroom. It's kind've freaking me out. Nothing scares you."

I walked out and closed the door behind me. "That's not true."

I wanted to add *First shows scare me* and *I'm afraid if I get close to you I'll do something girly and embarrassing and stupid. Like throw myself into your arms, kiss you until we can't breathe and tell you I've missed you. And still love you. And want to get back together.*

I grabbed a bottle of water off the first makeup table. I opened it, then took a big drink in the hopes it might settle my stomach. I did it a second time while feeling his eyes on me.

"Justin, I'm not made of stone."

"And I didn't mean it that way. I didn't know you were like this before your shows."

I shrugged and drank a little more water.

He gave me *his* smile. "I have something for you."

I finished my water and set the empty bottle down on the table.

I slowly approached him. When we were within touching

distance, he held out a pack of his favorite mint gum. I noticed him chewing a piece, too.

"Our first scene is coming up pretty quick. I know we can't chew the gum for long, but it might help your stomach, too."

"Oh. Thanks." I grabbed a piece, then another to be really safe.

He laughed, and I unwrapped a piece and put it in my mouth.

He held out his left hand. "Ready, Juliet?"

I put the second piece in my mouth, tossed the wrappers into a nearby trash can, and took his hand. And after another deep breath, I said, "Ready, Romeo."

Mr. Peters always did a pep talk before each show, then reminded us of areas that had been troublesome throughout the week. Like the sword fighting. And it seemed like no time later, Justin and I were standing backstage with our eyes on one another.

Our narrator, a sophomore, said to the full house, "Two households, both alike in dignity, in fair Verona where we lay our scene...from ancient grudge break to new mutiny...where civil blood makes civil hands unclean, from forth the fatal loins of these two foes...a pair of star-crossed lovers take their life—"

"Aren't you nervous?" I whispered.

"No," he whispered back. "Because we're gonna kill it."

Chapter Thirty-Eight

My cheeks ached from the smiling I couldn't stop. Because *all* of us had killed it.

"I'll be honest," Bree murmured as we wiggled our feet into our shoes, "it sucks Drew broke his elbow. But you and J.R..." She paused to look at me. "It sounded like you two were literally Romeo and Juliet, lost in your own world, during your few big scenes."

I giggled and started lacing up my shoes.

Being the actual show, the cast couldn't stand in the wings and watch. We were to stay on our sides of the stage, based on our entrances for upcoming scenes, and quietly melt into the darkness. Angelina and Mr. Lowry were no nonsense when it came to that.

It sounded like *Romeo and Juliet* had been a hit by the students' standards. There'd been some laughter and many had gotten into the sword-fight scenes. Of course. And Romeo and I received some ridiculous whistles during our heated kissing moments.

My smile grew at the memory of those moments.

"I'm not convinced there isn't something going on with you two."

Over a week ago, I had denied her question about us getting back together. But right now, and after the phenomenal show, all I did was continue smiling.

She smiled back. "Are you almost ready? I can wait."

"Go ahead. I need to finish tying my shoes." I also wanted to make sure I ran into him.

But maybe, just maybe, he was waiting for me in the house?

Her smile deepened, as if she could read my mind. "I'll see you tonight."

I finished lacing up my shoes and walked from behind the dressing screen.

Sloane and Maddie were still finishing up behind their screen. The four other girls were gathering up their stuff, but stopped to give me their huge smiles. I then picked up my backpack and slung it over my right shoulder.

I practically floated from the dressing room while I searched the quieter backstage. He couldn't still be changing, so I headed for the stage left stairs. Then I heard them talking—Justin, Shane, and Cody—beyond the Capulet's wall. They had to be sitting on the stage's edge. They were also laughing.

As I changed direction, now feeling my glow from the inside out because it seemed he *was* waiting for me, Cody's voice became a bit clearer.

"—and you two were looking pretty friendly for exes."

I stopped right behind the wall when I heard Justin's quick laugh.

Hmm. It sounded like they were talking about—

"I was being nice to her," he replied. "She's nuts. And I've dated enough crazy girls for one year. I'm done."

They shared one of those arrogant, I-totally-get-it boy laughs.

My face, my *everything*, became fiery hot and I backed away from the wall.

How many times had he called me crazy in the last several weeks?

Crazy behavior. Crazy head. Crazy Kassidy.

My heart landed in my stomach and I took a quick breath.

His behavior...the compliments, the obvious flirting, the chemistry on stage, the renewed closeness...had been for our truce. Not because he wanted us again. Or me. Now that the play was nearly finished he had no reason to continue the sham.

Justin Richardson really was a phony. A *fantastic* actor. And I'd fallen for it.

Tears hit my eyes. But I angrily blinked them away, stuck my chin in the air, and headed for the stairs. I, without looking in their direction, jogged down the steps.

"There's our Juliet," Shane said.

I ignored them and went for the auditorium doors. I had to go before my dam broke. Again. Dad tweaked his hours this week for the shows and picking me up after rehearsals. But thank goodness I hadn't needed him to pick me up today with it being only 3:30.

My phone buzzed in my backpack the moment I pushed, not-so nicely, through one of our auditorium's main entrance doors now unlocked because of the show. But I didn't go for my phone. It could be him, and I had to get away from him, the school, and my stupidity.

I'd made it steps beyond the school's already quiet main entrance and exit when I heard fast-approaching steps behind me.

I walked faster, but his long legs caught me.

"Wait a sec." He easily moved in front of me and stopped. "What happened?"

I tried going around him, but he blocked me.

"You were better than fine before you went and changed."

I glared up at him. "Will you let me by before I do something really *crazy*?" Striking his male parts with my right foot flashed through my mind.

He didn't move, but there went the lightbulb in his eyes that were narrowing. "You overheard that. And, as usual, jumped to conclusions and are acting—"

"Crazy. That's me. Crazy Kassidy Pashen. Nothing more than a DQ." I pointed to his right side. "Let me by. I want to go home."

He crossed his arms. "We were talking about the girl I broke up with in February because I wanted to be with *you*. And because she really is crazy."

The fight within lasted until my mind registered his words. Then it left me, as if my body were a balloon releasing air. Two emotions rapidly followed, the first being shock because he'd never—not ever—told me that. The second being total embarrassment.

"I ran into her at the basketball scrimmage last night."

I pressed my lips together and nodded once.

He had mentioned he'd be going to that yesterday after rehearsal, to support Owen and our basketball team. But I hadn't known the scrimmage was with her school and I did, despite being wrong, have a perfectly valid reason for my reaction.

"Well, how was I supposed to know you were talking about her? It's not like you haven't called me crazy a few times lately."

"I love your crazy. It challenges me. And makes me laugh," he quietly added.

That, too, was new information. But it had never come across as a compliment. I was about to say as much, too, when he ran his hands through his hair.

"Yeah, it pisses me off sometimes. Like right now." He

shook his head. "Why in the hell would you think I—we—were talking about you? Everyone in the play, with the exception of one person, loves you." He looked me straight in the eyes. "How can you not know by now that I'm still crazy in love with you?"

My mouth drifted open and I held our heated stare until embarrassment consumed me. I lowered my gaze and started playing with the hem of my sweater.

He still loved me, too. But then why—

I raised my head, our eyes connected and I asked, "Why did you choose her?"

"Yeah, you know what, let's talk about that night." He leaned forward. "Sloane was drunk and acting stupid. I was only...trying to be nice."

The fact he even flinched at that excuse caused me to cross my arms. "Really? That's what you're going with?"

"I know how lame it sounds." He shoved his hands into his pockets. "Okay, so I didn't handle it right and I'm sorry. We weren't getting along. Probably because we weren't ready for the summer—our summer—to end. I wasn't thinking."

"No." I also leaned forward. "You weren't. I can still see you two all cozied up on that hot tub. And you looking mad when I walked up. Like I was interrupting—"

"She wasn't backing off. I said I didn't handle it right and apologized. But you know something else? You broke *my* heart that night."

I straightened and my arms fell to my sides.

What on earth was he talking about?

"And how, exactly, did I do that?"

"You were so busy being pissed off, you never gave me a chance to explain my side of it. And then you said..." His eyes hardened. "Everything between us had happened too fast and we should've stayed friends."

I cringed since I had, lost in my humiliation and anger and

heartbreak, forgotten I'd said that to him. But they'd been nothing but angry, spiteful words.

"No matter what you've been hearing and thinking and saying since that screwed up night, Sloane was never my girlfriend."

"But—" I took a quick breath. "The evidence doesn't support that. You were together."

"Okay, so we went on some dates. One being Bryan's party." He shook his head. "But dating her was stupid. And I only did it because I was angry at you. And hurt."

"But..." None of this made sense. "She broke up with you."

"That's what she said to make herself look and feel better. I backed off after the whole picture thing. But she, for some reason, didn't get it. And when she flipped out because we danced that night, I was the one who told her we weren't together and never would be."

That explained so much. Especially his non-reaction following their "break-up." But it didn't explain why he let her get away with her wickedness on social media.

"How come you never told anyone the truth? She said some awful things about you."

"A few of my friends know the truth, but I told them not to say anything because Sloane wasn't worth it. And because it was partially my fault for dating her." He sighed. "Kass, all I've wanted to do our last few extra rehearsals is forget about the play and pick up where we left off. Before Owen's party. And the only reason I haven't is because I didn't really know how you felt and didn't want to chance ruining *Romeo and Juliet*."

That explained his distance at school, when we weren't rehearsing. It also explained his swift attitude change on Saturday afternoon and the obvious heat between us that night.

"It's no secret we've been *fantastic* together. If you'd eavesdropped a minute longer, you would've heard what Shane said about us. And my response to him."

Different tears hit my eyes. Guilt being the main emotion behind them. And a totally different type of stupidity. Justin Richardson wasn't a phony. At all. Despite the drama in August—and my nasty comment to him that night—we'd been on the same page for the last week up until, minutes ago, I'd again made the wrong assumptions. My crazy really was no better than Sloane's. Or that other girl's. Who he'd broken up with to be with...Oh. My. God.

What had I done?

"I was going to ask you," he mumbled, "if you might want to go to Cody's cast party tomorrow night. Together. But as us. Not as—" He fell silent and glared at the ground.

"Justin, I..." I scoured my brain for the right words. The words that would fix this newest mess I'd caused us. Him. A fantastic boy who had enough drama at home and didn't need this drama, too. And the guilt consumed me, then stole my voice.

"I told my mom I was walking you home and hoping to hang out with you until we had to be back." He shrugged. "I'd rather go home and drive myself back here later. But don't freak out. I won't let *this* latest fight effect tonight. And then we'll be almost done with this."

That stung every part of me. But at the same time, I knew I deserved it.

He turned from me and headed north.

I knew I should call out his name. Or sprint after him, tackle him, and kiss every inch of his face as an apology. But guilt had stolen my voice *and* ability to move.

Chapter Thirty-Nine

When Dad walked into our condo, I intercepted him. "I need to borrow the car."

After my walk home, and absorbing everything Justin said, I realized I had too much to say to him before our first, big night performance. We'd come way too far—as us and Romeo and Juliet—to let it end with his angry exit lines and me stupidly letting him walk away. Nothing would stop me from going to his house and saying what I needed to say. What he deserved to hear. Unless, of course, Dad refused to let me borrow the Volvo.

He, after closing and locking the door, walked around me and headed for the kitchen. "Hi, Dad," he said, and a bit sarcastically. "It's nice to see you. How was work today?"

Meg, who had walked over to not only fix my braid but also talk about what happened after my "I totally blew it" text, sat at the kitchen island with my sister.

"Hi, Dr. Mc—Dr. Pashen." She set her phone down. "How *was* your day?"

I gave my best friend a long, hard stare.

"It was okay, Meg." He smiled and opened the fridge. "Thank you."

"Dad, the car?"

He took out a bottle of water and shut the door. "Hi, Kassi. How was your day? And the matinee? Nice job with her hair, Meg."

"Thank you," she practically sang.

"It was awesome, but I really need the car. To go talk to Justin."

And he was wasting time. If I left, well, now, I could be at his house before five.

"Last time I heard he was Romeo. Means you'll see him tonight?"

"They had a fight," Michelle volunteered without looking up from her phone.

"And it has to be resolved right now? What time do you have to be back at school?"

"Daddy, we're Romeo and Juliet. Of course it has to be resolved right now. I'll be back in plenty of time for you to drop me and Meg off by six-thirty."

He looked at his watch and made it clear he disagreed.

"Please? It's terribly important or I wouldn't be asking."

He paused, then dug in his pocket, withdrew the key and tossed it to me.

I turned toward the door with an extremely grateful "Thanks."

"Wait a minute."

My shoulders drooped. I had to get out of here to make it back in time.

"Lauren's plans tonight with a couple of friends were cancelled. I guess one of them is really sick with that flu going around."

I looked at Meg and my sister, and back at Dad. Who was, as usual, grinning like a fool while talking about Dr. Lauren.

They'd since had their rescheduled second date and their third date last night.

"She knows about you being Juliet and the show tonight. She really wants to see it. Meet you girls. So, I invited her to go with me." He glanced at Michelle. "Us. Is that alright?"

"Dad, stop being soooo weird." My sister shrugged. "It's fine. I want to meet her."

"Me, too," Meg chirped.

Dad glanced back at me.

"I think that sounds great. Really. I can't wait to meet her. But I have to go."

"Okay. But please be careful."

I was about to open the door when Meg appeared at my right side.

"Kass, it's about freaking time you did this, and I'm proud of you."

I let her comments sink in before asking, "Did you know about him and Sloane and their break-up?"

"Only because Owen knew. And I had to work my magic to get him to tell me everything. After *that* Anti-Love Club meeting day. I guess J.R. told him not to say anything. To just forget it. Because Sloane wasn't worth the trouble."

That's almost exactly what he'd told me. Meg knowing also explained her wanting me to sit with them. And wanting me to talk to Justin. Give him a chance.

Meg smiled. "I thought about telling you. But then I felt you'd come around. After you started calling him by his name. And saying how well your extra rehearsals were going." She opened the door and pushed me out of the condo. "Please don't mess up your hair. I'll see you back here where you'll have to *immediately* tell me everything that happened."

* * *

"He's not here," Bethie said, finishing her Oreo cookie.

My heartbeat sped up as I stared at Bethie and Pearl, a heavyset, middle-aged woman with large glasses. They were standing in the Richardson's front doorway.

"What do you mean he's not here? He has to be here. Where else could he be?" Especially with it being just after five.

"Sweetie, he walked in here about an hour ago, said hi, went upstairs. I think he took a shower, then came back down and said he was—and this was so odd—going to the beach before heading back to school."

My lightbulb went on, and I stepped away from the door. "I know where he is. Thanks." Knowing where he was fueled me with encouragement, but even more haste.

"My husband and I are going to tomorrow night's show," Pearl said as I headed back to the car. "We're looking forward to it, too."

I smiled and waved my thanks while sliding into the driver's seat. As I looked both ways backing out of the short driveway, anger simmered inside me.

Pearl and her husband were going to a show, but Justin's parents couldn't be bothered?

I tapped the gas pedal a little too hard.

As I drove through traffic, trying to hurry without being one of those careless, new teenage drivers, I again went through what I would say to him. And I sensed I could get through it without resorting to desperation. Or begging. Because I loved him, and he loved me. Still. No matter my craziness and awful treatment of him before we'd agreed to our truce.

He hadn't, until calling the truce, been very nice, either. But then it never occurred to me I had hurt *him* deeply that night. I'd been too caught up in my insecurities and percep-tions of him sitting there with my theater rival that I'd refused to hear anything he had to say and lashed out. Then whole-body heartache had completely taken over, followed by the fury.

It really had been all about me. Something else I would address during my mini, please-forgive-me speech so we could start making up for lost time. But after our show.

I turned up the radio and tried, really hard, to focus on the songs. But as I got closer to Ocean Beach, I could only see him, in our spot, probably listening to music.

I hit the accelerator and whipped around a slow driver, then another.

If Dad knew I was driving like this, he'd sentence me to no more driving until I graduated. Possibly longer. Still, I made it in good time, and without hurting myself, anyone else or the Volvo. I even spotted the Richardson's SUV and parked a few spots away.

I wasted no time heading—more like sprinting—directly for our spot, not nearly as eerie during sunset. I swiftly rounded the slight dune and stopped at the sight of him.

He was stretched out on a towel and leaning against the tallest wall of sand. He had his eyes closed and was, like I pictured, listening to music. He looked adorable, too, barefoot, and in his jeans, and a long-sleeved gray shirt under a black T-shirt.

I wanted to jump on top of him, but I had to take this one step at a time.

I approached him, and when I reached his legs, I bent down to grab his phone, which rested on his stomach. That, as I suspected it would, caused his eyes to fly open.

As he yanked his Beats off, I pressed his phone's button to pause his music. But the song he'd been listening to made me halt and I caught his eyes—was he *embarrassed*?

"'All of Me' by John Legend. That's what you've been working on." I knelt beside him and gave him a shy smile.

I couldn't ignore he'd chosen the song since it could've been written about us.

He turned stoplight red and took back his phone.

"I can't believe you never told me you broke up with that girl to be with me."

"I thought it was obvious, but—" He shrugged. "How did you know I was here?"

"I forgot to tell you my newest superpower is clairvoyance."

He fought a smile, which I took as a good sign.

"I stopped by your house." I sighed. "I've been trying to work on not making it all about me since we got into it that day you joined the club. And I promise to also work on the whole jumping-to-conclusions, the other not-so wonderful part of me that brought us to this." I gestured at the distance between us. "I'm sorry. For everything. I should've given you a chance to explain. I don't know what happened that night. Maybe it was the arguing—because our summer was almost over?—then seeing you with my theater rival."

"Kass, she's not your rival. Sloane can sing, but she's got nothing on you when it comes to acting talent."

Just one more reason to love every single part of him.

He set his phone and headphones on the towel and shifted into a cross-legged position.

The sound of the busy and very near waves surrounded us until he said, "I know I was stupid that night. And after. I'm really sorry for all the trouble she's caused you, too. But what was I supposed to do? Throw her into the hot tub?"

"Yes. That would've been just fine with me."

He looked at me for a few seconds before laughing. He then gave me *his* smile. "I've really missed you. And your smart mouth."

"I've missed you, too." I started playing with the corner of his towel. "I'm still crazy in love with you, too. And I swear on my life I didn't mean what I said about everything moving too fast and staying friends. I was angry and hurt and couldn't—"

"Stop yourself."

"You know I'm working on that."

"But not too much. That's the part of you I fell for first."

I smiled, and he grasped my busy hand. I lifted my eyes, which met his instantly. "I love your idea of picking up where we left off in August. Before Owen's party?"

"Okay." He reached out, pulled me into his lap and I, very willingly, curled into his warm arms.

"All is forgiven? That easily? Even after all the mean things I said to you? I'm also very sorry about that," I added, remembering a few particularly nasty things I'd said.

"I wasn't very nice to you, either. But I'm glad you mentioned it." He started nuzzling *that* spot. "I think we can figure out ways to make it up to each other."

I giggled and angled my body enough I could wrap my arms around his neck. He replied by tightening his arms around my waist and we shared a long, tight hug. I, because I couldn't stop myself, released a girly, wistful sigh. I'd missed being with him.

Just. Like. This.

After a few seconds of simply holding each other, my mind went back to his apology about Sloane and I asked, "What did you say to Sloane when I was in my meeting that day?" I leaned back to look at him. "She's been ignoring me since then. For obvious reasons. But Meg told me you said something to her at lunch."

He laughed. "I told her when you *did* come back as Juliet she'd better back off or I'd make sure the entire school knew the truth about the break-up."

I nuzzled his nose. "My Prince Charming to the rescue. Again."

He pressed his forehead to mine. "I don't think you'll ever need to be really rescued. Another thing I love about you."

"Not true. And I love you're still my Prince Charming." I paused, then said, "Pearl said they're going to the show tomorrow. I'm sorry your parents totally—"

"Suck?"

"Yeah. But my dad and sister are going to be there tonight. For us. And the show. He's also bringing the doctor he's been dating."

"Really?" He kissed my forehead, and my eyes drifted shut at the oh-so familiar, affectionate gesture. "Sounds like they might be serious."

"I think so." I opened my eyes and snuggled the spot where his shoulder met his neck. "I'm looking forward to meeting her tonight—you smell so good." I loved that about him. "You're wearing the cologne I helped you pick out. You wore it to the dance, too."

"So you did notice that." He laughed quietly. "You smell good, too. And I meant to tell you earlier I like your hair like this."

"Thanks. But it's all Meg." Thinking of another thing I loved about him, I asked, "So, the John Legend song? Will I get to hear it?"

"Maybe. When it's ready."

He, again, nuzzled that spot, but now I felt his lips getting incredibly close to my skin. That's when reality hit me.

"We can't do this."

He lifted his head. "Why? What's wrong?"

I, very unwillingly, untangled myself from his arms and hauled myself from his lap.

"What are you doing?"

"*Romeo and Juliet*? Tonight? I have to go back home first, too. To drop off the car." I took two giant steps backward as he stood. "We also can't risk sabotaging our mojo."

"How is getting back together now going to sabotage our mojo?"

"We have to save these feelings for tonight. It'll be that much more intense. Trust me."

"Kass, wait. I'll leave with you."

"I'll see you at school. And we're going to beyond kill it tonight." I blew him a kiss and then sprinted back to the car.

Chapter Forty

I focused on my Romeo, lying beside me, having just swallowed his poison. "What's here? A vial...closed in my true love's hand?" I took the vial from his fingers. "Poison, I see, hath been his timeless end." I placed it to my lips, tilted my head back, then down, and stared at him. "Drunk all and left no friendly drop to help me after? I will kiss thy lips—" I dropped the vial between us and leaned down. "Haply some poison doth hang on them." I pressed my lips to his and stayed there a second before saying, "Thy lips are warm."

A loud noise off stage meant the Montagues, Capulets, Friar Laurence, and Prince Escalus were about to enter the scene.

I sat up. "Yea, noise? Then I'll be brief." I slid the prop dagger from its holder attached to his belt. "O, happy dagger." I angled it toward my heart. "This is thy sheath...there rust, and let me—" I pressed the dagger into me, which made the blade push into the handle. "Die." I fell, my head landed gently on his chest, and I kept a tight grip on the dagger.

A few seconds of silence followed, then the six other cast

members burst onto stage and launched into their dialogue that Prince Escalus started.

We laid together and I tried, really hard, to pay attention to the scene. But we were finished, and I allowed my blissful mind to wander. I wondered what we would do after the show. There was also a part of me that still couldn't believe we were back together.

I'd meant every word of my apology and that I wasn't perfect. I had my quirks. So did he. But I would never—not ever again—let myself be the crazy girl from earlier today and in August. Justin Richardson chose me twice and I wouldn't blow it by being a DQ.

Well, I would try very hard not to be that much of a DQ. Some things I couldn't help.

"Where be these enemies?" Prince Escalus said. "Capulet! Montague! See what a scourge is laid upon your hate, that heaven finds means to kill your joys with love. And I...for winking at your discords too...have lost a brace of kinsmen. *All* are punished."

Lords Capulet and Montague had their brief, "I'm sorry" dialogue. Then everyone left.

The stage darkened, except for a spotlight on us, and one on our narrator.

"A glooming peace this morning it brings. The sun for sorrow will not show his head. Go hence to have more talk of these sad things. Some shall be pardoned, and some punished. For never was a story of more woe...than this of Juliet...and her Romeo."

* * *

We actually received a standing ovation. And not just *us*, but the entire cast. Everyone was glowing when the curtain closed after our last group bow that included Mr. Peters.

He turned toward all of us and we formed a tight circle with him. We were all laughing from relief. And success.

"I have nothing but love for all of you right now. You're required to repeat what you did here tonight, tomorrow night." Mr. Peters looked at us. "Especially you two."

Which meant I'd get my Youth Summer Drama Session recommendation from him, and I thought of my mom. Who I'd felt was right here with me the entire night.

Justin and I glanced at each other and exchanged a for-us-to-understand-only smile. That's when family members and friends started appearing on stage, and everyone scattered.

I was about to throw myself into Justin's arms, but his attention caught on something behind me and I turned. And my eyes nearly popped out of my head. Because it was his dad, walking toward us with a woman I didn't know.

I looked back at Justin. His smile had turned into a glare.

"What the hell is this?" he muttered. "I'll be right back."

I watched him take long strides toward his dad and the unknown woman.

"Kass!"

I turned at the sound of Meg's excited voice and smiled. She was towing Owen, and Michelle, Dad and a really pretty brunette wiping her eyes were behind them.

Meg and Michelle immediately hugged me.

"You two made me cry," Michelle whined. "During your last scenes. And I think you made Dad cry."

I stepped out of their embrace, threw my arms around my dad and we shared a big hug. After a few seconds I pulled away and, based on the proud, yet tender look he was giving me, I knew he was thinking about my mom, too.

"You were breathtaking. Just like she was."

I gave him my best enthusiastic smile to stop myself from crying. I then faced Dr. Lauren, standing close beside Dad, and said, "Hi. I'm Kassidy. It's really nice to meet you."

She had one of those smiles that could light up a dark room and a melodic laugh.

"Lauren. I'm so happy to meet you, too. The show was amazing." She laughed again and sniffed. "I can't believe how talented all of you are. And you and the boy who played Romeo? Are you two an actual couple?"

I felt everyone's eyes as I looked over my left shoulder, but Justin, his dad, and the woman were gone.

Hmm. Hopefully the two showing up wouldn't ruin the high from our perfect show.

"We were together, then broke up. But we've…" I peeked at Dad. "Made up." Of course it wouldn't be official until we could be together, and not as Romeo and Juliet.

But that moment was so close.

Dad smiled. "I guess you'll want your curfew extended the next two nights?"

"Really?" The fact he had offered to extend my curfew nearly blew my mind.

"You've earned it. But midnight. Tell Romeo not a second later."

"I promise." And Snoopy started his happy dancing in my head.

"Let's get our picture." Dad pulled his cell from his jeans pocket and looked at Dr. Lauren. "The three of us get a picture after one of Kassi's shows, but before she changes."

She returned his smile. "Then let me do the honors."

He, after going into his phone to bring up the camera, handed it over. The three of us huddled together, with Dad in the middle. She took two pictures and handed over his phone.

"Thanks for doing that," he said, his smile growing.

Apparently, Cupid was working overtime with his love-tipped arrows. And that was just fine with me, *thankyou-verymuch*.

He took Dr. Lauren's hand and said to me, "Have fun tonight."

"It was very nice meeting you." She laughed. "Maybe next time it'll be longer than a few minutes? And maybe I'll get to meet your Romeo?"

I smiled. "I'd like that."

My sister gave me another hug and whispered in my ear, "Dr. Lauren's pretty cool. And Dad has it *soooo* bad for her." We laughed, and I waved goodbye as they left.

Meg smiled. "Text me tomorrow? I'll come over and redo your hair. And you can tell me how tonight went." She looked at Owen. "But you better not tell J.R. I said that."

He shrugged. "I didn't hear a thing."

We hugged, then she and Owen, also hand-in-hand, left the stage.

I headed for the dressing room. I still didn't see Justin anywhere, but I knew if his dad showing up with that woman had darkened his mood, I could bring him back.

* * *

I walked toward the stage since he'd, in a text, asked me to meet him there.

I felt a hundred pounds lighter now that I no longer had on my burial gown. I loved my costumes for this show, but my skinny jeans, black shirt, and black Converse was like wearing heaven in the form of clothing.

Mr. Lowry and a few tech-crew members were still backstage to get things ready for tomorrow night's show. Everyone else from the cast had left. It seemed they'd hurriedly changed to meet up with their families or friends, or boyfriends and girlfriends.

Justin, now back in his clothing, was staring out into the empty house.

My tummy did its somersaulting at just the sight of him. "How are you feeling?"

He turned and gave me *his* smile. "Invincible."

I stopped inches from him. "Great superpower. But I was talking about your dad."

"I know. And not even him or that woman—a *friend* who supposedly loves Shakespeare and had to see the show"—he rolled his eyes— "could ruin this day and night."

"And where's your mom tonight?"

"Supposedly a late rehearsal. They're getting ready for their Christmas season. But my dad said she was planning on coming tomorrow night with Pearl and her husband. Which was news to me." He shrugged. "I guess that's something."

I smiled, our arms went around each other, and I snuggled his chest. It's not like anyone could see us because of the set blocking the backstage.

"What did your dad have to say about your *fantastic* performance?"

"He seemed really impressed." He leaned away from me, and I looked up. "I guess in their own weird way they do care about us. Maybe if I concentrate on that it won't hurt as much when they're being stupid and selfish."

I nodded, then hugged him until I heard his breathless laugh.

"I don't want to think or talk about them anymore." He released me and gently cupped my face. "I have to kiss you right now. And not as Romeo."

"I want that, too. But just so you know, you're a pretty great Romeo kisser."

He smiled, and I went up on my tiptoes and our mouths fused. This kiss was naughtier and longer than his Romeo kisses. And I felt it all the way to my toes.

"I have to tell you something," he murmured after we, hearing voices from backstage, ended our kiss.

His arms went back around my waist, and I crossed mine behind his neck.

"I sort've lied about why I auditioned." His face flushed. "I mean, I did audition because of the extra credit. But I mainly did it because of you. Listening to you last year, talking about *The Crucible* and the cast, and the other plays you've been in made it sound awesome. And I really did think it would be fun to try out acting." He laughed. "But I swear I never thought Mr. Peters would give me a part. Especially what he did give me."

I gave him my best wicked smile. "So it kind've was about me."

"And there goes *your* big balloon head."

I laughed. "What was your audition piece?"

"Mercutio's Queen Mab monologue."

"That's why you always nailed that scene."

"You noticed that? Even back then?"

I forced myself not to roll my eyes. "Now that you've discovered this new talent, are you going to audition for next year's play? I'm so hoping Mr. Peters chooses a comedy."

"Yeah." His arms tightened around me. "I think I might do that."

I nuzzled his chest. And, suddenly thinking about superpowers and his x-ray vision comment from that Friday, quietly asked, "Did you join the club because of me? Of us?"

"Yes and no. I didn't go there that day to join, but you were pissing me off. And I realized I had every right to be there."

"Okay. But now that we're back together, you're going to leave the club. Right?"

"No."

I looked up at him.

"I promised that kid I'd help him with his game."

Now I had no choice but to roll my eyes.

"And everyone in there loves each other. If you get what I'm saying? Well, except Natalie. She's kind've mean. And scary."

"She can be. But I promise she has a huge heart. And I do know what you're saying."

"Speaking of love." He pulled away from me. "I have to do this while we're on the stage, because it's the main reason we're back together, and I have the room." He went down on bended knee and took my left hand.

"Justin," I mumbled, "what are you doing?"

"Kassidy Pashen." He dramatically raised my hand. "Will you do me the honor of being my date tomorrow night for the cast party? And for the Snowflake Formal? And prom?"

Something about this scene, and him saying Snowflake Formal, made me giggle.

I bent down to better look him in his eyes. "And I'm the crazy one?"

He lowered our hands. "I learned from the best. Is that a yes?"

"Yes. But only if you promise to never stop *this* crazy side of you from coming out."

We leaned closer to each other and stopped when our noses were barely touching.

"It's a deal."

Then we shared a Romeo-and-Juliet-worthy kiss.

He stood, and I threw my arms around his neck. Which made him laugh.

"Where to, Juliet?"

"Surprise me, Romeo."

Author's Note

I hope you enjoyed Book One in the Pacifica Academy Drama Series that will continue with Natalie's story, *The '68 Camaro Between Kenickie and Me*. Though each book can stand alone, it's recommended the books are read in series order for maximum enjoyment.

And if you have a moment, please feel free to leave a rating and brief review at wherever you purchased the book. Authors always appreciate and need honest, reader reviews.

Acknowledgments

Writing has been in my blood since I was eleven or twelve, and I've worked on other projects here and there throughout the years. But it wasn't until I became an avid reader of contemporary YA romance and an English teacher that I decided to stop treating my writing as a hobby. So thank you to the fantastic writers of YA romance and, again, to my former students for inspiring the *Romeo and Juliet* storyline. I'll never forget how they jumped into their roles and powered through reading Shakespeare. For most of them, it was their first, real introduction to Shakespeare, too. They so rocked!

As do Brittany, Kelly, Loretta, and Mary for reading early, pretty rough drafts of this story. And still walking away with nothing but encouraging feedback. Thank you, ladies.

A huge thanks to The Killion Group for creating such a cute cover (and everything else you did to make the story an actual book), and being so patient with a new Indie author.

To my mom, thank you for putting up with me those two weeks in July while I scrambled to finish the first draft. Sorry for waking you up at 5:00 in the morning.

About the Author

Christine Miles is a full-time writer living in Albuquerque, New Mexico.

An avid reader and writer since elementary school, her passion for literature inspired her to pursue a BA in English and an MA in Creative Writing. She writes YA and Adult Contemporary Romances with sassy, independent heroines and swoony heroes who love them for their strength.

When not writing romances, she loves traveling, binge-watching shows on streaming apps, reading mysteries and thrillers, listening to music, and spending quality time with her family, friends, and dog.

You can find her on Facebook and Instagram. Sign up for her newsletter to get ARC's and updates at www.christine-milesauthor.com.

www.ingramcontent.com/pod-product-compliance
Lightning Source LLC
Chambersburg PA
CBHW061603190726
48288CB00007B/2159